the inconvenient unraveling of gemma sinclair

the inconvenient unraveling of gemma sinclair

a novel

meg myers morgan

Published by GFB™, Seattle
www.girlfridayproductions.com

Produced by Girl Friday Productions

Cover design: Lauren Smith
Production editorial: Kylee Hayes
Project management: Sara Addicott

Image credits: cover © iStock/Yulia Sanatina

ISBN (paperback): 978-1-964721-90-3
ISBN (ebook): 978-1-964721-91-0

Library of Congress Control Number: 2025907311

First edition

*For the mothers.
Yours. Mine. Theirs.*

How can I be a mom when I still feel so much like a daughter? —Gemma Sinclair

CHAPTER 1

Gemma Sinclair jerked awake, her eyes snapping open to see the crack on the ceiling straight above the bed. Her heart was beating fast. She lay still, working to find the details of the dream she was just having. There was a tightness in her chest, but she couldn't remember the cause. She rolled over, opened her eyes, and grabbed instinctively for her phone, unplugging it from the charger and bringing it close to her face. Without her glasses on or her contacts in, she had to close her right eye to focus as she swiped her thumb across the screen. The phone illuminated with an image of her son holding his newborn brother in the hospital—a picture taken four days earlier. The time was 5:18 a.m. She'd only been asleep for an hour.

Without thought she opened Instagram, her eyes suddenly flooded with images and icons and text, her thumb mindlessly rubbing the phone's screen in upward strokes. She let out a disgruntled sigh when she scrolled over a friend's anniversary post. "Thank you for putting up with me!" the caption read. *Have some self-worth,* Gemma thought. She closed the app and carelessly tossed her phone on the bed as Anthony stepped slowly into the room.

"Hey there, Mama," he said softly from the side of the bed. He handed her a cup of steaming coffee. "Did you get any sleep?"

"Oh, you know," she said, awkwardly taking her first sip, still horizontal. "How was your shift?"

"Good. He's such a sweet baby."

"After nineteen hours of labor, he'd better be."

Anthony smiled as he lowered himself onto the bed beside her. "Are you feeling up for today?"

Gemma looked at him with her eyebrows knitted. "Why wouldn't I be?"

He sighed, looking up at the ceiling. "Oh, I don't know. Maybe because you had a baby four days ago?"

She smirked. "Oh, that."

Anthony looked at her for a beat, his concern showing. "This just feels like a lot for the state you're in."

"What state is that? Insanity?"

He winked. "You said it, not me."

She leaned her head back on the pillow, her hand carefully balancing the coffee mug beside her on the bed. "The timing isn't great. I'll give you that. But I'm looking forward to it."

"You sure?"

"Totally."

Even with her eyes closed, Gemma could feel Anthony studying her face.

"I'll be down in just a minute," she said lightly.

"Take your time," he said, rising from the bed and walking toward the hall.

As she watched him close the door, Gemma had a gnawing, uncomfortable feeling. *As to be expected with postpartum,* she thought. The subtle sadness. The erratic emotions. The overwhelming numbness. Well, not *overwhelming* numbness; she could certainly feel every inch of her vagina. The nine stitches—which her doctor had told her wasn't that bad given the size of Calvin's head—were throbbing, and the rocket-sized maxi pad shoved into her hospital-issue mesh panties was clearly full. She shifted her body slightly to put the coffee mug on the nightstand. She gripped the edge of the mattress, tucked her body, rolled off the bed, hunched over, and shuffled to the bathroom, knees together.

She made it to the toilet with just a trickle running down her leg. Working fast, she slid down the mesh underwear, sopped up the blood, and disposed of the pad. *Do I medicate the stitches now, or after the shower?* she wondered. Deciding to wait, she folded toilet paper on her palm in layers and placed it between her legs to catch any new blood while she prepared fresh underwear with a clean pad. Shuffling so as not to disturb the toilet paper lasagna between her thighs, she laid the padded contraption on the sink and reached up into the medicine cabinet for the numbing spray and ointment. Setting those beside the underwear, she inched over to the tub, leaned in, and turned on the faucet. While she waited for the water to heat, she extracted the paper from between her legs: It was fully soaked. This validated Gemma's long-held theory that there were just as many female serial killers as there were males, but women never got caught because they were experts at cleaning up blood.

As she scrubbed her hands under the scalding water in the sink, she began mentally working through the day's tasks that stretched before her. There were so many things to do, the enormity of the day was stripping her of what little energy she had. Calvin was sleeping well, at least two-hour stretches at a time, but Gemma was struggling to sleep, even with Anthony taking turns with the feedings. Sleep always seemed to evade her, and when she found it, it was often punctuated with vivid dreams.

With all there was to do, she wouldn't have time for a nap today, so she needed to focus on waking up. She knew it would have to be a quick shower and an even quicker breakfast. The thought of a bowl of Lucky Charms sent a flutter of excitement through her chest.

In the shower she was careful to turn away from the stream of hot water. She had suffered such terrible breastfeeding woes with her older son that she had confidently decided she would never put herself (or another child) through that again. Besides, two different doctors *and* a lactation consultant had concluded that she simply couldn't make milk. Like she was some medical anomaly. And yet, after the liberating declaration this time that she wouldn't do it—didn't *need* to do it!—her breasts had become tender and prickly in a way they never had the first time around.

She cried as she worked shampoo into her scalp. She knew it wasn't just because of guilt over her untapped milk. But she let herself cry with abandon, refusing to acknowledge why she needed to. As she rinsed the shampoo, she forced her mind back to her task list and, as she always did, assigned each task an allotment of time. Getting Bo up and fed and in front of a cartoon would take about twelve minutes, if he didn't throw a fit about which bowl his oatmeal was served in. And if he didn't throw a fit about eating oatmeal in the first place. Getting Calvin's diaper, making and giving him a bottle, burping him, and changing his clothes would take another twenty-two minutes. She would need to get herself dressed, with full makeup and hair blown out. She'd need at least forty-five minutes for that. And the house. The house had to be perfect. She was hoping for an hour and a half, minimum. And the food, and the setting of the table. Maybe a half hour. If she had time, she'd sweep the front porch.

As she stepped out of the shower, Gemma heard a soft knock at the door.

"Yeah?" she responded.

"Can I come in?" Anthony asked.

"Give me a sec," she said, pulling the mesh underwear and pad up around her damp legs. She wrapped a towel around herself and opened the bathroom door to see him standing there. His sandy-blond hair in wild curls, his baby face adorned with round gold-rimmed glasses. He was short but surprisingly muscular beneath his rolled-collared sweater. Anthony had always exuded approachability and warmth.

"How can I help you?" he asked.

Help me? You aren't my assistant, Gemma thought. "You know as well as I do what needs to be done," she said flatly.

The smile left his face. "I just meant, is there something specific you want me to prioritize?"

Gemma stared at him. In moments like this, she couldn't help but feel the inherent imbalance between them. No matter how good a partner Anthony was, his goodness was relative. As her mother always said to her, "He does more around the house than your father ever did!" Sure, her father never did the grocery shopping, but when Anthony did, Gemma still had to make him a list. She was supposed to be grateful for any closing of the gender gap, even though the gap still felt quite large in moments like these.

She swallowed her frustration. "We have so much to get done."

"Just tell me what you need me to do."

She shifted on her feet in an attempt to relieve the pain in her lower back. "Well, we need to get Bo up and fed."

"I was letting him sleep as long as he would. But I can go get him up and ready."

"If you can do that, I'll get dressed and give Calvin his bottle."

"Your voice," he said, softer.

"What?"

"There's always a slight tremor in your voice on days like this."

Gemma worked to control the irritation rising in her throat. "Days like what?"

"When you're stressed."

"I'm not stressed. I'm bleeding."

He shook his head and laughed. "Maybe that's it."

"It is. Promise. And there's just so much to do. Can you just please go get Bo up and ready? I'm worried about getting everything done."

"Absolutely," he said as he headed through their bedroom and into the hallway.

She closed the door behind him and opened her closet. She knew what she wanted to wear. She had thought about it even before the baby was born. Hours she'd spent in the last few weeks of pregnancy scouring the websites of her favorite clothing stores, searching for the perfect outfit for today. It needed to look effortless. As though she were just naturally put together. But it also had to be loose fitting; she had only gained twenty-four pounds during the pregnancy, and she was already down twelve of those, but her stomach was hollowed out and sagging, flapping a little over the top of her pubic hair. Whatever she wore, even if somewhat loose, also needed to be structured; she couldn't look frumpy. Gemma couldn't bear the look on her mother's face if she looked frumpy.

She had settled on a navy T-shirt dress and had bought it in two sizes, not knowing how far postpartum she'd be today, and paid extra for overnight shipping. She had found a lime-green infinity scarf and metallic sandals on sale a few weeks earlier. The dress and scarf would pair nicely with the white teardrop earrings Anthony had given her last year for her birthday.

As she finished blow-drying her hair and began inserting her earrings, Anthony came back into the room.

"Did you clean the kitchen last night?" he asked, changing out of his pajamas.

Gemma stared into the mirror while threading an earring in. "Yes."

"It looks amazing."

"Oh," she said, turning toward him. "Thank you."

He smiled at her and pulled his T-shirt over his head. She looked at his bare chest for a moment before casting her eyes down.

"Shut it down," he said playfully.

She forced a smile, but knew it was so weak it didn't even reach her eyes. "Okay, I'm going to get Calvin and do a final sweep through the house," she said.

"It looks perfect. There's nothing left to do."

But Gemma didn't agree. She always felt as if she had not done enough.

She looked over herself in the mirror with disappointment. Her naturally wavy hair, which she usually blow-dried straight, looked frizzier than normal. Her eyes looked dark underneath, despite all the concealer. She felt short and dumpy and full of dread. She walked out of their room and into the hallway to adjust the thermostat six degrees higher than normal. Her sister and mother always complained about how chilly her house was. Their grousing made her feel left out, somehow. Two skinny women huddled together on her couch, shivering under her cable-knit throw, while she was alone—and possibly fat—for not being the least bit chilled.

The day before she went into labor she had made a trip to the liquor store, taking rebellious joy in the judging looks of the shoppers watching her waddle down the aisles with her arms full of glass bottles. She had wanted to get just the right imported beer, though she was never sure exactly which one her father preferred, so she always bought four or five different kinds, which she and Anthony would take months to finish. Beer and coffee: that's where she was able to show her father love. She had also stopped at a local coffee shop downtown to buy beans. She hated that place. The coffee was good, sure, but she hardly felt it was worth all the pretense. The tattooed arms of the barista, the pink hair of the owner, the way they served coffee in chemistry beakers. She abhorred that kind of snobbery. She didn't much care for big coffee chains either, but she appreciated how they didn't make her feel bad for not composting her coffee grounds. She had made the extra trip, despite how freakishly swollen her feet were that day, and despite the fact that she was technically on bed rest, in hopes that her father would appreciate the gesture. And she knew her brother, Eddie, would comment on the coffee if she dared to buy it at the grocery store.

As Gemma walked to the bedroom door, she turned back to Anthony. "You arranged for the food, right?"

"Yep. I'm picking up a deli tray from Juniper's."

A beautiful tray from Bloomington's most popular deli would certainly please her mother. "Thank you."

"You bet. I'll pick it up an hour before they get here so the meat and condiments are still cold."

"Wow."

"I know," he said with a grin. "A decade with you and look how much I've learned about hosting."

"You could never be me," she said under her breath as she walked out of the room and toward the nursery.

The last task she would need to complete—in between feeding the baby, doctoring her stitches one more time, and vacuuming the stairs—would be to set up the guest room. She had been surprised to learn that Eddie was coming into town, and downright floored that he wanted to stay with her. Given how long it had been since Eddie had come back to Bloomington, she had assumed he'd want to stay at a hotel, or maybe even crash with an old high school friend. But he had emailed her to say he'd be flying in on the fifth to meet up with his running buddies as they were traveling en masse to a marathon in Indianapolis. She had been thrilled to hear from him, her hands shaking as she texted her sister what was happening.

Eddie hadn't been home in over ten years. The times the family had seen him in the last decade were when they met him and his wife somewhere during their extensive traveling. Gemma's sister once saw him at the Seattle airport when their business travel happened to sync up. And her parents planned some of their vacations to correspond with trips Eddie and Kat were on, so they could at least share one meal together. During Gemma and Anthony's first getaway as a couple, she made them take a slight detour to connect with Eddie and Kat at a national park to go hiking. But Eddie never came to them.

Gemma thought it would be healing for Eddie to stay at her place; perhaps they could have some quality time together, and of course he could finally meet Bo. He'd never stayed with her, not even once, so she had taken this as a sign that they were good again. Or, more accurately, good for the first time since the day of his football tryouts. Perhaps something had shifted in Eddie after three decades of keeping his distance.

While all this was exciting, perhaps even confounding, it also meant she had to hurriedly prep the guest room. They had moved into the house just over a year earlier, a decision Anthony wasn't quite on board with given the size of both the footprint and the mortgage payment. But Gemma had pushed for it, desperate to move out of their cheap new-construction home in the suburbs and into the expansive historical colonial, which was full of charm and cracks. She was excited to have four bedrooms, although all the closets were tiny—a problem in older homes that suburbanites never faced. They had decided to use the fourth room as their home office, but it also had to double as Bo's playroom and triple as the guest room. Given that they had yet to have visitors, it had never been set up for overnight guests. But since Eddie had told her he would be coming to stay, just three days before she went into labor, she had called a local furniture store, ordered a couch that pulled out into a bed, and paid extra for next-day delivery. She had been eyeing the couch for some time, waiting for it to go on sale, but with Eddie coming she felt it was okay to go ahead and buy it. She'd rather purchase an expensive piece she really wanted than a cheap air mattress as a temporary fix. She had put it on the credit card, telling Anthony that she would pay it off quickly. She had taken on several new patients in the past few months, so they were doing better financially anyway. "Therapists have built-in job security," she always said with a laugh. So what was $2,500 more?

As Gemma savored the initial bite of Lucky Charms, her first taste of sugar since her gestational diabetes diagnosis, her phone lit up with a text. It was Eddie. Her heart jumped and she dropped her spoon, which landed loudly in the bowl, startling Calvin awake upstairs. *Man, he's a light sleeper,* thought Gemma, annoyed. Despite the baby's whimpers, she focused on the text.

We need someone to come get us from the airport.

We? Gemma thought. She hadn't known that her sister-in-law was coming too. Kat traveled so much for her job that Gemma never once assumed she'd be part of this trip. She was excited Kat would be coming, though it was strange she was just learning about it now. She immediately pushed that thought aside to respond to the text:

No problem. I'll send Anthony.

Gemma watched as the bubbles pulsed on the screen.

We'll also need to borrow a car. We didn't get a rental, but we'll be visiting a few friends while we're in town.

Gemma stared at the phone with her eyebrows furrowed. When would Eddie and Kat have time to visit friends around town? They were only staying for two days. She shook her head and tapped her thumbs onto the screen.

Of course. You can borrow one of ours.

Gemma watched the screen, waiting for bubbles, but none came. Her shoulders felt tight as she analyzed their brief text exchange. Eddie always wrote with a cool detachment that Gemma struggled to match. She sat back, preparing herself to tell Anthony that he now needed to fill up the tank, vacuum the Goldfish crumbs out of the floorboards, remove the car seats, and pump up that left-front tire before handing Eddie the keys.

Calvin's cries began to grow in intensity. She gave the phone one last look before locking it, slowly stood—so as not to pull the stitches—and made her way to the stairs. With each step up she could feel that her pad was already soaked again. She needed to have a bowel movement too, but she was terrified. She remembered how painful that had been after giving birth to Bo. Of course, she had also torn six ways to Sunday with Bo, which had made that first shit worse than the birth itself. As she reached the top of the stairs, she made a decision not to defecate until Eddie and Kat were gone. And with that, she felt her insides arrange themselves to fit her plan. She shuffled into the nursery and picked up her crying, red-faced baby. Her half-eaten bowl of cereal, still sitting on the kitchen table downstairs, had gone soggy.

CHAPTER 2

Gemma was lost in her thoughts while diapering Calvin. His glorious bald head was round as a cue ball. She rubbed it lovingly, her crotch throbbing, and she wondered, for what felt like the millionth time, about the age difference between him and Bo. *What was the point of such planning when I still doubt my decision?*

Gemma had nearly made herself sick contemplating how far apart to space the kids—a question Anthony always seemed to shrug his shoulders at, not because he wasn't invested, but because he was an only child. He could bring no insight to the table. Whereas well-meaning friends, coworkers, and strangers had filled her head with such pearls of wisdom as "Space them close together so you're out of diapers quicker!" or "Keep at least four years between them so you aren't paying for college at the same time!" These same people also had a lot to say about the pros and cons of breastfeeding, the humanity—or inhumanity—of sleep training, and the perfect age for a child to go to Disney World. Of course, the last one was heavily contingent on how far apart her children were spaced, which reinforced to Gemma that their age gap would undoubtably be the single most important decision she would make as a parent.

She knew that her own birth order, and spacing therein, was a substantial piece of this. Eddie was eleven years older than Gemma and two years older than Mary. Growing up, Mary and Eddie had a typical dynamic, one of inside jokes, mutual friends, and shared memories. By the time Gemma came along—a clear malfunction of their parents' contraceptive choice—her siblings had moved on and out of true childhood, no longer patient with or interested in diaper changes, playing with blocks, or being gentle with a creature that could provide them nothing in return but spit-up.

Anthony appeared in the doorway, startling Gemma out of her thoughts. "Okay, babe, I'm headed to get Eddie and Kat."

She snapped the onesie between Calvin's legs and gingerly lifted him to her shoulder. "Perfect. Thank you."

"How's he doing?" Anthony asked as he came to stroke the baby's back.

"Just the sweetest little baby there ever was," Gemma said.

"I can't get over this head of his."

Gemma crossed her left leg over her right and bent forward with a groan. "Neither can I."

Anthony's nose scrunched in reaction. "I'll bet."

"It's the very definition of a round peg out of a square hole."

"Square?"

"Well, no telling what shape it's in now."

Anthony let out a laugh as he wrapped his arms around both Gemma and the baby. The three swayed slightly. At five nine, Anthony still towered over Gemma, who got none of the height gifted to Mary and Eddie from their tall parents. Anthony's grin, with its tiny gap between the two front teeth, and the way he constantly lifted the bridge of his glasses with his index finger, meant no one ever seemed surprised that he was a librarian. Director of the downtown branch, actually.

"I'm just gonna ask one more time. Are you sure you're up for Eddie's visit?"

"Of course," she said, backing away from him and squaring her eyes. "Why do you keep asking that?"

"I don't know, Gem. This just feels kind of weird to me. The timing and all. And you *just* had a baby."

"I'm fully aware I *just* had a baby."

Anthony laughed. Gemma didn't.

"Okay, okay." He put up his hands. "I just want to make sure you know we can send him to a hotel if that's easier on you. You know, emotionally."

Gemma let out a sigh, partly in frustration at Anthony and partly in acknowledgment that what he was saying wasn't entirely wrong. "Look, I'd do the hotel if he were being like he usually is. But this time is different."

"You keep saying that. But how? How is it different this time?" Anthony crossed his arms but the side of his mouth lifted.

"Because he emailed me. He wants to meet our kids. He's making a special trip."

"He's coming in for a marathon. Our kids are not the reason for the trip."

"Dammit, Anthony!" Gemma yelped, making Calvin shudder in a newborn reflex. Tears began to well up in her eyes. "He's making an effort, so I am too."

"Hey, okay, okay. Sorry, Gem. Don't cry." He edged in to hold her again. "I'm just trying to protect you."

"I know, I'm just tired," she said. "You remember how the tears just come constantly after birth. Remember that time I cried when I couldn't open the pickle jar after Bo was born?"

"Of course I do. But that was warranted. Pickles are great."

Gemma laughed before getting quiet for a beat. "Look, I know you're not the biggest Eddie fan."

"Not true. I just don't know him."

Gemma pulled away from Anthony again and lightly slapped his shoulder. "You don't try!"

"How can I? He's never around."

"That's fair," Gemma said, nodding. "But he's here now. Or, you know, he will be."

Anthony smiled. "Well then I need to get to the airport so I can start being his biggest fan."

Gemma shook her head with a smile, then pursed her lips and leaned in for a kiss. "Love you."

"I love you more," he said before responding to her pucker. He gently rubbed Calvin's head. "And you too, Charlie Brown."

"His body will catch up to his head, right?"

Anthony nuzzled the baby's neck. "We will love him even if it doesn't."

"But will we though?"

"I think so, yes."

"Tell Bo bye and explain what you're doing before you go. He'll ask me a thousand questions otherwise."

"Right. Okay. I'll do that and then I'm off. Be back in about two hours with my absolute idol."

Gemma picked up a diaper from the changing table and threw it at Anthony, who ducked behind the door frame just in time.

Laying the baby in the crib, Gemma worked to swaddle him. He yawned and she smiled in delight at his beauty. Big, round bald head and all. Her chest pulsed in a way that was nearly painful. It wasn't for the reason she'd expect—the warm, visceral ache of love a mother feels for her child. This was more a panicked feeling. About what, she didn't quite know.

She gave Calvin's head one more stroke and went downstairs to check on Bo. He was sitting in the middle of the living room surrounded by a circle of metal cars. "Bang! Bang!" he yelled as he collided them over and over.

"Hey, bud," Gemma said softly. "Baby brother is sleeping

again, so we need to stay quieter." Bo looked up at her with his big green eyes—the same color and shape as Anthony's—and smiled, revealing the faint dimple in his left cheek. She laughed, bent down, and tousled his dark-brown hair.

"Okay, Mommy!" he said, and then went back to ramming the cars into each other and whisper-screaming, "Bang! Bang! Bang!"

Gemma rolled her eyes as she stood, feeling the weight of her mesh underwear drooping. She heard a car door slam. Her heart quickened as she walked to the window to peer out onto the street. She sighed when she saw her sister emerge from her stark-white Mercedes.

"Why is she here early?" Gemma groaned to herself as she watched Mary extract a large platter from the back seat of her SUV. Gemma marveled at Mary's hair, which wasn't even blowing in the breeze. It didn't matter the weather, it could be pouring down rain and Mary wouldn't have a hair out of place. Her bright-blond hair was always expertly coifed into a painfully perfect bob that hung just below her earlobes. Gemma couldn't remember a time when Mary hadn't had that hairstyle.

One of Gemma's favorite memories of her sister, who was nearly a decade older, had been watching Mary get ready for prom. Gemma had sat cross-legged on Mary's bed while she applied the faintest bit of blush to her cheeks. Even back then Mary wore her hair in her signature bob, but she placed one rhinestone barrette on the left side. Mary's prom date was Greg, the boy who had lived three doors down from them and been Mary's best friend since childhood. "Do you like Greg as a boyfriend?" nine-year-old Gemma had asked Mary in that moment. "No," Mary had said sternly. "I have no need for a boyfriend."

Mary carried that sentiment through high school, college, law school, and up to the moment her tight fist rapped three times on Gemma's door.

"Hello!" Gemma forced out as she opened the door.

"Hi! How are you?" Mary said with a wide smile.

"Tired, but good!"

Mary nodded as she slipped past Gemma into the living room, where Bo was running toward her. She placed the platter of cookies on the coffee table just in time to scoop him up. "My Little Bo Peep!" She kissed his forehead.

Bo giggled and laid his head on her shoulder.

Gemma loved how Mary was with Bo. Such a natural for someone who had never had—and didn't want—kids of her own. On some level, Gemma felt a profound insecurity that Mary should have been the one to have kids instead of her. It was not as though Gemma wasn't in love with her children, but she didn't have the ease with kids that Mary did. It was as though Mary could transform into a child momentarily to meet them, greet them, and play with them. Gemma never felt childlike. Childish, sure. But childlike? That was Mary's strong suit. Even though, on the face of it, Mary was as adult and uptight as they came. After all, only Bo was allowed to touch her hair.

Having snuggled with Bo until he was ready to get back to his cars, Mary joined Gemma in the kitchen. "So how are you really doing?"

Gemma shrugged her shoulders, mildly miffed at Mary's air of pity. "Completely fine. I just wasn't expecting you this early, so you'll have to help me with all these dishes."

The sisters worked quietly side by side, one with perfect hair and no body fat, and the other with loose, somewhat frizzy waves, and a roll of sagging belly flap jiggling atop her mesh—and full—underwear.

When they finished assembling a spread of platters across Gemma's dining room table, they stepped back to admire their work. The entire table was covered—first with a white linen tablecloth Gemma had ironed last night, then with every serving dish Gemma and Anthony received ten years ago at their wedding shower, and then with piles upon piles of fruit, dips, crackers, cheeses, and pastries.

Gemma scanned the table. "Oh shit! Where will we put the deli tray Anthony's picking up?"

"No, no, no," Mary said. "There isn't room for anything else on this table."

Gemma looked at the table, confused. "Just push those trays down a little and it can slide in right there."

Mary shook her head. "That will mess up the balance."

"Too bad. I want everyone to have what they want."

"But right now, the platters are evenly spaced. Look how symmetrical it all is."

The women looked at each other for a beat before bursting into laughter.

"Wow," Gemma said, shaking her head. "My people pleasing and your fastidiousness are really on display today, huh?"

Mary groaned and pulled out one of the six chairs around the table. She gestured for Gemma to take a seat too. Gemma leaned back to check the time on the oven before pulling out a chair. She gently lowered herself, feeling the cold thickness between her thighs. "Ah, ow," she whispered.

"Oh. Right. You okay?" Mary said. And before Gemma could answer, tears were sliding down her face.

Mary leaned forward and took Gemma's elbows in her hands. "Gemma, what? What's wrong?"

Gemma's head tilted forward, and she pressed her fingertips into her forehead and cried while Mary sat quietly, her hands still at Gemma's elbows. When Gemma finally managed to keep her tears from falling, she did what she always told her patients to do in moments of great anxiety—blow out the candles on your birthday cake. And assume you're fifty, so there are *a lot* of candles. She took five deep breaths, enjoying the way Mary's hair refused to flutter when she exhaled.

"Okay," Gemma finally said.

"What's going on?" Mary pressed.

Gemma waved a hand and with an embarrassed smile sat back in her chair, prompting Mary to do the same. "It's nothing. Just the regular postpartum blues. Crying is very common."

"Yeah, that's what I want to talk to you about. That's why I came a little early today."

Gemma felt a pang in her chest, the kind she always felt when she was in trouble as a kid. "Oh?"

"Mom and Dad and I were talking about all of this last night."

Gemma's eyes narrowed as they watered again. "All of what?"

"Of Eddie coming in."

"And Kat too."

Mary's eyes widened. Gemma nodded.

"When did you find *that* out?"

Gemma rolled her eyes. "Literally five minutes ago."

Mary threw up her hands.

Gemma's eyebrows furrowed. "You were all talking about Eddie without me?"

"You know how they are," Mary said with a shake of her head. "I had called Mom to ask about the cookie recipe and she put me on speakerphone and Dad was in the room, and suddenly it's all about Eddie."

Gemma nodded and shrugged but felt the pang of being left out. Yet again.

"They are just a little confused about why he's visiting. And now to learn Kat is coming too? And that he wants to stay with you. I get their concern, I guess. I mean, you *just* had a baby."

"I *just* had a baby?" Gemma snapped, aiming for sarcasm, but it came out much more biting.

Mary looked confused at Gemma's response. "I was

wondering if it would be easier if he—if they—stayed at my house."

"*You* were thinking that, or Mom and Dad were thinking that?"

"I was. It just seems like way too much to ask you to host someone not even a week after giving birth."

"I know, but maybe he wants to be in my life?" Gemma cringed at how childlike and innocent that sounded.

Mary tilted her head and smiled sadly. "That could be it."

"Or?"

Mary bit her nail. "I don't know. Part of me thinks he has news?"

"Like what?"

Mary shook her head and shrugged.

"Well, whatever it is, we should just be excited he's coming."

"Yeah . . . It's just that you know how it can be between you two."

Gemma's first clear memory of Eddie was the day he tried out for the varsity football team. Which was the same day she broke her collarbone. She was five years old, and for the next thirty years she'd keep revisiting the memory of being in those hot bleachers, because she was certain it was when things between her and Eddie turned.

"I think if I just didn't come on so strong, or was just less, I dunno, annoying? Maybe we could get along better than we have in the past."

"Is this the best time for you to be 'less annoying'?" Mary asked.

Gemma rolled her eyes. Even when Mary was the one who brought him up, she often deflected conversations about Eddie. For years, when Gemma tried to talk to Mary about the day of football tryouts, Mary would either clam up or laugh it off. Gemma shifted her gaze downward before lifting her eyes to the window and focusing on the ginkgo tree she and Anthony had planted when they moved in. She watched the leaves blow gently in the breeze and thought back to the last time she had seen Eddie. It was a few years after she married Anthony—and before Bo was born—that she spoke to Eddie on a FaceTime call. He had called to congratulate her on graduating with her doctorate. And though he did text her right after Bo was born, more of an acknowledgment than congratulations, she hadn't spoken to him since. As far as she knew, he had the same dynamic with their parents and Mary. But she never confirmed that because they never collectively talked about Eddie—a habit the family had seemingly agreed to thirty years ago.

"Gemma," Mary said, reaching a hand out to her across the table. "I'm just afraid this is all too much, and you need to focus on Calvin right now."

Gemma slowly pushed her chair back and stood up. "You don't think I know where to put my focus?"

"No, no. That's not what I mean. It's more that I'm just confused what Eddie's motivations are."

"Geez, Mary, he's not a defendant in one of your trials. Maybe Eddie just misses me. Wants to meet my kids. Is that such an insane motivation for our brother to have?"

Mary was quiet for a minute. "No. I guess not."

"Are you and Mom and Dad just mad that he reached out to me and not you all? That after decades of ignoring me, he's finally paying attention to me, and it what—? Makes you all jealous?"

"We aren't jealous, Gemma."

"Oh, I'll bet it's driving you all a little crazy that I know more about Eddie's visit than any of you."

"You don't think it's odd? Him contacting only you? Wanting to stay with you?"

Gemma took in a big breath. Of course it was odd. Even though Eddie was distant with everyone in the family, he was especially so with Gemma. He would text Mary somewhat frequently. They even spoke on the phone with some regularity. He talked with their parents every other month or so. But yes, he and Gemma rarely spoke. It had been that way since the day of his football tryouts.

"Well, perhaps everyone could be a little less interested in understanding Eddie's reason for visiting now and instead call him out for never showing up in the first place. Why does no one schedule a conference call to talk about how Eddie never participates in this family?" Gemma walked back into the kitchen without a real plan for what to do once she was in there.

Mary followed her in a few seconds later. "This is kind of what I'm trying to say, Gem. We can't control Eddie."

"No shit," Gemma said under her breath, her head deep in the fridge, needlessly moving jars around.

"And there's no telling how he's going to be this trip."

Gemma stood up straight, closed the fridge door, and spun around to face Mary. "Ah, okay. I get it. Everyone's worried I'm going to fuck this up somehow."

"That's exactly the opposite of what I'm saying." Mary's voice was pleading. "I'm saying since we *can't* know why Eddie is coming or what he's going to be like, maybe he should stay with me."

"He asked to stay with me." As she said it, Gemma felt like a petulant child refusing to share a toy.

"Yeah, I know he did," Mary said, as if she knew something further.

Gemma got a sinking feeling that she was about to be surprised. "What? What don't I know?"

"Nothing, Gemma. Not a thing. We are all just a little surprised he asked to stay with you. And we are worried about it."

"Damn, Mary."

Gemma hated the feeling of being left out of a conversation, or worse, being talked about behind her back. When she was first dating Anthony, her mother had been concerned about how quiet he was. She texted Mary, who confessed this to Gemma. Gemma still felt the betrayal from that. And now, despite her best efforts, she was always hyperaware of how much, or how little, Anthony talked when they were with the McAlisters.

"What?" Mary's eyes and tone were softer.

"You all discussed, behind my back, the level to which you are surprised my own brother would want to stay with me so he can spend time with me and meet—*finally* meet—my children?"

"Yeah, Gemma." Mary shrugged as she held Gemma's gaze for a beat. "I guess we did."

Gemma nervously shifted her weight back and forth on her feet, uncomfortably aware that she needed to change her pad again. "And so, what? What did you and the planning committee decide is behind this?"

"Gemma, this isn't a conspiracy *against* you. It's a family in support *of* you."

"Funny how everyone likes to support me behind my back, but never to my face."

"It wasn't a planned call. I told you that! Did you want me to patch you in while you were on bed rest to talk about Eddie's visit?"

"Why not!? That's when Eddie called!"

"Right!" Mary shot back, but then stopped before saying again, lower, "Right."

"What?"

"I dunno, Gemma. The stakes are just so high because Bo and Calvin are involved, and frankly, I'm afraid the kids are a good excuse to see Eddie and forget all that could go wrong."

"Oh, I see," Gemma said softly. "I'm a mother who uses her kids to manipulate others."

Mary crossed her arms. "That's not what I said. Why are you so determined to take offense at everything I'm saying?"

Gemma sighed. "You're right. I don't know. I think I'm just tired."

"Of course you are!"

"And I'm excited to see Eddie. It's so hard to be excited and exhausted at the same time."

"That's all I'm getting at."

Gemma nodded.

"Gemma, you're a great mother. And you're a proud mother. And of course you would want Eddie to meet your kids."

"His nephews."

"His nephews, yes. But I can also see how your optimism could leave you wide open for heartbreak."

Gemma exhaled. She knew Mary had a point, which just made her all the madder. Mary always had a point, always saw the logical progression of situations rather than their emotional core. That logic had made Mary one of the top litigators in the region. Maybe even all of Indiana. Gemma was only vaguely aware of what kind of law Mary practiced, but she did know that Mary made more money than she and Anthony combined. Gemma was so proud of her sister's success—never jealous, despite how prone to jealousy she was. She believed her feelings for Mary were so pure because the two of them were very different. It wasn't as if Gemma had a mind for the law. And she knew Mary absolutely did not have a mind for human emotions. Gemma had chosen her profession because it steered deep into the very thing her family seemed to struggle with—*feelings*. In most interactions with her family, Gemma displayed wild emotions in contrast to their indifference. She hated how loud, or emotional, or unhinged she felt compared to them—but it was a compulsion of hers. The more logical or aloof they became, the more Gemma would spin out.

Even now, in this moment, Mary was playing out the logic of Eddie's visit. *Gemma just gave birth, birth is hard, Gemma is tired. Gemma should not be hosting Eddie. Eddie is arriving without us knowing why, or what he wants. Party of the first part, party of the second part, and all the* whys *and* wherefores.

And the more Mary pressed on that, the more Gemma felt herself escalating. As if she needed to defend Eddie's choice to stay with her. To prove she and Eddie were fine. Close even. Gemma simply didn't care about the logic of it. It's not that she didn't understand it, of course. She knew that most women probably wouldn't try hosting their estranged brother, and his wife, four days after giving birth. But Gemma was different. She knew how to sink the pain and tiredness down deep so she could show up and show off. And what Eddie had done, or how he had behaved in the past, didn't matter. It had never mattered. Gemma knew she was a puppy when it came to her desperate need for his attention and affection. And sometimes, merely his acknowledgment. Sure, Eddie had always been what Anthony referred to as "bemusedly removed" from the entire McAlister family. Somehow away and above the four of them, and only mildly interested in how all their lives were playing out. But that left Gemma craving her brother's interest all the more.

"Look," Mary said, her voice softening, "I just know he upsets you. And I know how badly you want this to go well—how much you want any interaction between you and Eddie to go well." Her eyes scanned Gemma's face. "But I also know that there are three people who are in line *ahead* of Eddie for your attention."

Gemma nodded while she wiped away the tears that were slowly streaking her cheeks.

"See?" Mary said, wrapping her arms around Gemma. "This is what I'm worried about."

"But *you're* the one making me cry." Gemma sniffed.

Mary laughed. "Fair enough, Gem."

With Mary's arms around her, Gemma gave in and rested her cheek on her sister's shoulder, her arms hanging at her sides. "I just want him to know my kids," she whispered.

"I know, I know," Mary whispered back. "But you also want him to know *you*."

Gemma took in a big breath of air through her nose before stepping out of Mary's embrace and looking at her with a smile.

Mary put her hands on Gemma's shoulders. "We good?"

Gemma shrugged and nodded her head. Just as the tension began to lift between the sisters, the chime of the doorbell reverberated through the house. Upstairs, a startled but quiet cry escaped Calvin's lips, raced out of the nursery, down the stairs, around the corner, through the living room and past Bo's pileup of cars, and into the kitchen, and landed deep within Gemma's ears, a sound so faint only a mother would detect it.

"Dammit!" Gemma cried out. "What assholes ring the doorbell knowing there's a newborn inside?!"

Mary patted Gemma once on the shoulder. "Our parents. That's who."

CHAPTER 3

Gemma felt the cold, sharp edge of her mother's pendant earring against her cheek. Irene McAlister was known for her earrings. As a handmade jewelry designer, her top-selling item, which shipped all over the country, was a pair of copper and tourmaline earrings. Not only did she have a shop in downtown Bloomington where she sold her highly coveted earrings (and necklaces, bracelets, and rings), but she also had hundreds of pairs packed inside four standing jewelry boxes lined across the far wall of the bedroom she and Gemma's father, Jack, had shared for fifty years. During Anthony and Gemma's fourth date—a night that ended in glorious, spontaneous, lusty sex on the floor of his small apartment kitchen—she told him that if he ever met her mother, he would notice the earrings first. "So, I'll be meeting your parents, huh?" he had asked, breathing heavily, as they sprawled naked on the cold tile floor.

"It's looking likely," Gemma had said, throwing her arm across his chest.

"What about these earrings is so special?"

"Oh, you'll see. I'd hate to ruin the surprise."

Now here was Irene, standing in the doorway, embracing

her younger daughter so tightly that her earrings were digging into the side of Gemma's face. They were emerald green, with a sparkly stud that attached to a hammered-copper V adorned on the bottom with tassels made of tiny gold chains. They went perfectly with her cream-colored turtleneck. And her turtleneck—worn in summer, no less—perfectly accentuated Irene's long, slender neck and sharp blond pixie cut, a look only a few famous actresses, and Irene McAlister, could make sexy. Irene was a sight, for sure. Her beauty was startling to everyone Gemma introduced her to. But Anthony hadn't seemed thrown by it. When he met Irene for the first time, about three months after the sweaty kitchen encounter, he looked at her as if she were just any other woman. He didn't seem shocked or entranced or beguiled by Irene's long, lanky body; her platinum hair, slender neck, and sharp chin; or her perfectly symmetrical face. He was polite, of course, and even hugged her. But his face didn't contort into the usual face of those seeing Irene for the first time. In that moment, Gemma had decided she would marry Anthony.

As their embrace broke, Irene said, "All right, now give me that baby!"

Gemma opened the door wider and moved her body to clear a pathway to the stairs. "He's awake now, so he's all yours." With her purse still over her shoulder, Irene grabbed Mary's hand and they ascended the stairs like lionesses on the hunt.

"Don't you just feel like chopped liver?" Jack asked, still standing on the threshold as Gemma pulled him into a hug.

Jack was a beast of a man. Broad shoulders, square jaw. Stoic. He almost always wore a hat of some kind, for many years simply a part of his look, now an excellent cover for his receding hairline. Today it was an Indiana University ball cap. Gemma liked his sports hats best. They made him look much more approachable. Casual even. And Jack was the antithesis of casual. Like Mary, he was a lawyer. Mary was a partner at the firm Jack started. But while Mary was the kind of lawyer that mostly settled disputes in large boardrooms, Jack was the very intimidating kind that took on major cases, often landing him in televised courtrooms.

Gemma had long wished she had gotten Jack's height and strong jawline, or her mother's metabolism and delicate features. But alas, all those characteristics had gone to Eddie and Mary; by the time Gemma came along, Jack and Irene's genes had given enough of themselves. Gemma often thought she looked nothing like her parents. She even worried others thought that as well. But when Jack, Irene, and Gemma were side by side in shorts, it was obvious Gemma's knees and feet came from her father, and her freckly, sunburn-prone skin from her mother. *Of all the features to get,* Gemma would grumble to herself every summer.

Jack kept his cap on as he stepped into the living room, slowly scanning the space before looking back at Gemma. Though he didn't ask where Bo was, Gemma knew that's what he was wondering. This was how her father communicated: with grunts, groans, and looks. Gemma loved that she was the only one in the family to speak this language. Irene would roll her eyes and raise her voice an octave: "What, Jack? What do you need?!" But Gemma always seemed to know instinctively what Jack meant. A small, secret language that they alone spoke made her feel special.

"Bo's around here somewhere," she said. "He might be upstairs with Gram."

Jack nodded once and then looked back at her with the slightest of head tilts.

"I'm fine, Dad." She smiled. "Just a little tired. They say giving birth is easier the second time around. And it was. But the exhaustion is the same."

Jack nodded.

"You hungry? Can I get you a drink?" Gemma asked.

Jack shifted his body to better see the dining room table covered with food.

"Beer? Scotch?" Gemma probed.

"Just water," he responded as Irene descended the stairs with Mary. Calvin was wrapped up tightly in Irene's arms, and Bo was chatting enthusiastically to Mary from the comfort of her left hip.

As if just then coming alive, Jack clapped once. "There's my boy!"

"Gramps!" Bo shouted, wriggling out of Mary's arms when she reached the bottom step. He ran to Jack and jumped into his arms, then grabbed the bill of Jack's cap and twisted it back and forth across his forehead. Jack laughed, and the crinkles around his eyes exposed themselves, betraying his age.

"Oh Gemma, this food looks great!" exclaimed Irene as she carried the baby into the dining room. "Did we decide against cold cuts?"

Gemma and Mary exchanged a look they had shared endless times before. There was always something Gemma could have done better. "Anthony's bringing the tray," Gemma said.

"Oh! Right! Where *is* Anthony?" Irene asked, her free hand, its long, thin fingers jeweled with rings, landing on her chest dramatically.

"He went to pick up Eddie and Kat from the airport," Mary responded.

"Oh! Good. Flying is exhausting. I'd hate for them to have to take an Uber," Irene said.

"Why don't you all move to the couch," Gemma said, gesturing. "I need to excuse myself for just a minute." She left Mary, Irene, and Jack to wander slowly into the living room.

As Gemma climbed the stairs, she could feel a dribble of moisture seeping down her leg. She tried to squeeze her thighs tighter together as she climbed, but her heart started to pound. She couldn't ruin her dress. Her mind raced through her closet. What else could go with this scarf, sandals, and earrings? She realized that nothing else in her closet would work. She was so misshapen right now. Her stomach was too flappy for anything formfitting. Pants were out of the question. She shook her head slightly to muster her resolve. She would assess the damage in the bathroom and make it work. She had no other option.

Just as she predicted, blood was seeping out of the pad and had created a Rorschach effect on her thighs. She worked quickly, dabbing toilet paper with water and scrubbing. "Dammit!" she whispered, sweating. She could tell the front of her dress was now stained. "Jesus," she spit angrily. She lifted the infinity scarf over her head and hung it on the hook on the back of the door. Then she did the same with her dress. She could get the stain out. She just had to think about the steps. *Okay, you're okay, you're okay. You can do this,* she said to herself. She placed her hands on either side of the sink, balanced herself, and closed her eyes. *Okay. First, change your pad. Then spot clean the dress. Next, get the hairdryer out and dry the wet spot. Put the dress back on, then the scarf. You're fine. You're okay. No one will be the wiser.*

As she opened her eyes, she looked at herself in the mirror. Her eyes were dull, but her skin was surprisingly clear. Her hair still looked good—her mother hadn't said anything about it, which had been a relief—and her makeup was still visible. With the intensity and precision of a soldier shining boots in the barracks, she executed the necessary steps. When she was done, she reassessed herself in the mirror, adjusting the infinity scarf just so. She was overcome with a pain down low in her gut. *I really need to take a shit.* She leaned forward slightly, fists clenched, and eyes closed. She took three big breaths. The pain subsided with a low bellow from deep within her bowels. *Okay, all good now.* And with that, she opened the door, turned the corner of her bedroom, and walked back down the stairs.

In the living room, Jack and Mary sat on the couch with Bo between them. Gemma couldn't help but smile at how much the two of them doted on Bo. The first grandkid was truly be-loved, and he knew it. He was showing Mary his latest car—a present Gemma and Anthony had given him before heading to the hospital days earlier. Gemma took a seat in the chair adja-cent to the low-slung armless chair Irene had sunk into with Calvin. She was giving him a bottle.

"Aren't you so glad you didn't even try to breastfeed?" Irene asked without looking up.

Gemma smiled slightly, the swelling in her breasts still throbbing faintly. "Yes, that way *you* can feed him."

Irene turned her head to look at Gemma, probably to check that she was joking and not in tears. "Exactly!" she said. "No one should feed this child except Grammy!"

"Challenge accepted," Gemma said lightly.

Irene shifted her body around to face Gemma. "This chair," Irene fussed as she worked her body without the ability to use her hands.

"Is my favorite piece of furniture in the house," Gemma said.

"It's just so cushy. I feel like I'm sitting in a bed!"

"That's the point, Mom."

"Well, a chair without arms and a seat this deep *is* a bed."

"Anyway . . . ," Gemma said, hoping to end the most recent of many complaints Irene had about Gemma's choice in home decor.

"Fine, fine," Irene said, gazing at Calvin, who was dozing off with the bottle in his mouth. "I cannot believe how much he looks like you."

Gemma beamed. It was true. The moment he emerged and the doctor held him up for her to see, both she and Anthony audibly gasped. It was as if she were looking in a mirror. Mostly, the nose and lips. They were Gemma's, without question. The tiniest button nose ever to grace a face, a thin upper lip, and an overly puffed bottom one. This had always made Gemma look much younger than she was, but it had also made Gemma cute—not beautiful, certainly not sexy, but cute.

"But was my head that big and round as a baby?"

"Oh dear, that was twenty-five years ago!"

"Thirty-five."

"Well, whatever. Yes, I remember you were hairless for two years, so it might not have been that your head was so round and big as much as it was just, well, *visible*." And she threw her head back in laughter.

"Maybe that's it," Gemma said, tilting her head to the side as she looked at her baby. "He just doesn't have hair. . . ."

"Bo came out already needing a haircut!" Irene trilled.

Gemma laughed. Bo had been born with so much hair it surprised her. "That explains all the heartburn," she had said when the doctor placed him in her arms for the first time.

"That's a myth, Gemma," the doctor said.

"Give me this, doc," she had replied. "I need a reason to forgive him."

Irene gently took the bottle out of Calvin's slack mouth, set it beside the chair, and adjusted him in her arms. "I see you haven't put the bumpers on the coffee table yet," she said, looking at the large white square table between herself and the couch. Gemma held her breath. She compulsively did this when she felt criticized. "Jack, help Gemma put those bumpers we got her on the coffee table."

Jack looked up from Bo and lifted his eyebrows. Gemma knew this look to mean he needed what had been said to him repeated. "She wants you to do something I should have already done," Gemma said flatly.

"No, no, no." Irene shook her head at Gemma. "I'm trying

to help you out." She turned back to Jack. "Get those bumpers we got her and let's put them on before Eddie gets here."

"Ah, worried Eddie will bump his head?" Gemma quipped, which made Mary laugh.

"No, Gemma," Irene said in a serious tone. "I'm worried about Bo getting hurt."

"Of course, of course." Gemma sighed. "You know, he'll be six in February and has never hurt himself on those corners yet."

Irene ignored Gemma's comment. "Where did you put those bumpers, anyway?"

Gemma looked at Mary, who was back engaged with Bo. She looked at her father, who was gazing at her with an expectant look. She tilted her head down a beat before standing, slowly. "I don't know where Anthony put them. Most likely in the basement."

"Okay," Irene said, looking pointedly at Gemma. "Do you want your dad to help you find them?"

"Anthony will be here any minute. Do we really want to mess with that right now?" Gemma asked, her voice more pleading than she would have hoped.

"It will only take a minute," Irene insisted, looking at Jack and jerking her head toward the basement door. "They have adhesive on the back, so you just peel off the paper and stick them on. Two minutes, tops."

Gemma looked at her mom for a measure, unaware she was holding her breath. "Okay." She rose and Jack mirrored her, following quietly behind her to the basement door and down the stairs.

"It will make her feel better," Jack offered in what Gemma took to be a response to a comment she hadn't made.

Gemma shrugged as she opened the closet door at the base of the steps. She pulled an overhead chain, and a dim light flicked on. Her eyes scanned the crowded shelves before relaxing when they landed on two boxes up high. Without saying anything, she stepped out of the closet and pointed up. Her father nodded once and, without even having to extend his arm fully, pulled them off the shelf.

They looked at each other and Jack started laughing. Gemma did too, their unspoken language fluently communicating so much.

"Oh good!" Irene chirped as Jack emerged from the basement carrying the two boxes. "I also think you should do this edge," she said, pointing to the brick hearth that surrounded the fireplace. It was the perfect height to serve as additional seating when Anthony and Gemma had friends over. "These bricks are even sharper than the coffee table!" she exclaimed, reaching her hand down the side of the armless chair and inspecting the hearth.

Jack looked at Gemma, and she knew he was awaiting her go-ahead. Despite how deeply aligned Jack was with Irene, he was also always on Gemma's side in a quiet way that she appreciated.

Before Gemma could nod back in response, she heard a car pulling into the driveway. All the McAlisters reacted to the sound. Gemma was shocked to see how quickly her mother lifted herself up and out of the cushy chair without disturbing Calvin in her arms.

She strode toward Gemma to hand off the baby. "Eddie's here!"

Gemma brought Calvin close to her body in a movement that was less to comfort him and more to steel herself for whatever was coming next. She felt a touch on her elbow. She turned to see her father beside her with one of the boxes still in his hand.

She smiled at him. "Those edges have waited years. What's one more day?"

He looked toward the window where they could see

Anthony's, Kat's, and Eddie's feet sliding out from under the open car doors. He looked back at Gemma, smiled, and gave a subtle wink. A wink that gave Gemma the strength to take her first step toward the front door.

CHAPTER 4

Gemma's breath always caught in her throat when she saw them together. They were a striking couple, both tall, both well above average in looks. Such a beautiful contrast in their skin tones—Kat's dark-brown, Eddie's pink and pale—and both always with their chins raised ever so slightly. She noticed Eddie's dark waves had grown out and were halfway down his neck. And he had grown a beard. Kat's microbraids were twisted up into a high topknot with a teal scarf secured around it. These two would have been intimidating to anyone, but there was something particularly tricky for Gemma about Kat—an unreadable, aloof woman who held the keys to the wall around Eddie. Keys she seemed uninterested in letting any of the McAlisters have a copy of.

For the briefest moment, Gemma forgot she was holding a newborn baby, *her* newborn baby. She was walking zombielike toward the front door, her eyes like lasers on the front window, watching Eddie and Kat move around the car, unloading luggage. Seeing Eddie and Kat together always amazed Gemma. The attention and affection Eddie showed his wife looked so natural from a distance. But Gemma didn't know what it felt like up close—what it was like to experience Eddie's focus, his acts of love.

Gemma was snapped back into the moment, back into acknowledging Calvin in her arms, when Jack put a hand on her shoulder. She flinched before realizing he was prompting her to walk a bit faster toward the door. Mary and Irene—holding Bo's hand—were already outside, rushing to Eddie's side. Everyone was rushing out to Eddie like the ducks at the pond ran to Bo when Gemma let him throw them grains. Gemma moved her body so slightly that only her father would have noticed, so he seized the opportunity to step around her and out the door. This left Gemma just inside, peering out, watching her mother introduce Bo to her brother for the very first time. Her eyes went hot. *She didn't mean to steal the moment,* Gemma thought. *She just rushed out in her excitement.* Gemma moved Calvin to her left arm, her right arm tingling from having held the same position for so long. The numbness extended to her fingertips as she pushed the glass door open. She stepped out into the Indiana afternoon, making eye contact with Kat, who nodded once before placing her arm around Eddie's lower back.

At Kat's touch, Eddie jerked his head up to meet Gemma's gaze. "Well, there she is!" he exclaimed, setting down his bag and walking up the brick path to embrace Gemma. She put her tingling right arm around him as he squeezed her tight. She didn't even think about how it might be squishing Calvin's face until they broke their embrace and she glanced down to see him opening his mouth as if for air.

"How was your flight?" Gemma asked more loudly than she intended as she patted the baby's chest in an apology.

"Good, good." He nodded, looking down at his feet, a tic of their father's. "So, this is the new guy, huh?" he said, smiling with one side of his mouth as he stroked Calvin's bare head.

"Yep, this is Calvin," Gemma said, not taking her eyes off Eddie. "And I see you met Bo."

"Yeah, that's a really cute kid there, Gem," he said, looking over his shoulder at Bo, who had crawled up onto Mary's hip. It was only then that Gemma noticed Mary, Irene, Jack, Kat, and Anthony were all lined up in a row beside the car, watching her and Eddie. After a beat, Jack cleared his throat, which made everyone else start moving again.

Anthony caught Gemma's gaze and mouthed, "You okay?" Gemma nodded slightly and smiled. Anthony was attentive during moments like these, although he also seemed to disappear, fading into the background when all the McAlisters were together. And it didn't matter how much she recognized it and tried to make it less so the *next* time, the outcome was always the same. Anthony receded into the background while the McAlisters talked, gossiped, laughed, and generally took over any space they were in. Gemma wanted Anthony to join them. "Be a McAlister!" she'd joke afterward. "I'm a Sinclair," he'd retort with a grin. "And lest you forget, so are you."

As Gemma watched Anthony continue to help with the luggage, only then taking inventory of just how many bags there were, she saw Kat approaching.

"Nice work making these humans," she said flatly, even though she was smiling.

"Hi Kat!" Gemma exclaimed. "I love your shirt." She cursed herself. *You're pathetic, Gemma.*

Kat frowned and looked down at the cropped white silk shirt she was wearing—a shirt that no woman with children could ever wear, not with all the snot and spaghetti that would inevitably end up there—and said, "This? Thanks, I've had it forever."

"Well, it's beautiful," Gemma said too quickly in response. "How's life in Boston?"

"Busy!" Kat sighed with a laugh. "And with how much I'm gone, it's more of a home base than a home."

"I can't imagine," Gemma said, truly struggling to imagine what Kat's life was like. She vaguely knew that Kat did something in consulting that took her around the world, but Gemma had never gotten a good read on what that meant or where specifically she went. "Let's get you both inside! I've got lots of food and drinks in there!" She turned, opened the glass door, and went back inside, her lower belly gripped like a tight fist, desperate for release. *Nope,* Gemma thought to her bowels. *Not a chance.*

Once inside, Irene did what she did best—took over. "Gemma, hon," she called from the kitchen. "Did you happen to grab any of the craft beer Eddie loves?"

"Yep! I'll come get it!" Gemma hollered from the living room, where she was laying Calvin down in the pack and play they had received as a gift from Anthony's parents when Bo was born.

"No need, dear, just tell me where it is! I can't find a thing in this fridge of yours!"

Anthony was halfway through the front door, juggling all the luggage, but he caught Irene's biting comment. Gemma saw him roll his eyes and narrowed hers at him. He saw her catch him and shrugged, mouthing "I'm a Sinclair" before dropping all the bags in a pile at the base of the stairs.

"Anthony," Gemma said after tucking a blanket under Calvin's feet. "Can you go down to the basement and get the beer I bought?" He nodded once and swiftly walked toward the basement door.

"Nice house, Gemma," Kat said as her head turned slowly in all directions, admiring the professionally framed pictures, crisp and colorful curtains, and cushy throw pillows.

"Thanks!" Gemma said, happy to be momentarily free of her baby. She didn't even wonder where Bo was. It was one of the nice things about having family over: her anxiety about where Bo was at all times was tempered by the number of eyes on him. "Would you and Eddie like a tour?"

Kat looked toward Eddie, who smiled. "Sure thing. But let's wait on Tony to come back up with the beer," he said with a wink.

Anthony hated being called Tony. And he especially hated that Eddie called him that. But Gemma insisted that because they'd never corrected Eddie early on, it was too awkward to do it now. As if on cue, Anthony emerged from the basement carrying the necks of four beers between his fingers. Irene came around the corner just in time to intercept Anthony, extract the bottles from his grasp, duck back into the kitchen to open one, then round the corner again to deliver Eddie his. The rest were left unopened on the counter.

"Eddie," Irene cooed, "you must be hungry. Why don't you come make a plate of food?" She pushed softly on Eddie's lower back, guiding him into the dining room. The tour would have to wait, it seemed.

Gemma followed Irene, Eddie, and Kat into the dining room, surprised and softened to see that Anthony had brought in the deli tray, without her even noticing, and arranged it with the other platters in such a way that Mary's symmetry somehow remained intact. He had even removed and discarded the plastic lid. She made a mental note to thank him for that later. Mary and Bo were sitting at the bench beneath the windows in the dining room, and Jack, she could only assume, was in the bathroom. For a moment, Gemma felt herself relax. Everyone seemed in good spirits. Eddie had given her what felt like a heartier than normal embrace. Anthony didn't seem resentful, though Gemma knew that could still come later. Mary was managing Bo well. Calvin was sleeping in the other room. *I knew it,* Gemma thought. *Everyone was worried for nothing.*

———

By early evening, Gemma felt almost giddy. After filling their plates in the dining room, everyone had moved back to the living room, Eddie and Kat opting for the big, armless chair her mother hated.

"Damn, this thing is awesome!" Eddie had said as he sank into it. "And it gives such easy access to my beer, which I can put right here on this handy hearth." He smiled, acting out just that, before reclining back in the seat and allowing Kat to nestle in against him. The conversation among the seven of them wove in and out of the usual family fodder—weather, travel, politics, and sports. Gemma told stories of Bo's adventures, Mary talked of her latest case, Irene complained about the rising cost of gold, Kat mentioned that her latest consulting client would be taking her to Prague, and Anthony and Jack did what they always did, stayed engaged but quiet. Gemma had excused herself once to change diapers—hers and Calvin's—and once to get a bottle—hers and Calvin's. If Eddie had news, he hadn't shared it. This confirmed to Gemma he was just there to be with her.

As the living room was blanketed in gloom from the darkening sky outside, Jack looked at his watch and cleared his throat. Instinctively, every McAlister stood up, turning to each other for hugs. "I know Gemma's going to need to get her boys some dinner," Irene said, narrating what was already known. "So, we are going to go."

Mary gave Eddie a soft punch on the shoulder. "Will I see you after the marathon?"

"Nah, we're going to go straight from Indy back home."

"Oh," Irene said. "You aren't coming back through town?"

Eddie shook his head and looked down. "Kat has a thing, and we need to get back."

"Well," Jack said, as if to stop the discussion, "great seeing you both."

"Yes, always nice to see you, Jack," Kat said, extending her arms for a hug.

"I'm going to order that book you suggested," Jack said as he patted Kat's back in their embrace.

"And I'll text you the link to that interview with the author. Fascinating."

Jack nodded as Mary stepped in to hug Kat. "Have fun watching the run. Let us know how he does."

Kat nodded, moving toward Irene to hug her. "I will, I will."

The McAlisters shuffled slowly together—a shoal of fish—toward the front door. It always seemed to take hours, as each member said goodbye to one another; additional hugs were given; Mary tickled Bo one more time; Irene reminded Gemma, yet again, how best to store the deli meats; Jack fist-bumped Anthony; Eddie put his arm around Mary and squeezed her roughly; and on and on until finally Irene, Jack, and Mary were officially over the threshold and Gemma was able to close and lock the door behind them.

She turned around to find Eddie back in the chair, Kat looking intently at her phone, Anthony holding Calvin, and Bo back to playing with his cars on the floor.

"So?" Eddie asked. "Should we catch a movie?"

Gemma laughed out loud, as did Anthony, before they realized Eddie wasn't kidding.

Kat looked up from her phone, pointing at the screen. "There's a film on honey extraction down at a place called The Crest."

Of course she'd mention a documentary, Gemma thought, *and of course it would be playing at the only independent movie theater in town. Do these people ever allow themselves the joy of Michael Bay and Junior Mints?* Gemma looked at Anthony, at a loss as to what to say.

"Well," Anthony started. "If you all want to go, I can stay with the kids."

Gemma's heart quickened with excitement at the thought of getting out of the house and just being with her brother—even if Kat was there too.

Eddie's brow furrowed. "The movie isn't R-rated or anything."

Anthony opened his mouth to respond, but Gemma interjected. "Oh, of course. It sounds fascinating."

"And I would imagine being exposed to this type of film would be good for Bo," Kat pitched in, taking a seat next to Eddie.

"Right," Gemma said, trying hard to make sure her face wasn't wearing an expression that could be interpreted as combative. "It's just that Bo isn't to where he can sit through a movie. He's still too young to last very long."

"Well how long do you think he *could* last?" Eddie pressed.

Gemma felt her chest tighten. Eddie's tone made it seem like he was getting frustrated. *Does he know other kids Bo's age who* can *sit through a movie?*

"Look," Anthony said in a commanding voice that startled Gemma. "Bo goes to bed at seven thirty." He glanced down at his watch before adding, "That's an hour from now. I think it's best if we just get some dinner—if you two are even hungry—before we have to start getting the kids to bed."

Gemma felt a flash of anger at Anthony.

"Or, like Anthony said, we can go, and he can stay here," she stammered. Anthony frowned in confusion for a beat before shrugging.

"You go to bed at seven thirty?" Eddie asked in Bo's direction.

"Yeah, but I don't fall asleep then!" Bo exclaimed, making everyone laugh.

"So he *could* stay up later?" Eddie asked in a tone that Gemma felt was pointed.

"Gemma is strict about their bedtimes, so—" Anthony said before Gemma cut him off.

"I'm not strict," she said. "I just have Bo on this schedule that helps keep the tantrums milder. The more sleep he gets, the better behaved he is during the day."

Eddie looked at Gemma and then over to Anthony and raised his eyebrows. "Well, alright then." He smiled and grabbed his beer off the fireplace ledge. "No movie."

"But you all can go see it if you want!" Gemma added eagerly, trying to fix what felt like the night crumbling.

"How about we get our stuff upstairs to our room and get settled in?" Kat suggested, before patting Eddie's leg once and standing. "Then we can figure out what we're going to do tonight."

"Oh," Gemma said. "We're happy to just hang out here with you."

Kat and Eddie looked at each other. "Well," Eddie said, "we wanted to visit some of our friends tonight. Go see Mark and Lori and their kids. We haven't seen them since Christmas."

"Hold up," Anthony said with a hint of annoyance in his voice. "Were you going to do that after the movies? Or were they coming with us?"

Gemma laughed nervously, swatting a hand in Anthony's direction. "Sure, yes, I can see why you'd want to go see them. How are the twins, anyway? They must be, what, twelve now?"

"Twelve on February eleventh," Eddie said, sinking Gemma's stomach. He'd never called Bo on his birthday. Anthony was convinced he didn't know when it was.

"But Mark is going to the run with you tomorrow, right?" Anthony pressed. Gemma shot him a look, but he seemed to ignore it.

"Yep," Eddie said, looking at Anthony as if to challenge him. They stared at each other a beat longer before Kat interrupted. "Eddie, let's go upstairs and get settled."

Eddie stood, put his empty beer bottle down on the table, and walked over and grabbed their bags. "Which room?" he asked.

"Top of the stairs, first door to the left," Gemma said.

She watched the two ascend, her bowels clenching in a knot so painful she had to gasp for air.

CHAPTER 5

Gemma was lying on her back across their bed when Anthony walked in.

"How you holding up?" he asked, stretching out on his stomach next to her.

"I'm fine," she said, not taking her eyes off the crack in the ceiling.

Anthony studied her face. "Are you mad at me?"

Gemma jerked her head toward him. "Nope. Just frustrated."

Anthony pulled his body up to sit. "What did I do?"

"You were so weird about Eddie and Kat wanting to go to the movies," she said, working slowly to lift her own body, ever mindful of blood seeping and stitches pulling.

"No I wasn't, Gemma," he said flatly. "He was being ridiculous. He wanted us to take a five-year-old and a *newborn baby* downtown to watch a documentary?"

"They don't have kids. Don't blame him for not knowing that's difficult for children."

"But he *was* a child, right?" Anthony asked, his hand sweeping through his hair. "Did he enjoy documentaries when *he* was five?"

Gemma stared at him for a second before bursting into laughter. Her laugh overtook her; it was the first time she'd laughed, truly laughed, since going into labor. Her loose belly shook so hard she grabbed her torso to stabilize it. Anthony, who could never resist his wife's laugh, abandoned his own stern expression and joined her with his trademark chuckle, the air escaping his nose sounding like a horse whinnying.

"Oh . . . ," Gemma said, catching her breath as she wiped a tear from her left eye. "Yeah, what a fucking idiotic request. . . ." And she laughed all over again.

When they finally stopped laughing, Gemma's face got serious. "I'm sorry. I didn't mean to be weird or frustrated at you. It's just . . . I just feel . . ." She trailed off.

"Tired? Sore? Emotional? Insane?" Anthony offered with a smile.

Gemma smiled back weakly. "Desperate, actually."

Anthony's face twisted as it did when he was either confused or disgusted. Gemma wondered which one he was. Probably both.

"Desperate how?"

"I shouldn't have said that. I just want this to go well. Mom and Dad and Mary are so curious why he's here and can't fathom it's just to see me. To meet the kids," she said, fingering the flap of her pillowcase. "I just want everything to be perfect."

"Gemma. You just had a baby. Eddie's an adult. I need you to take care of yourself right now."

"I am. I'm fine. You know how rarely I see him, and even though the timing isn't ideal, I want to make the most of it."

Anthony opened his mouth to say something but then seemed to change his mind.

"I know you don't like him," Gemma said quietly.

"It's not that I don't like him," Anthony said, shaking his head. "But the guy is awfully self-centered."

"No he isn't."

"He's here four days after you gave birth and hasn't asked you a single question."

Gemma frowned. "That's not true!" she protested, her mind racing over the afternoon's conversation, searching for a question Eddie asked her.

"Yes, it is, Gemma," Anthony said. "We spent two hours giving them food and craft beer—which you bought when you should have been resting—and listening to him and Kat talk about all their travels and work stories. But he didn't ask one question about your job. Or Bo. Or me. Or about you *giving birth*."

Gemma turned her head toward the window and exhaled a long breath.

"Gemma, I'm not trying to upset you. I'm just saying, don't bend over backward for him right now. Or ever, really . . . ," he added, his voice fading.

"I think sibling dynamics are lost on you as an only child," Gemma finally said, turning back to him.

Anthony's gaze fell to his hands. Gemma watched as his face seemed to reflect several thoughts before settling into a neutral expression.

"Okay," he said. "You're right. This is your family. I'm just protective of you." He reached a hand across the mattress to grab hers. She squeezed back, but as she opened her mouth to respond, there were three firm knocks on their bedroom door. Gemma and Anthony looked at each other, confused. Anthony got up and opened the door to see Kat standing in the hall.

"Hi," she said with a pained expression on her face. "The baby is crying."

His name is Calvin, Gemma thought, annoyed. "Oh, okay!" she said, rising slowly from the bed. "I'll come get him. It's time for his next bottle."

"Is Bo still in your room?" Anthony asked. Bo had followed

them up the stairs earlier, and Gemma had heard him chatting away to Eddie as he unpacked.

Kat made the face one makes after accidently touching something hot. "He is," she said. "Could you take him so we can get changed?"

"Oh, of course!" Gemma chirped. "So sorry, Kat! I hope he wasn't bothering you."

Kat shrugged. "He's fine. We just need some privacy now."

Anthony nodded and pushed past Kat. Gemma heard him tell Bo to follow him. Gemma smoothed the blankets on her bed before walking toward the door, surprised to see Kat still standing there. "What's up?" Gemma asked, working hard to stay casual.

Kat shifted her weight on her feet. "Gemma, I appreciate all you did setting up the guest room."

Gemma smiled and swatted a hand. "Of course. Not a big deal."

"And the pullout looks like it's really nice and all. . . ." Her voice trailed off and her expression was pained.

"Okay . . . ?" Gemma said, confused.

"I'm just such a weird and light sleeper, and I'm worried that trying to sleep on a couch with a baby crying all night will be tricky for me."

"Oh!" Gemma exclaimed. "Calvin sleeps in here at night," she said, moving her body back to expose the small pack and play set up beside their bed.

Kat lifted her chin and extended on her tiptoes to gaze in at it. Then her eyes shifted back to Gemma. "That's sweet. And, again, I appreciate that."

"Oh, that's not because you're here. It's just common to do with babies for the first few weeks."

Kat's face twisted, as if she were offended.

"I mean, I know you know that," Gemma stammered, her heart fluttering. "Sorry. I just mean, I didn't want you to feel like we had gone out of our way by putting him in here. I just meant to say that since he's in here, I get him the second he cries, so he shouldn't disturb you."

Kat's lips pursed. "I understand that, Gemma. But truly, I'm the worst sleeper. You should see me at home: eye mask, humidifier, memory foam mattress, eighteen-hundred-thread-count sheets, and a sleeping pill the size of my fist!" She threw her head back in laughter.

Gemma laughed mechanically, confused about what Kat was getting at. "Okay, so . . . ?"

"So anyway, I'm thinking it's best for all that I stay with Mark and Lori tonight," Kat said with a syrupy smile across her face.

"Oh," Gemma said, surprised and hurt, but hoping her face didn't betray either. "So you and Eddie are staying there instead of here?"

Kat looked over her shoulder toward the guest room. "Well, Eddie hasn't decided."

"I'm just a little confused here, Kat," Gemma said, unable to make sense of this conversation and feeling the pressure in her bowels amplifying with each purse of Kat's lips.

"Eddie and I are going to have dinner at Mark and Lori's—give you and your family some privacy, and get those kids to bed without us being in the way!"

Gemma blinked to hold back what she feared would be a geyser of tears. "Fun!" she said, an octave higher to help hide her hurt.

"Eddie thinks he will probably come back here, but he might also decide to stay over there with me. He doesn't want to decide just yet."

"Okay!" Gemma said, sounding as peppy as she could. "That sounds like a plan! You just might have Eddie text me so I know whether or not to leave the front door unlocked."

"Awesome," Kat said.

"You'll have to excuse me, Kat, I have to go to the bathroom and it's always a bit of an ordeal," Gemma said with a mild laugh, hoping Kat couldn't see the budding tears.

Kat scrunched up her nose. "This is why I could never have kids!" She laughed. "Just one more thing before you do that, Gemma."

Gemma's nails dug into the doorframe behind her back. "Yes?"

"We will need the car to get to Mark's."

"Oh, right. Anthony has the keys."

"Cool. And if Eddie does end up staying with me, you'll need to come get the car from Mark and Lori's tomorrow."

Gemma thought as fast as she could before responding. "Wait, couldn't Mark follow you all over here tomorrow to drop it off? I know we'd like to say goodbye." Gemma felt certain her body was about to give out—every bodily fluid was going to come pouring out of her if she didn't finish this conversation.

"Oooh," Kat said, baring her teeth while sucking in air. "I don't know if that will work. Mark and Lori really like to get up and around early, and we need to be on the road before eight."

"Tell you what," Gemma said, on the verge of screaming but working hard to keep her voice from shaking. "Let me go to the bathroom, and then I'll meet you two downstairs and we can talk it out."

"Perfect," Kat said, nodding her head once before finally turning to walk away.

Gemma quickly closed the door, and with her hand still on the knob, fell to her knees and began to sob. As quietly as she could she cried and cried, snot dripping onto her bent knees, her head hanging and heavy. With her left hand still clenching the smooth crystal of the doorknob, her knuckles white and shaking, she wrapped her right arm around her abdomen. "Ow, ow, ow, ow, ow," she whispered to herself, the pain in her abdomen so severe she thought she might pass out. *Blow out the candles, Gemma. Blow them out now,* she thought, willing herself to inhale and exhale large gulps of air until she could unpeel her fingers from the knob. She wrapped both arms around herself, feeling herself shake as she kept quiet through her deep breaths. Her mouth opened into a silent scream, her eyes squeezed tight. When her lips joined each other again, she felt her body relax. She remained still, kneeling in front of the door, holding herself, until she was confident in her strength to rise, make it to the bathroom, change her pad, reapply her makeup, and find her smile in the mirror, all of which took longer than she would have liked.

"All right!" Gemma said as she descended the stairs to see Eddie and Kat standing by the front door. She turned to look into the dining room, where Bo was perched on a chair, eating an assortment of whatever Anthony had found to cut up. Anthony was in the chair next to Bo, feeding Calvin a bottle. She saw a look of concern wash across Anthony's face as he saw her. *Oh shit. Can he tell I've been crying? Can they?* Gemma worried as she turned back to Kat and Eddie.

"What's the plan?" Gemma asked, clapping like a camp counselor excited for the day's activities.

Eddie cleared his throat and looked at his shoes. "We've got the keys from Anthony and are headed over to Mark's for a quick dinner."

Gemma glanced down to see Eddie was holding only one bag and her heart lightened. It was Kat's Louis Vuitton duffel bag. Eddie's ripped and faded canvas bag and scratched leather messenger bag were nowhere in sight.

"Cool," Gemma said, smiling as brightly as she could. "And you'll be back later, Eddie?" she asked, trying to hide her hope. Disgusted, she heard Irene's voice asking teenage Eddie if he'd be coming home after the football game or staying the night with one of his teammates.

"Yep," Eddie said. "Gotta get in some more time with the

boys." He smiled, looking into the dining room at Bo shoveling up bits of pasta.

"Yes! Uncle Eddie is gonna teach me to play football!" Bo said, bits of food flying from his mouth.

"Oh is he?" Gemma turned back to her brother. "When would that happen?"

Eddie shrugged with a shake of his head and a smile. "Oh, you know."

Gemma blinked, willing herself to let it go. "I'll be up late—I take the first shift with Calvin, so I'll be here when you get back."

"Oh, cool . . . ," said Eddie, scratching at his beard. "I mean, don't wait up or anything."

"I won't!" Gemma said, shaking her head, hoping to convince him. "I just meant that I stay up late to do Calvin's feeding and let Anthony sleep. Then we switch."

Eddie raised his eyebrows. "Wow."

Gemma couldn't quite discern what that meant. Did he think Anthony was a pushover? Did he think doing shifts was a bad idea? Was he implying she should be doing all the feedings? Not using formula, but instead nursing Calvin morning, noon, and night? Gemma shook her head to get herself back to the conversation.

"Anyway," she said, as casually as she could muster, "if I'm up, I'll see you. If not, I'll catch you in the morning before you take off."

"Sounds good," Eddie said, nodding thoughtfully as if Gemma had suggested something very impressive.

"It was great to see you all!" Kat said, her excitement to leave not in the least bit hidden.

"Yes! Always great to see you, Kat," Gemma said, walking toward her for a hug.

As they finished their hug, Kat raised her voice to Anthony

in the dining room, "Don't get up, Anthony, your hands are full! But good seeing you!"

Anthony raised a hand and nodded. "Take care, Kat. And Eddie, I'll see you in the morning. I'll have the coffee ready."

"Awesome, man, thanks," Eddie said, smiling. "I'll need some energy for the trip."

And with that, Kat and Eddie opened the glass door and let it slam back without attempting to catch it. Gemma watched as they opened the door to Anthony's car.

"You vacuumed it out, right?" Gemma asked, still watching the car.

Anthony sighed. "Yes. The car is spotless. Come eat."

Gemma waved as the car backed into the street and the headlights came on. She closed the door behind her but made sure to leave it unlocked.

"Want me to make you a sandwich?" Anthony asked, bringing Calvin to her.

"That sounds great," she said, taking the baby into her arms. "Then I might try to take a quick nap when we put Bo down."

Anthony tucked her hair behind her left ear. "Good plan. How are you feeling? You look like you've been crying."

"Oh, just a little weepy. Hormones. I'm completely fine."

"Okay . . . ," Anthony said in a soft tone. "I just want to make sure you're getting enough rest."

Bo crawled down off his chair and walked over to join Gemma, Anthony, and the baby.

"Uncle Eddie is silly," he said, looking up at them.

Anthony leaned down to pull Bo up on his hip.

"Yes he is," Gemma said, running her free hand through Bo's thick hair.

"Kat is not," Bo said. Gemma and Anthony looked at each other before breaking into laughter.

"No she is not," Anthony said. "Now, let's get you a bath, buddy."

"Do you like Uncle Eddie?" Bo asked, looking at Gemma.

Gemma looked at Anthony with surprise. "What, honey? Of *course*. He's my brother. I love him, sweetheart."

"Oh," Bo said, looking confused.

Anthony bounced Bo up and down a few times in his arms. "Why do you ask that, bud?"

Bo looked at his dad and then at his mom. "I dunno." He shrugged. "Your voice gets really weird when you talk to him."

Gemma stared at Bo before looking at Anthony and stammering, "How so?"

"Like Katerina on *Daniel Tiger*!" Bo said, laughing. Anthony glanced at Gemma with a look that told her to drop it.

She let out a sigh and weakly swatted a hand in dismissal, then leaned forward to kiss Bo's cheek. "All right, little man, go take your bath and I'll be up in a bit."

"That's the voice!" Bo said, still cackling. But before he could say anything else, Anthony lowered him onto the stairs and tapped his bottom to encourage him to go up.

CHAPTER 6

Gemma was nestled into the couch—Calvin asleep in her arms—watching an episode of *Bob's Burgers* on mute. The house was quiet, save the gentle grumbling of the dishwasher. Her eyes were fixed on the television in a dry gaze. She blinked a few times to add moisture but couldn't will herself to do much more than that. As the bright colors continued to flicker on the screen, her mind felt gray and still. Her thoughts wandered across the past few hours.

Anthony had gone to bed at nine, the start of his sleeping shift. The shifts had been the brilliant idea of seasoned parents. "This time let's split the night into two shifts," Anthony had said while she was in the hospital bed, still waiting to dilate. "I could take nine to, say, three in the morning. Then you could take three to seven or eight." Gemma nodded through clenched teeth and measured breathing, her contractions stronger than her cervix was wide. "Then we'd at least each get an uninterrupted five hours of sleep," Anthony said, adjusting the cold washcloth on her head. "Yet another advantage of skipping that whole breastfeeding nightmare from last time." Gemma glanced up at him to see if he was joking. But she could tell from his face he was as earnest as always. She had nodded once more before returning her focus to another rising contraction.

And to Anthony's credit, the sleep shifts were an unexpected gift to Gemma. It gave her time alone with her baby and her thoughts. Time without having to answer Bo's unending questions. Time without having to clean, or cook, or work. Time without having to perform, really. While this was only their second night of the sleep shifts, she had looked forward to it all day. A chance to be alone, quiet, calm.

She looked down at Calvin. His full bottom lip, his long lashes. Her thoughts were filled with love for this child—though she was concerned that she thought it more than she felt it. It was a conflict within herself: she could think something, but she couldn't feel it. Her heart felt foggy and somehow not her own. She'd look at Calvin and think about how much she loved him, but when she tried to force her chest to swell with the feeling, her body refused to react.

She shook her head to snap herself back into the moment, this quiet moment in the dark house, illuminated only by the flashes from the TV. She picked up her phone, which was on Calvin's chest—the mark of modern motherhood—and worked her thumbs around the screen until Instagram images filled it. She clicked the plus sign on the bottom of the screen, pulling up her phone's camera roll, selected a picture of herself holding Calvin in the hospital bed, then chose a different one that was more flattering of her, even though Calvin was technically blurry in it. "I love this kid!" she wrote on the caption after adjusting the lighting, zooming in to crop out the trappings of the hospital around her, and adding a filter that made her hair look lighter than it was. She hit share and immediately pulled her thumb down the length of the screen to refresh the page. No likes yet. She did it again. One like from a former classmate at Penn. She smiled at it before pressing the button on the side of the phone and laying it back on Calvin's chest.

Her mind curved around a replay of the evening, as if she were a player watching video after a game, analyzing her performance. She had felt good about everything in real time, but as her anxiety was wont to do, it was now forcing her to second-guess every word she had spoken. This pattern played out after most social interactions, but with anything involving Eddie, everything was intensified. Everything was high stakes. After all, she was convinced that whatever happened that day of his football tryouts had made their relationship weird for three decades, even though she couldn't remember what it was. If she didn't know what caused the rift so long ago, how could she possibly prevent it from happening again?

But now, with the dishwasher keeping rhythm to her thoughts, she had to agree with a belief Anthony had long held: Gemma was not to blame. Whatever had happened that day, Gemma was just a child. Only five years old. Though Eddie's issues with Gemma, whatever they were, had never made sense to Anthony, they felt oddly justified to Gemma. She'd spent thirty years trying to get her mind to conjure any useful memories of that day, to answer questions her family seemed to avoid. Given how tight-lipped everyone had always been about that day, Gemma had accepted that whatever had happened, she must have been to blame.

Gemma's thoughts were broken by the sudden illumination of her phone. It was a text message from her mother.

How are Eddie and Kat?

Gemma rolled her eyes but felt a pang of guilt.

They went to see Mark and Lori for a bit!

She hoped the exclamation point would calm any concern Irene might have.

Oh?

Gemma stared at the one-word question and felt her pulse

quicken. She sat up, stood carefully, and laid Calvin in the bassinet. She would need to tamp these embers before they ignited fully.

Yep! He will be back later tonight.

Eddie will? But what about Kat?

She wanted to stay with Lori. Makes sense—she hasn't seen her in a while.

There was a pause. No pulsing bubbles. Gemma began writing Irene's response in her head: *What did you do, Gemma? Did you upset Eddie? Did you say something to Kat that made her feel bad for not having children? What happened after we left? I knew we should have stayed longer.*

But instead she got this text almost two minutes later:

I wondered if that pullout would be comfortable enough.

Gemma read and reread the text in disbelief. No matter how much Gemma braced herself for her mother's criticism, and no matter how harsh she imagined it being in preparation for the unavoidable shame she'd feel from it, Irene had the magical skill of delivering a blow both crushing and simple. This time, the message was clear: Gemma hadn't done enough to make Eddie and Kat comfortable.

Gemma wrote back quickly, her thumbs moving to keep the shame at bay.

Eddie's coming back to stay here. I think it was more about Eddie wanting time alone with me.

The bubbles illuminated quickly, which Gemma knew from experience was worse than when Irene sat for a minute to respond. As Anthony always said, "Irene has cutting remarks locked and loaded."

I'm sure that's true!

Gemma looked at Irene's response, confused. *What the hell was that supposed to mean? Is she being sarcastic? Genuine?*

Gemma thought as she lowered herself down onto the couch again.

She was too tired to respond. The phone showed it was nearly eleven. She was starting to lose hope Eddie was coming back. Even if he did, Anthony would be up soon after, leaving them little time to talk. Gemma looked over at Calvin in the bassinet. He was sleeping soundly. Then she sank further into the couch, pulling the fuzzy blanket over herself. And before she could fully unfold the blanket to cover her feet, she was sound asleep, the familiar flashes of dreams as vivid and distracting as the muted scenes of *Bob's Burgers* still playing on the TV.

——

Gemma was jolted awake by the sound of the doorknob turning. She sat up quickly, a sharp pain in her lower half making her wince. She stood, looking back to see if there was a stain where she'd been sitting. She exhaled with relief and turned her attention to the door swinging open.

Her chest tightened, and she glanced down at Calvin, who was still sleeping, before snapping her eyes back to the door. From the darkness a figure emerged.

She stared at him for a beat, trying to place him. Her mind was still in her slumber and her blood and her child. She couldn't get her thoughts together quickly enough. *What's happening? Who is this?* She stared at him as his head tilted to the side.

"Gemma? It's me."

Her eyes went wide before she laughed, hoping to hit the right tone of a silly younger sister just being flaky and not a deranged woman who couldn't recognize faces. She swatted her hand in a casual fashion. "Yes, yes, of course!"

He looked confused. "Did I wake you?"

"No, no. I may have dozed slightly, but I'm awake! Come in, come in! Can I get you something to drink?"

"Actually," he said, "I could really use something to eat."

"Of course!" Gemma said, doing another quick check on Calvin. "I've got loads in the fridge. What can I get you?"

"What do you have?"

"Well, let's go see." She motioned for him to follow her. Instead of trailing her through the living room and into the kitchen, he went around through the dining room. "I've got stuff to make sandwiches, all the leftover food from today, frozen pizzas . . . ," Gemma said, continuing to move stuff around on the refrigerator's shelves.

Eddie looked in over Gemma's shoulder and pointed to a foil casserole pan.

"What's that?"

"Oh that?" Gemma said, a little hesitant. "That's my favorite dish from this restaurant downtown. My boss sent it when Calvin was born."

"What is it?" Eddie asked again.

She turned to face him. "It's this baked pasta dish with all this seafood in it from this place in town called Rick's. It's my favorite restaurant."

"Sounds perfect!" Eddie clapped his hands together. "Where are the bowls?" he asked, turning his attention to the cabinets behind him.

"Oh, okay. Just to the left of the sink." She reached in to grab the silver pan. On the top, in Dr. Heinz's distinctive handwriting, was a message scribbled in Sharpie: *Congrats! Eat up and hurry back to work!*

She brought the pan to the counter and watched as Eddie—who had found both a bowl and a spoon—dug out five scoops.

He opened the microwave door. "How long do you think?"

Gemma shrugged. "Maybe forty-five seconds, then check it?"

Once his food was heated, he walked into the living room and plopped down in the armless chair. Gemma lowered herself carefully onto the couch. "So how was Mark? And the kids?"

With a mouth full of pasta, Eddie had to chew a few bites before clearing enough room to talk. "Good. The twins are so smart."

"Remind me where they go? What grade?"

"Sixth grade at Washington," he said automatically, as if they were his own family.

"That's a good school." Gemma nodded, wanting to stop talking about this but sensing Eddie didn't.

"They raise their kids in a really cool way."

"How so?"

Eddie shrugged. "It's just super calm and open and, kind of hard to explain, but it's just so easygoing over there."

Gemma nodded slowly, at a loss for how to respond.

"And I'll say this," he added, then chewed a few more bites. "Lori's gotta be the best mother I've ever seen." And he lowered his spoon into the bowl for more.

Gemma felt something deep within her clench. *Just my bowels,* she thought, as her eyes stung with tears. Before they could spill over, she rose from the couch.

"Hang on, Eddie, I have to go to the bathroom."

As she turned to leave before he could see her face, he called out, "Grab me a beer on the way back?"

"Sure!" she said, as upbeat as she could manage, rushing to the small half bath beside the back door. She closed the bathroom door and slapped a hand across her mouth just in time to stifle a painful sob. The kind a bear might let out after being shot with a tranquilizer dart. She kept her hand across her mouth as tears rolled quickly but quietly down her cheeks. *Gemma, what is happening? You're fine. You're fine.* Her free hand was clutching the porcelain pedestal sink as her body trembled. *Not now. You cannot do this now.* She worked to swallow the sobs, breathing slowly and carefully until she regained control. But as she did, her lower stomach growled, a noise so loud she was certain it could be heard from the living room. She snapped the water on quickly to drown out the noise. Air was escaping her from below, and the pressure of her bowels was sitting right at the opening. She needed to poop. She could feel it working its way, so she squeezed her butt cheeks as tightly as she could while the water ran, her stomach wailed, her left hand gripped the sink, and her right hand gripped her mouth.

Within a few minutes, all her bodily noises stopped. Her tears dried. She released her grip on the sink and turned off the water. She breathed in deeply before turning the knob, opening the door, walking into the kitchen to get a beer, popping it open, walking back into the living room, and handing it to Eddie.

"Here you go!" she said with a perkiness more appropriate for the middle of the day, not the middle of the night.

Eddie reached for the beer with one hand and used the other to set his empty bowl on the coffee table. "Thanks, man."

"No problem!" Gemma chirped, walking over to retrieve Calvin, who was stirring.

"Does he want some of the pasta?" Eddie asked, smiling.

"More likely, the beer," Gemma quipped as she hoisted Calvin onto her shoulder.

"He's a cute one, Gem."

"Thankfully. Would have been a shame to have had to leave him at the hospital," Gemma said as she paced around the room.

"Is it hard?"

Gemma perked up at the recognition of Eddie asking her a question. "Which part?"

Eddie shrugged. "I dunno. All of it?"

Gemma laughed. "Yep." She realized Eddie's face was suddenly more serious than she had expected. "Why do you ask?"

Eddie took a drink of beer, sighed, and said, "Oh, I dunno. I think I sometimes like to hear it's hard."

"So you don't feel that you've missed out?"

Eddie nodded, his eyes moving from Calvin to the floor.

Gemma smiled at him. "I think there's something really magical about being an uncle without having to be a dad."

He smiled back lightly. "Oh yeah?"

"For sure. You get all the fun of the kids without any of the hard stuff—the diapers, the crying, the paying for college."

Eddie nodded with a laugh. Gemma looked at him for a moment before asking a question she knew Irene would scold her for.

"Is the door closed on kids for you and Kat?"

Eddie leaned back in the chair and put his beer on the fireplace ledge before responding. "Closed, and locked."

Gemma felt the energy in the room was more open than it had ever been with her brother. There was no tension. She wasn't scared or worried. She was just with him. She pressed on. "Closed by choice?" she asked as she stood swinging her body side to side to soothe Calvin, who was very close to needing a bottle.

"A little bit of choice. A little bit of chance," Eddie said, looking off into the dark room.

Gemma watched his face twist slightly. She gave his answer some air before speaking again. "Well, I don't know if you knew this about me, but I love ice skating."

Eddie turned his head toward her.

"And no matter how hard I try," she continued, "I just can't skate."

Eddie tilted his head.

"I make Anthony take me every year to skate at Frank

Southern, and every year I fall. One year I fractured my wrist. Truly. It's like watching a bird ride a bike."

Eddie laughed.

"One year Anthony got me skating lessons for my birthday. I took six weeks and still *nothing*. I think the teacher had to retire after working with me."

Eddie laughed again.

"But you know what? I still love it. I can't *be* a skater, but I love watching it during the Olympics. I love watching ice dancing. I love going down to the rink and watching others skate. I even play *The Cutting Edge* on repeat around here."

Eddie smirked. "Your point?"

Gemma shifted Calvin to keep him hidden, to keep him out of the middle of what was happening between her and Eddie. "Sometimes it's just as fun—maybe even *more* fun— being a spectator."

Eddie kept his eye contact with Gemma for a bit before nodding. "I like that, actually," he finally said. "Even though I was always conditioned to be a player."

Gemma had a sudden flash to the day of Eddie's high school varsity football tryouts. Watching him from the stands, her legs burning on the metal bleachers, as she scanned a *Where's Waldo?* book while sitting next to her father. "You didn't spend much time watching others play, huh?"

"Nope," he said, taking a swig of beer.

"Well, there's some fun to be had enjoying the game from afar," she said, though she remembered being quite bored that day in the hot sun. "And, at least for me, there's some relief in not having to be the one *on* the ice."

"Or on the field."

"Or in the day care director's office when your kid bites another kid."

A genuine laugh escaped from Eddie, one that showed off the dimples he got from Jack.

"You might be onto something."

There was a nice, comfortable silence as Gemma continued to swing Calvin, and Eddie watched her as if she were an ice skater sticking the landing.

"Eddie, would you like to hold Calvin for a bit?"

Eddie nodded. Gemma lowered Calvin into his arms. "I'm going to make his bottle. Hang tight with him for a bit."

In the kitchen, Gemma noticed the dishwasher was done and decided to unload it while Eddie was holding Calvin. She worked diligently to unload each dish quietly, so as not to wake Anthony before his shift ended. She wiped down the counter, reloaded the dishwasher, put the pasta pan back in the refrigerator, and made a bottle.

When she walked back into the living room, her breath caught in her throat at the beautiful scene before her. Eddie had fallen asleep holding Calvin, who had also drifted off. She stared at the two of them sleeping peacefully. She put the bottle down and leaned over the couch quietly to grab her phone. She opened the camera and walked slowly toward Eddie to snap a picture of the two of them. Eddie's chin was touching his chest and he was breathing deeply. Calvin's little eyes were fluttering under the lids. It was a moment Gemma didn't know she had wanted, but now that it was here, she was mesmerized. And grateful. And for a brief moment, her heart seemed to clear.

After capturing at least two dozen images, she walked back to the couch, sat down, and admired the pictures she had just taken. She opened Instagram. She couldn't wait to post this. What a perfect moment to share with others. As she messed with filters and contrast, she didn't see Eddie's hand relax. She didn't see his arm drop to the side of the chair, she didn't see Calvin start to roll, slowly at first, but then at warp speed, and she didn't see his face plummet toward the hearth, the bricks Irene had long nagged Gemma about—as though the sharp corner had been waiting patiently all this time for the softness of a baby's face. No, Gemma didn't see anything. She just heard her child's piercing scream, which didn't even wake Eddie, whose arm remained extended, as if showing her where the tragedy occurred.

CHAPTER 7

Before her left foot was even untucked from her right leg, before she dropped her phone beside her on the couch, before her palms pressed into the cushion to propel herself up, Gemma's voice exploded in her chest, up her throat, through her teeth, and out her lips in a scream of Anthony's name. And while her voice sounded slow and low within her head, her body felt fast and light as she sprang from the couch, leapt over the coffee table, dug her hands under her infant, and thrust him at her husband, whose right foot had just joined his left one on the living room floor after his rapid descent of the stairs.

She couldn't fix her eyes on Calvin. The instant she rescued him she pushed him away. Instead of looking at him, her eyes darted around the room, scanning for blood or any other evidence that would let her know how bad this was before she could bear to look at her baby for the verdict.

Even in the blur of blood and screaming and confusion, Eddie didn't wake. He had slid low within the chair, his chin on his chest, sleeping as if on a quiet beach in a remote tropical village rather than in Indiana with the piercing scream of his infant nephew filling the house with terror.

With her eyes fixed on Eddie, Gemma retrieved her phone and dialed 911. She could barely find the words to explain to the dispatcher that her son had been dropped and had landed on his face on the sharp corner of a fireplace hearth. When she was told the ambulance was on its way, Gemma locked her phone, still staring at Eddie, unable to bring herself to look at her son.

Only two minutes had transpired, but to Gemma it felt like ten, and Eddie still wasn't stirring. The thought flashed in her mind that Eddie might not be breathing. As her younger son bellowed, she reached out and pressed her brother lightly on the shoulder. At the gentlest of touches, he jerked. His eyes opened on Gemma's, dilated in the darkness, and then his brows stitched together as though he were working to understand the noise and tension within the room.

"Eddie," Gemma said in a soft tone, a tone she was sure Anthony would grill her about later, "I need you to wake up and watch Bo."

"What's going on?" he stammered, jumping out of the low chair and running his hands through his dark hair.

"Calvin fell and an ambulance is on its way—"

Anthony, who was working furiously to soothe Calvin's screams, cut Gemma off.

"Eddie! You need to wake up and pay attention." His tone was what he used at the zoo when Bo would run out of sight.

"What have *I* done?" Eddie said, his hands up as if defending himself from a fight. Gemma shot Anthony a glance, which she immediately regretted, because instead of catching his gaze, she caught a glimpse of her newborn son's face for the first time and could see the damage.

"Eddie, I can't explain now," Gemma said, her voice hissing in panic. "I need to pack a bag and get changed. Bo is upstairs sleeping and shouldn't wake up until around six." Gemma glanced down at her phone to see it was just now three in the morning. "We will be back before he gets up."

"We don't know that," Anthony exclaimed, moving toward the door to open it. Gemma ran up the stairs. As she passed Bo's room, she paused for a moment. His sound machine hummed quietly; the nightlight cast a glow over his sleeping face, his hair matted in sweat. His flawless young face, somehow perfectly swept up in sleep despite the horrifying screams from his brother below.

Snapping back to the urgency of the moment, she shut Bo's door, ran down the hallway, and burst into her bedroom. She was wearing an old U of Penn T-shirt and pajama bottoms. Her head darted in all directions, looking for something to throw on. Deciding to change into sweats, she hooked on an old bra. As she ran back toward the stairs, she heard the faint sound of an ambulance in the distance.

When she reached the bottom step, Gemma was disappointed to see Eddie standing in the exact same spot, looking just as confused as when she woke him up. She didn't know what she had expected. Perhaps that he would join Anthony outside to check on Calvin? Or help pack the diaper bag? Or put a few snacks and bottles of water in a backpack? *Yeah,* Gemma thought. *Any of those.*

Gemma pulled her shoes on by the front door. "Take care of Bo, and we'll call when we know more." She looked through the glass storm door and could see Anthony outside with Calvin. It appeared he had managed to both sop up the blood on their son's face—with the fuzzy blanket she had been lying under earlier—and pack the diaper bag, despite holding Calvin with one arm. And based on his body language, Gemma knew Anthony had no intention of changing out of the T-shirt and running shorts he always slept in.

Eddie looked at her. "Did I do something?"

His expression was so pitiful, innocent even, that Gemma had to swallow the instinctive and intense desire to make him feel better. She thrust the baby monitor into Eddie's hands.

"Watch Bo and I'll call you later. Get some sleep." And with that, she walked quickly out the door and to the ambulance just in time to see her four-day-old son being strapped onto a gurney big enough for a linebacker.

The two EMTs—one overweight bald man and one skinny Black woman—looked at Gemma as they finished securing Calvin. The man, whose large frame filled up the entire ambulance, nodded at her in such a kind way that it made her stomach turn. He looked back at Calvin one last time before hopping out of the ambulance and allowing Gemma room to climb in.

"Steve," said the female EMT, who was now sitting on the bench inside the ambulance next to Anthony, "let's get going." Gemma sat down on the opposite side of her husband—closest to Calvin—and Steve slammed shut the heavy doors. Gemma soon heard the engine rev and the sirens sound, and the big metal box lurched forward as they accelerated down the street.

Gemma gripped Calvin's little fingers tightly now. Forcing herself to look at his face. Willing herself to stare at the product of her neglect. Demanding she acknowledge that what she had focused on during her child's desperate and terrified screams was Eddie.

Calvin's cries turned to whimpering as the ambulance rattled its way toward IU Health. His face didn't look right. *It barely looks like Calvin,* Gemma thought. She realized she hadn't stared at him as much as she had at Bo when he was this little, so she hadn't yet committed every angle and hair follicle to memory. It wasn't because she hadn't had the time, of course; she had just given most of the time she could have spent enthralled with his newness to preparing for Eddie and Kat's arrival. Her chest grew tight with anger at herself. *How could I be so stupid? So needy? So desperately focused on the wrong piece of my life at every single moment of it?*

She lifted her wet gaze to Anthony, whose eyes were dark

and hollow in a way she'd never seen before. Her lips parted to say something, but he just shook his head.

"He was born four days ago," the female EMT said, startling Gemma, which caused Calvin to begin whimpering again. Out of the corner of her eye Gemma thought she saw Anthony shake his head in anger.

I've disappointed every man I've ever loved.

"And there were no complications at birth? No emergency surgery? No ICU?" the EMT continued.

"No." Gemma stroked the side of Calvin's head. "It was all perfect. He was perfect," she whispered as sobs took over and she laid her head beside Calvin on the gurney to which his tiny body was strapped.

"He *is* perfect," Anthony said with a coolness that felt physical to Gemma.

She snapped her head up and glared at Anthony. "I didn't mean he wasn't."

The EMT moved her eyes back and forth between Gemma and Anthony, her clipboard resting on her lap, before clearing her throat gently. "This little guy is going to be okay."

"How do you know that?" Anthony asked in a tone more confrontational than curious.

"His vitals are fine," she said in a kind voice but without smiling. "Babies are much more resilient than you think. And you two need to remain calm." She held up her clipboard and began to write before finishing her thought: "For him."

Anthony's eyes narrowed at her for a beat before shifting to Gemma. She gave him a look only parents can use or recognize. A look that spoke every apology, every concern, every need. A look she had first given him during her miscarriage in the hotel where they were staying for their second anniversary. A look she had given him when Bo ran off at the zoo and it took them six excruciating minutes to find him. His eyes relaxed and he mouthed, "I love you." Gemma released her breath for the first time since she heard the scream escape her baby's lips.

Since she felt the scream escape her own.

——

Gemma's phone vibrated in her pocket. It hadn't stopped buzzing for hours. Eddie had clearly let Mary and her parents know. Maybe Eddie was also texting to ask a question about Bo. But she couldn't look at the phone. If she so much as pulled it out of her pocket and glanced at the screen, her face would be illuminated by a barrage of questions she wasn't ready—or able—to answer.

She didn't know if Calvin's eye was okay.

She didn't know if there was internal bleeding.

She didn't know if his skull was fractured.

She didn't know what tests they were running.

And she certainly didn't know how long they could expect to be at the hospital.

All she really knew was that, in that moment, she was standing at the head of a gurney, looking down on an upside-down angle of her four-day-old son and his battered face. She and Anthony did as the ER doctor had instructed them—Gemma held Calvin's head and shoulders while Anthony held his hips and legs. The doctor held up a needle so long and thin, Gemma wasn't entirely convinced it existed. Trying to focus on the needle felt like an optical illusion, and Gemma felt tired trying to keep her eyes on it. The doctor's stern demeanor was as terrifying to Gemma as the time she had watched a flight attendant bow her head in prayer during turbulence.

To her credit, the doctor's hand was steady as she brought the needle closer to Calvin's head. "We'll put the IV here," she said without shifting her gaze. "This is best for babies this young, so they don't accidently pull it out."

A lump formed in Gemma's throat at the words *babies this young*. She kept telling herself that none of this should be happening to a child, ever, and certainly not to one she had just taken home from that very hospital only days earlier.

"Their heads also have the best veins," the doctor said in a slightly more casual tone, which gave Gemma an odd sense of calm. "Mom, Dad, you ready?"

But before Gemma or Anthony could respond, the doctor bent low and pressed the thin filament of a needle into the faintest blue line running along the uninjured side of Calvin's head. As the needle pierced his skin, he awoke with a wail so full of pain and betrayal, Gemma began crying with abandon, the space between her legs filling up with blood and hurt and worry and shame, pulsing in time to her son's woeful screams.

CHAPTER 8

Gemma watched Anthony's head bob up and down as he dozed in a plastic chair in the corner of the dark hospital room. She knew he was angry. She knew him well enough to understand that anger was how he handled stress. But even after a decade of marriage, she couldn't quite figure out when he was angry with her.

Anthony was generally reserved, a quality that contrasted nicely with Gemma's more demonstrative personality. But when they first began dating, she had trouble reading him. Once, at a birthday party for a mutual friend, a balloon burst. The sound startled Anthony, who ducked. Everyone in the room burst into laughter, including Gemma, and his face had gone so serious, it confused her. She couldn't believe he would be mad—everyone was just ribbing him. On the drive home, she asked if he was mad at her. He was truly perplexed by her question, explaining that he wasn't mad; he was embarrassed. Since then, Gemma had struggled to read Anthony's more nuanced emotions as anything but anger, no matter how many times she had been proven wrong.

Calvin was finally resting, thanks to a mild sedative and the exhaustion of trauma. He was on his back in the tiny plastic bassinet—the same kind he had slept in after delivery, less than a week earlier. Now, however, he was surrounded by machines that beeped out some small measure of reassurance. Even though she knew those strong vitals weren't telling the full story.

Calvin's orbital bones, three of the seven that surround the eye, appeared to have shattered with his fall on the unprotected bricks. The X-rays had revealed this horrifying image to Gemma and Anthony in stark black and white. Neither had said a word. The doctor explained that a CT scan might help determine what long-term damage this may have caused his left eye. The CT scan would also help them better prepare for the necessary surgery, which would take place the next afternoon, when the pediatric ophthalmologist was available. The ER doctor made a point to Gemma and Anthony, though Gemma noticed she only looked at Anthony, that the ophthalmologist would need to reschedule a routine surgery because, with Calvin's case, time was of the essence. "He could go blind in that eye," she had said, so casually Gemma's stomach had lurched.

But for now, given that Calvin was sedated and his vitals were fine, and there was no indication of internal bleeding, the medical team thought it best to let him rest for a few hours before the scan. This had given Gemma and Anthony the chance for three hours of sleep, should sleep come to either of them, before they would need to offer their alert parent faces, the only faces doctors seemed to accept.

Gemma wanted to text Eddie—partly to check on Bo, though she doubted he was awake yet, but also because she wanted to gauge Eddie's mood. He had seemed so unaware of what was happening. How was that possible? Did he not remember holding Calvin before he fell asleep? She shook her head in anger. In disbelief. *What a selfish asshole,* Gemma thought, unsure if she meant Eddie or herself.

And yet she couldn't get Eddie's expression out of her head. The way he had said "What have *I* done?" in response to Anthony had stirred in her a physiological response in the moment. Remembering it now did so again as she sat in the dark, watching her husband doze. Eddie's reaction had felt so familiar and yet was impossible to place, like perhaps she'd experienced it in a dream. He had looked so innocent in that moment, so childlike. But his voice, his tone, had pressed a button deep within her. She closed her eyes and ran her fingers across her eyebrows with pressure. *Blow out the candles,* she thought. She straightened her back, lowered her shoulders, placed her phone in her lap, and focused on her breath. In and out. In and out. And on and on she breathed, almost able to push the question Eddie had asked, "What have *I* done," out of her head, past the large hospital room door, and down the hallway, the question slowly floating away like a semideflated balloon.

"You need to get sleep," Anthony said with such firmness that she flinched in her seat, causing her phone to drop on the floor with a loud thump. Her eyes snapped open and she looked at her husband, who was sitting in the chair with his arms crossed. Without dropping his gaze, she bent forward, tapping around on the ground until her hand found her phone.

As she shifted her body back into a sitting position, she hissed, "How can I sleep right now?"

He shrugged, as if unwilling to help her find the answer. "We need to be ready to go in a few hours."

"I'm aware of that, Anthony."

He stared at her without blinking. Then he inhaled through his nose, puckered his lips as if to whistle, and exhaled slowly. "Gemma." Then he paused.

"I know you're pissed at me."

"What the hell?" he said, uncrossing his arms.

"You think this is my fault."

"Jesus Christ, Gemma," he said, running his fingers through his hair.

"You're not denying it."

"I'm not pissed, Gemma. I'm terrified."

Gemma rose from the chair and walked swiftly to the large door, opening it just enough to squeeze her aching body through it. Once in the hallway, her eyes squinted in the fluorescent glow. She looked both ways, trying to decide where to go. She wanted to get away from the tension, but she felt the fullness between her legs. She needed a new pad, and some pain meds, both of which she had forgotten to pack in the rush to get in the ambulance. The halls were vacant, but two nurses sat at a nearby station, talking quietly. Gemma approached it gingerly, cleared her throat, and addressed them both.

"Hi, excuse me," she said with a faint smile. "I need a pad and some pain meds."

The nurses looked at each other and then back at her.

"Oh, I'm not on my period." Gemma smiled lightly. "I just had a baby."

"Okay . . . ," one nurse said.

"Well, four days ago. Actually, five days ago." Gemma looked at them, assuming this clarified the situation.

"This is the pediatric wing," the other nurse responded, as if in explanation.

Gemma tapped her fingers nervously on the counter. "Right, I get that, but it's also a hospital."

The nurse smiled slightly. "We can find something for your bleeding. But not for your pain."

Gemma nodded. "Fair enough."

"But then you'll need to go buy what you need," said the first nurse flatly, before turning to her computer and shaking the mouse to wake the screen. Gemma turned her back to the desk so the nurse wouldn't see her eyes fill with tears.

Thankfully, the second nurse returned quickly with two large pads in her hand. "Ma'am?"

Gemma sniffed and wiped her eyes before turning back around. She extended her hand to grab the pads. "Thank you," she mouthed noiselessly. The nurse winked at her and pointed to the restroom across the hall. Gemma nodded, crossed to the restroom, and locked the door.

She pulled her sweats down and breathed a sigh of relief to see she hadn't leaked. The mesh underwear felt damp from sweat, but overall, the bloodshed in her pants wasn't what it could have been after that many hours.

She was, however, in tremendous pain. Her groin was pulsing and tender, and she needed the assortment of sprays and medicated pads her ob-gyn had sent her home with. She needed her pain meds. She needed sleep. And, above all, she needed to shit.

She felt the pressure of her bowels. It felt for all the world like the moment five days earlier when her doctor had instructed, "It's time to push!" Her hand reached up automatically and grabbed hold of the rail beside the toilet. She squeezed with such might it forced tremors throughout her body. "You can do this," she whisper-screamed in the cold, sterile room. And with one hand gripping the railing, and the other on the edge of the toilet seat, she lifted her bottom just enough to give herself leverage to push. But as the poop came, as it knocked on the door of her rectum, the pressure pierced her vagina with such a sharp pain that she screamed, her voice reverberating against the tiled walls.

There was a gentle knock at the door.

"Someone's in here!" Gemma called out.

"I know," said the nurse from the other side of the door. "All okay?"

Gemma bit down on her lip until she could find her voice. "Yep. All good."

She lowered her butt cheek back down onto the seat, then clenched every muscle in her body until she felt the pressure subside within her. She held on to the railing for a few more breaths, sweat beading on her forehead. *Not yet,* she thought to herself. *Maybe tomorrow.* She wiped her forehead with the back of her hand, swallowing sobs. Then she worked her hands with such swiftness, the product of the mastery women develop over years of tending to blood between their legs. As she finished, flushed, and washed her hands and her face, she began to feel a little bit better. This was always the case when she was on her period too. A fresh pad, a new tampon, a rinsed-out Diva cup—it didn't matter the mechanism. It always made her feel a little bit more assured. As if the clock had been reset.

She came out of the bathroom, catching the eye of the helpful nurse. Gemma nodded at her without smiling, and the nurse returned an identical nod. Back at Calvin's room, she found Anthony standing at the window.

He turned quickly to face her with an expression that told Gemma he had been standing there in agony for the few minutes she had been gone. They walked quickly toward each other and embraced. His body shook in a way that let her know he was crying. For whatever reason, when he cried, Gemma didn't. She couldn't. It was as if her body reset itself to be of service to him. She stroked the back of his head while he softly cried into the nape of her neck.

"I'm just scared, Gemma," he said, lifting his head up and back to meet her gaze.

"Me too," she said.

"But in no way do I think any of this is your fault," he said so earnestly that tears began to well up. She felt such relief to not be blamed. More accurately, she felt such relief to not be in trouble.

"And I hate to ask, because I don't want you thinking I blame you," he said softly. "But what *did* happen? How did he land on the fireplace like that?"

Gemma wriggled free of their embrace. Her body was overcome with sharp tingles. "It all happened really fast," she said, her voice trailing off.

With all the rushing, first in the ambulance and then to get Calvin's IV started, the only question that had been asked of them about the accident was what exactly his face had hit, and from what height. Gemma, in panicked shock, had mumbled that he'd fallen onto the corner of a brick fireplace from about a two-foot height. After that, there was so much to do for Calvin that no one—not even Anthony—had pressed further for the specifics.

"Tell me what you remember."

They were standing so close she could smell his breath. Gemma sucked in air, unsure what to say. Anthony and Eddie already had a strained relationship. In fact, Gemma and Anthony's first fight had been about Eddie—a fight that felt to Gemma so unfounded. She'd never before been called out for the strange dynamics between her and Eddie. When she and Anthony had planned their road trip, she'd convinced him to add a stop in Wyoming to catch up with Eddie and Kat, who were staying with a group of friends in Casper for a marathon. Her brother and sister-in-law invited them for drinks at the lodge where the group was staying. Anthony remarked at the time that Eddie and Kat could have met them somewhere in town, so they didn't have to trek up into the mountains, but Gemma had brushed it off. When they arrived at the lodge, they found Eddie surrounded by his running buddies—a few Gemma recognized as his high school classmates, but most had been friends of Eddie's from college or beyond. When Eddie finally broke free of his huddle of friends, he walked up and extended his hand to Anthony. "You must be Tony!" he exclaimed, grabbing his hand and pumping it aggressively. Before Anthony could correct him, Eddie had motioned to Kat across the room to join them at a table in the back corner.

Later that evening, back at the hotel where Gemma and Anthony were staying—miles from the mountain lodge— Anthony mentioned his frustration with Eddie. "He barely sat with us all evening."

"What are you talking about? We ate dinner together."

"Yeah, and in between bites he was up and talking to his friends."

Gemma rolled her eyes. "You're exaggerating. Besides, we're the ones who interrupted *his* vacation."

"He invited us!"

Gemma shrugged.

"We drive this far and he can't even meet us in town? We have to go *all the way* to him? And then he can't even sit with us for a solid hour?"

Gemma felt tension in her shoulders. She didn't know what to say in the moment. This was her boyfriend, and the man she wanted to marry, having a very strong reaction to her brother, the man she'd spent her whole life trying to have a relationship with.

Anthony threw his bag on the bed and unzipped it. "And Tony? *Tony*?"

"I know. I'm sorry."

Anthony stopped in the moment and looked at her. He walked over to where she was sitting on the other bed and knelt in front of her. His tone was soft. "Gemma, you don't have anything to be sorry for. I'm not frustrated at you. I'm frustrated *for* you."

Gemma smiled at him and leaned in for a kiss. She had

misinterpreted his anger. Though she felt slight relief at this, her chest was still gripped with the realization that Anthony and Eddie might never get on. *A jock and a nerd rarely do,* Gemma thought as Anthony rose to get ready for bed.

The next morning, Gemma awoke with her chest still tight. And though she should have just let the previous night go, she couldn't. For the next two days of the road trip, she and Anthony fought over Eddie, and what Anthony saw as Eddie's selfish and dismissive behavior, and what Gemma saw as Anthony being a snob. Hundreds of miles later, the fight turned into Anthony feeling like Gemma was taking Eddie's side over his. And finally, a hundred miles after that, they had exhausted themselves on their very first fight as a couple, even pulling onto the side of the road to climb into the back seat for a sweaty release of pleasure.

After that encounter on the shoulder of a two-lane highway, with both of them giggling as they buttoned up their shirts and pants, Gemma didn't think she'd ever fight with Anthony about Eddie again. But in truth, that fight would repeat itself over and over throughout their relationship—Gemma constantly trying to explain to an only child how sibling dynamics worked, and Anthony trying to tell a smart, independent woman how pathetic it was to see her pander to any man, especially Eddie. The day before they got married—when Mary informed Gemma and Anthony that Eddie wouldn't be making the wedding after all—they fought again. And now, standing in a hospital room with their newborn hooked to machines and tubes, Gemma felt that same tension building again.

Anthony would never forgive this. Not ever. If she told him the truth, it would end any hope for a relationship between Eddie and Anthony. Between her and Eddie. Saying what really happened would be the end of something Gemma had spent her whole life trying to get started, and her whole relationship with Anthony trying to explain and be understood.

Still, in the moment, even Gemma was surprised to hear herself so casually, so effortlessly, so convincingly say, "I was holding Calvin and I tripped."

CHAPTER 9

Gemma watched Anthony's face cloud with confusion and anger, yet she felt an odd wave of relief. He had every right to be angry. But if his fury was directed at her, at least it wouldn't be directed at Eddie. Why this was of importance in the moment was a question Gemma was not ready to face.

"He was sleeping in my arms, and I tripped and dropped him," she repeated.

Anthony moved backward so slightly that only a couple in the most intimate of relationships would detect it. The shift was undetectable to the untrained eye, but it felt cavernous to Gemma. His strong hands, which had been resting on her hips, dropped from their post in what felt like slow motion.

"It's okay," he whispered. "It could have happened to anyone."

He cleared his throat lightly and moved to face Calvin, who was still sleeping soundly in the bassinet, the beeps of the monitors so rhythmic they made Gemma sleepy, and her eyes began to close.

"I'm so sorry," she whispered.

Anthony put up a hand, rejecting the apology. "Gemma, it was an accident. There is nothing to apologize for."

Gemma opened her mouth to say something, to try to bridge the ravine forming between them, but she didn't have a way back to him. She couldn't tell the truth. Not yet, not before they knew what would happen to Calvin. And she couldn't explain much more because it was a lie, and she was far too tired to weave a plausible tale that would make all of this even remotely okay.

All she could do was stand there, inches from her husband, who was watching their infant son sleep, tracing the outline of Anthony's face with her eyes. His profile was very angular—the sharpness of his nose, the point of his chin. Even his forehead slanted in a way that seemed geometric rather than organic. She had told him, while they were lying in bed one night talking, that his profile always looked angry, but the front of his face was tender and joyful. "Give me your face!" she would say if he was lying on his back. And he would laugh and then dramatically flip over on his side to face her with a wide grin. "This better?" he would ask. "Much!" she would say, always happy to see the creases around his eyes and his dimple on display. The angles of his face softened with the shift in perspective.

But right now, in the dark hospital room, his profile was illuminated by the single beam of light coming in through the crack in the door. Though they were standing close enough to hear one another's heartbeats, he wasn't giving her his face.

Not at that moment.

At that moment, it was clear to Gemma that he had to look away.

———

Gemma managed to fall asleep on the bench under the window in Calvin's room. One minute she had been watching Anthony stare at their son, whose swollen face looked worse with each passing hour, the swelling so pronounced it looked as though his eye might explode. The next minute she was asleep in the same position she had lowered herself into when she felt her knees might buckle. And in that pretzel shape, the shape of a woman who was trying to stay awake but whose body was giving way, Gemma fell into a deep sleep for the first time in nearly twenty-four hours.

Her eyes fluttered as her brain began its nightly performance of wildly vivid dreams. Her dreams were always so detailed and vibrant that she often jolted awake, breathing heavily. For a brief period in college, she had gone to the effort of keeping a dream journal, but after a few months, she grew bored by the task. It felt like writing down the fantasies of a toddler. Besides, she'd had one too many of her psych professors equate dream interpretation to numerology or astrology.

But tonight, lying on a hard vinyl bench and covered by a thin, scratchy blanket, Gemma was visited by a series of images both mundanely familiar and captivatingly new.

She heard sirens.

Her legs were burning.

Eddie was yelling.

She couldn't find her dad.

She ran toward Eddie's truck.

His screams got softer.

She was at the football stadium.

She fell to the ground.

She saw flashing lights.

She heard a faint scream, "What have I done!?"

What have I done?

Gemma jerked awake to see Anthony above her. He was pressing on her arm.

"They're ready to take Calvin for the scan." She reached up to rub her eyes. "I've fed him, and he seems calm and relatively comfortable."

Gemma sat upright, feeling a pinch in her neck. "How long was I asleep?"

Anthony glanced down at his watch. "Twenty minutes."

Instinctively, Gemma reached under her to check for a leak. She was dry. Only then did she realize the room was full of nurses, moving monitors and rolling Calvin's bassinet away from the wall. Gemma jumped up and rushed to his side. When she looked down at him, she gasped. His face had turned from red to a deeply violet purple. Her hand shot up to her mouth.

Anthony stepped up beside her, his hand on her back. "It's okay, Gemma."

Gemma bent down to kiss Calvin's head. "In what world is any of this okay?"

"We will take him for the scan and then bring him right back," said a short man with thick glasses and orange scrubs, a color that Gemma thought would have looked like a prison jumpsuit if not for the embroidered name across the left side of his chest: *Tomás*.

"How long will he be gone?" she asked.

"The machine is free, and we are headed there now," said Tomás. "We should be back within thirty minutes." He looked at Anthony for a beat and then back at Gemma. "Might I suggest you take this time to get some breakfast?"

Anthony nodded. Gemma's stomach clenched in refusal at the mention of food. She hadn't eaten any of the deli tray at home—she didn't want any more food in her stomach until she could make a bowel movement.

Tomás and the team of scrubbed soldiers filed out of the room, pushing the plastic bassinet in which her bruised and battered son was sleeping. As she watched him being wheeled out, Gemma noticed a shadow move just outside the door. The shadow shortened until it was replaced by her mother, standing in the doorway.

"Mom!" Gemma rushed to Irene, who embraced her. With her mother's arms around her, Gemma began to cry, realizing that was all she ever did anymore. They held each other for a full minute, both women crying in the sun-soaked hospital room.

Then, without speaking, they walked arm in arm to the bench and sat down, looking up at Anthony expectedly.

He took the cue. "I'm going to get us all some coffee and breakfast."

Gemma nodded but said nothing as Anthony glided out of the room. *Even in a crisis, my husband is a graceful man,* Gemma thought.

She rubbed away snot with the back of her hand and turned to Irene. "How did you know we were here?"

Irene wiped her eyes. "Eddie called us."

"Have you let Mary know?"

"Of course. She's on her way to your house to be with Bo when he wakes up."

Gemma hung her head. "Bo . . . ," she whispered.

"Bo isn't even awake. And when he does wake up, Mary and Eddie are going to take him for pancakes."

"Well, at least one of my kids is okay."

Irene stroked her daughter's hand with her own. "Both of your kids are okay. I spoke with the nurses' station. They said the doctor should meet with us just a little before noon"—she glanced at her phone—"which is in five hours."

Gemma shook her head in confusion. *How did she know this before I did?* she wondered. She quickly pushed the thought aside because she was just happy to have her mother there. Because, at that moment, *being* a mother was too much. Too hard. Gemma wanted more than anything to go back to her own childhood, where the adults around her took on all the stress and she ran through the sprinklers in the yard.

Her shoulders slumped as the tears rolled down her face. "I'm a terrible mother."

Irene rubbed the curve of Gemma's back. "You are a wonderful mother," she whispered.

"You haven't seen him."

"That's true," Irene said. "But according to the nurses, everyone is optimistic."

Gemma sat up straight to face her mother. "What the hell, Mom?"

"What?"

"How is it possible you had conversations with these people—*helpful* conversations?" Gemma stood up to distance herself from her mother. "I can't even get those assholes to give me a fucking maxi pad!" She began to pace.

"Gemma," Irene said in a soothing tone.

Gemma crossed her arms. "What, Mom? What do you want from me? What do I need to be doing that I am not?" she demanded, her voice raised and cracked with sobs.

Irene stared at Gemma, blinking a few times before finally saying, "I need you to come sit down and let me take care of you."

Gemma sighed, letting out a cathartic breath, and rejoined her mother on the bench. "Mom, I am terrified."

"I know."

Gemma buried her face in her hands. "And I can't . . . I can't bring myself to look much at my baby."

"It's okay."

"Every time I look at him, it physically hurts."

"What even happened? Eddie said he didn't know. Said he woke up to the baby screaming and you all sprinting out the door."

Gemma looked at her mother, feeling young beside her.

Feeling vulnerable. She wanted to tell her the truth. To talk about the image she couldn't unsee—Eddie's extended arm and the curve of her newborn son lying on the floor screaming. She needed to share it, to relieve herself of the image. Of the truth.

But as her lips parted to speak, a realization hit her. She couldn't tell her mother the truth when she had told her husband a lie. Which is why, sitting in the hospital room now with her mother, despite how much she wanted to say what really happened—that Eddie had fallen asleep and let go of Calvin—she looked her mother dead in the eyes and said, "I tripped over the rug and dropped him."

"Did he hit the coffee table?"

"The fireplace."

Irene nodded. A nod so knowing Gemma thought she might punch her own mother in the throat. A nod that said, *If you had just put the bumpers on like I said, we could be back at your place enjoying Eddie, rather than here with you in the hospital.*

"It's completely my fault," Gemma said with finality.

"Oh honey!" Irene said, shaking her head. "Not at all! This was an accident!"

"Does that make it any less horrifying? Do you think Calvin cares whether it was an accident or on purpose?"

"Gemma . . ."

"Just let me be, Mom."

Irene's hand went up. "Fair enough."

"Sorry. I'm just so fucking tired."

"Tell me what you need."

Gemma rubbed her temples as she thought. She needed so many things. A shower. A nap. Her pain meds. The list was so long that she wasn't sure where to start. Defeated, she looked up at the ceiling and said: "I need to take a shit, Mom."

She glanced over at her mother to see her eyes twinkling.

The corners of Irene's mouth began to curl. Her nostrils flared before her chest jumped and she was overcome with laughter.

Gemma stared at her in disbelief. "Dammit, Mom!"

Which only made Irene laugh louder.

"Mother," Gemma said firmly, but she felt a lightness bubble up in her stomach. "Mom," she said again as a smile spread across her face. And together the women laughed, softly at first, and then picking up steam, the laughter rolling out of the room and down the hall, meeting Anthony, who walked in carrying a holder full of coffee cups, a stack of Styrofoam boxes, and an expression that made Gemma immediately stop laughing.

"What could possibly be funny?" he asked, setting the cups and food down on the counter. He didn't just look confused; he looked disappointed.

Irene stood to greet him in a hug. "Hi, Anthony. It was nothing."

"No, seriously," he said, barely returning his mother-in-law's embrace. "What could possibly make you laugh at a time like this?"

"Jesus, Anthony," Gemma said. "I just told Mom that I have not taken a shit since before I gave birth."

Anthony lowered his head and turned his attention to the coffee cups. He handed Irene one with a weak smile, and then sat beside Gemma, handing over hers.

"You really haven't pooped since you gave birth?" Anthony asked with a face so full of concern that Gemma realized how much she yearned to be taken care of.

But her eyes caught the empty space in the room where the bassinet had been, and she was reminded that there were bigger concerns facing her than her bowels.

"You must be uncomfortable," Anthony said. "Is there something we can do?"

Gemma shrugged, taking a cautious sip of her coffee. "No,

it will come. I just need to heal down there a little bit more and then I can push it out."

"Unless you're constipated," Irene said so casually that Anthony raised his eyebrows. "If you're taking pain meds but not having any movements, that's likely why."

Gemma noticed Irene's earrings for the first time since she had entered the room. *My son is in the hospital, and you had the forethought and time to put on earrings?* Gemma marveled.

"I can go to the store in the lobby and get some laxatives," Anthony suggested.

"I think I'm okay," Gemma said softly.

But she could tell Anthony was already thinking through this option. "No, I'm going to go get you some."

"Anthony."

"Gemma, I can't risk the possibility of you being admitted while Calvin is."

Gemma sat up straight, turned to face Anthony, and threw her hands up. "I'm sorry my immense pain is a problem for *you.*"

"Gemma," he responded, shaking his head.

"But I *am* fine."

"I just want to get on top of this for you—for me and Calvin and Bo and you—before it turns into something more serious."

"I'm not sure laxatives will do much at this point," Irene said, reminding Anthony and Gemma she was in the room.

"Why not?" Anthony snapped.

"If she hasn't gone in a week, and she's had pain meds, and likely not drinking much water . . . ," Irene trailed off before saying, "We are past the point of laxatives."

Gemma looked at her mother in confusion, until her brows unknitted in realization. "No fucking way, Mom."

"What?" Anthony said. "What? What am I missing?"

Irene took a sip of her coffee. "It will be easy and effective."

"For who, Mom?" Gemma shot at her.

"We have time. I can get one across the street at the pharmacy, and we can do it right here in the room."

"Tell me what the hell you are talking about!" Anthony demanded.

"Oh yeah?" Gemma yelped. "Right here in this room?"

"Yes, ma'am." Irene nodded. "You'll be good as new before Calvin goes into surgery."

"For the love of God, what the hell are you talking about?" Anthony asked so loudly both women turned from glaring at each other to look at him.

In unison they shouted, "An enema!"

———

Calvin's scan went well, and the surgeon came to speak to Gemma and Anthony and Irene. While it was true the orbital bones looked damaged, he couldn't tell to what extent. But as it looked, he did not think the damage would cause long-term problems for Calvin's left eye. The ER doctor, it seemed, had inadvertently exaggerated the injury.

"I can't know for sure until we are in the OR, but you have every reason to be hopeful," the surgeon said, and was met with the sigh of three adults craving relief.

"What will happen in this surgery?" Gemma asked, more alert given the large coffee she had consumed.

"And how long will it take?" Anthony added.

"The procedure is about two hours long," said the surgeon. "And until I get in there, I'm not exactly sure what will need to be done. As I mentioned, a CT scan on this type of injury isn't always as clear with an infant as it is with an adult because an infant's face is so small, making all the bones much more compact. If it's his nasal bone, I'll perform what's called transnasal wiring, which is essentially like sewing his bones back in place with metal thread. We do that if it looks like the nasal bridge needs support. Now, if it's an orbital wall blowout—that's the bones under and on the outside of his eye—I'll potentially need to replace any bones that shattered with a tiny polyurethane piece."

"Wait, what?" Gemma asked, her voice cracking. "You're putting *metal* in my baby?"

The surgeon nodded. "Or plastic."

"Is there any alternative?" Irene asked.

"I understand it sounds intense," said the surgeon, his graying mustache providing a good place for Gemma's eyes to fixate while she processed the news. "But this is common for orbital bone breaks. And keep in mind, kids get these broken a lot. Mostly in sports, but still."

"Certainly not in infants," Irene said in a way that made Gemma shudder with shame.

The surgeon shifted his weight, a sadness spreading across his face. "We get abuse cases from time to time. But relative to those kinds of injuries, what we have here is very manageable, and you can be optimistic."

Gemma looked at the doctor, fresh waves of guilt rushing over her. Until that moment, it had never crossed her mind that anyone might look at what happened to her baby and suspect abuse.

"Whether it's sports injuries or cases like this, the process is the same," he continued. "The only difference is that, given Calvin's age, he may need this surgery again when he's six or so."

"Why?" Anthony asked.

"Well, as the skull grows, there may be a need to rethread the wiring or replace any poly piece."

"That means we are looking at at least two surgeries?" Gemma asked.

"No." The surgeon smiled slightly. "We are looking at just the one right now. And we will reassess around age five or six—at that point the skull is about ninety percent of the size it will be as an adult—and determine then if another surgery is necessary."

The three adults, all lined up in a row in front of the doctor, stared at him, none able to find the next question.

The surgeon aided them. "Now, you may be wondering about a scar."

Gemma squeezed her eyes shut. She hadn't thought about that either.

"There will be a scar, but given how young he is, it will likely not even be noticeable as he ages. And in fact, the incision we make follows the natural curve under the eye," he said, gesturing with his pinky to his own eye, "so the scar blends in with the natural creases formed over time."

Again, there was silence in the room.

"I'm not feeling well," Gemma finally said, surprising herself.

The surgeon looked at her with concern. "Have you spoken to your ob-gyn?"

Gemma bent over and wrapped her arms across her lower stomach.

The surgeon looked at Anthony, then at Irene, before addressing them both. "This is a lot for any parent." Irene and Anthony nodded. "But," he said, lowering his voice, "Calvin's not the one I'm most worried about." Gemma walked a few steps away from the huddle and leaned over, resting her hands on her knees, but continued to listen intently. "Keep an eye on her," he said, gathering up his clipboard. "Your son is in excellent hands. We'll come get him in an hour, and by this afternoon things will be much better." Gemma looked up to see the doctor nod to Anthony, then to Irene, before walking out of the room.

"It's time," Irene announced.

Gemma watched as Anthony walked over to the counter and grabbed a plastic CVS bag. He pulled out a box and read the label. "It doesn't seem like a good sign that this is a two pack."

Irene smiled lightly and extended her hand for the box.

"Gemma," she said. "It's time." To both Anthony and Irene's surprise, Gemma nodded. A defeated nod.

"Anthony," Irene said, "do you want to go out in the hall for a little bit?"

"I'm not leaving her," he said.

Gemma, who had curled up on the bench, her knees up to her chin, looked at Anthony and her chest filled with gratitude. "I'm not leaving you," he said when she looked at him.

Gemma smiled, tears dripping over her nose and onto the bench. "Thank you," she said softly. "Can you guard the door?"

Anthony grabbed the plastic chair beside Calvin's bassinet, carried it across the room, and set it down facing the door.

"Okay," Irene said to Gemma. "You'll need to take your pants off."

Gemma stood slowly, removed her sweats, and folded them in a way she never did at home when there wasn't a need to stall. "What about my mesh underwear?" she called to her mother, who was at the sink filling the enema bottle.

"I can work around it," Irene called back.

Gemma, wearing nothing but the stained sweatshirt, sports bra, and mesh underwear containing a half-full maxi pad, turned to face the window, giving her bottom to the room. To her mother. To her sleeping baby. To the back of Anthony. She shut her eyes and whispered to herself, "You're okay. Just blow out the candles."

She felt her mother's cold fingers separate her cheeks—which she instinctively clenched—then the pressure of the nozzle, and finally the bubbling feeling of her body filling with fluid.

"Wow," Irene exclaimed as she squeezed tighter and tighter around the bottle, pushing the warm liquid into her youngest child.

"What?" Gemma grunted through held breath.

"Your hemorrhoids don't look bad at all."

Gemma felt the release of the nozzle being extracted, and the immediate gurgle of her lower stomach. She sat up, gently at first, before realizing she really needed to sit on a toilet, which was at least three feet away, and she was suddenly convinced she couldn't make it and would indeed shit on the floor. Irene stifled a giggle as Gemma quickly waddled to the toilet and slammed down on it.

She swatted her hand at Irene, a sign for her to close the bathroom door. "Oh my god, oh my god, I can't do this!" she grunted. "It's going to hurt! I can't do this!" She began sobbing and shaking, her hands gripping the toilet seat under her legs. Her body shook as she watched her mother approach the bathroom door, wink at her, and then close it slowly. The moment the door clicked, the movement came over Gemma strong and fast, ripping through her. She screamed out in anguish, her voice rising at the rate of the pain. And as the last bit of excrement left her body, she felt her voice give way. She started laughing despite her bottom, her vagina, her stomach clenching in agony. The suddenly empty sensation felt as heroic as when Calvin's massive head emerged from between her legs. Relief overcame Gemma, and she was crying and laughing and sweating, her fingers still clenched around the toilet seat. She worked to slow her breathing down, wanting to soak in the feeling—the same feeling every good poop gives, but with added layers of physical achievement and immense relief. When her breath finally slowed and her rectum stopped pulsing, she lifted a hand to the toilet paper holder, slowly unrolling a large amount before tearing it off and balling it up in her fist. Then a thought hit her. Her smile faded and her brows furrowed.

"Wait," she called out. "I have hemorrhoids?"

CHAPTER 10

Gemma's phone rang. "Boss" flashed across the screen. Dr. Heinz hated when Gemma called him Boss, but she loved the way he rolled his eyes when she did, so she'd put him in her contacts that way. She swiped her thumb and brought the phone up to her ear.

"Hey, Boss," she said in a voice she hoped would mask her stress.

"Have I caught you at a bad time?"

Gemma worked to swallow her tears, to not even make a sniffing sound. But she was talking to a highly trained psychoanalyst.

"Tell me more," he said softly but firmly.

"It's Ca-Calvin," Gemma sputtered, her tears spilling out.

"Tell me more."

"He's in surgery. His eye. His eye is . . ."

"Tell me more."

"He fell on his eye and the bone is broken and he's in surgery, I haven't had any sleep, or anything to eat, really, and my brother is in town, and the nurse was rude to me when I asked for a pad, and my mom just gave me a fucking enema in front of Anthony!"

There were several seconds of silence.

"Tell me . . . less."

Gemma yelped with a single laugh, tears still rolling down her face. She felt free to laugh in the quiet room she had found at the end of the hallway. It was a corner common area, where floor-to-ceiling windows came together in a forty-five-degree angle. In the triangular space was a couch and two chairs. It was clearly designed for stressed parents to find a moment of solitude amid the chaos.

She had gone in there about an hour into Calvin's surgery. Her father showed up fifteen minutes before they wheeled Calvin out, and Gemma felt a strong desire to cry, but she knew it would make her father squirm. So instead she smiled brightly, embraced him, and pushed her tears down. She noticed Jack didn't get within three feet of the bassinet. It shouldn't have bothered her—this was how her father was in the most vulnerable moments—but his intentional distance from her son filled her with sadness. Even though it was just the four of them—Gemma, Anthony, Irene and Jack—the room felt packed despite everyone being spread out against the walls. It was mostly small talk; Anthony refused to participate, leaving Gemma to smile and feign optimism.

At a certain point in the conversation, when Jack brought up the chance of rain, she felt an inescapable lump boiling up inside her throat. "Excuse me for a minute," she said, her index finger raised and a forced smile across her face. Anthony looked at her to check for tears—an expression she knew all too well—which made the force of her emotions all the stronger.

She just made it out of Calvin's room and down the hall, into the pie-shaped glass room, before she was down on her knees gasping for air through tears. She was so grateful to be alone and yet yearned for a hug. Or a Kleenex. After a few minutes on the floor, she was able to rise and seat herself on the couch, thrilled to find it was actually cushy and not like the hard vinyl bench in Calvin's room.

She was able to calm herself using breathing exercises. And during those exercises she started to think of work. Of her beautiful, sunny office downtown. Of the coffee shop across the street from their building. Of Betty, her newest patient, who gave her such terrible anxiety—a clear instance of countertransference. Of the broken air conditioner in the break room, which made it too hot to want to get a snack. As her mind swirled around all the pleasant and annoying aspects of her job, she felt herself longing—growing homesick, even— for the routine she had given up, even if only temporarily, for maternity leave.

During that thought, that feeling of wanting to go back to a routine that she had been so excited to trade for maternity leave just a few weeks ago, her phone's screen had illuminated with "Boss."

"I believe I'm falling apart," she said with a sigh.

"You are facing a lot," he replied.

Gemma bit hard on her lip, swallowing the intense distress. She shifted her emotions, as if shuffling a deck of cards, until she found a better one to play.

"So, what's up?"

"Gemma."

"No, no, distract me. Why are you calling?"

"I was calling to check on you. Ask how things are going. Hear about your new son. See if you got the pasta from Rick's."

This reminder that she had just given birth but was not sitting at home with Calvin on her lap, having this conversation with a colleague about her baby's big head and cute chin dimple, ripped through her body like a bolt of anger. And yet that anger was replaced almost immediately with overwhelming resentment that Eddie had eaten half the pasta dish.

"He's perfect," she whispered. "But I've ruined everything."

"Gemma," he said firmly. "Tell me what's going on."

Gemma told him that Calvin had accidently landed on the bricks, that they had come to the hospital in an ambulance. She described how swollen and bruised Calvin was. The way he had screamed. The foreign piece that was to be inserted into his new, tiny face. Her mother's earrings. Every detail she could think of from the past twenty-four hours—except exactly how Calvin had been catapulted onto the bricks.

"What do you need?" he asked.

"I have no idea." She sighed. "I'm exploding and dissolving. All at once."

"Feel the feelings."

"I'd rather not, thank you."

"Gemma, you know how trauma works."

"I know how it works for other people."

Dr. Heinz chuckled lightly. "You need to be present, to know what's happening. To gather facts and process the feelings those facts evoke in you."

"That's just the bullshit we tell our patients."

"Bullshit it may be," Dr. Heinz said. "But it pays the bills. And it can work."

"I think I know what will help."

"Oh?"

"Assuming the surgery goes well, and that the recovery really is just sleep, which is all a newborn does anyway, I think I want to cut my maternity leave short."

"Gemma—"

"No, hear me out. Twelve weeks felt excessive when I asked for it. I'm thinking just eight."

"Gemma, it hasn't even been *one*."

"You asked what I needed."

"Okay, okay. Maybe let's come back to this idea when you're home and settled."

Gemma knew this trick. It was what every parent, every schoolteacher, every babysitter did to a kid who was begging for something they shouldn't have. How often had she done this to Bo when they went to the zoo and passed the gift shop? "The stuffed tiger will still be there on the way out, Bo. Let's look at the animals first." Then Bo would pass out in his stroller after the penguins, and home their family went—tiger-free. Yes, Gemma knew Dr. Heinz was treating her like a child, hoping she'd wear herself out on a want and burn the desire like fuel until she had no power left.

"Okay, Boss, I gotta go and check on my child. He should be getting out of surgery soon."

"Gemma—"

And with the sound of her name coming out of his mouth, she pressed her thumb hard on the red button. "Asshole," she muttered, standing up to leave the triangular space. As she turned fully around, she saw Anthony on the other side of the glass. His face looked crushed.

As if something terrible had happened.

As if the surgeon had bad news.

As if Calvin's eye was damaged beyond repair.

"What?" she mouthed, her heart racing.

He just shook his head.

She rushed to the door, pulled it open forcefully. "Is Calvin all right?"

"He's still in surgery," Anthony said, pushing past her and into the room.

Gemma breathed a sigh of relief. "Then what's with the face?"

Anthony stood at the apex of the room, looking out, his hands resting on the wood railing that wrapped around the room. "You left me back there with your parents."

"I was about to lose it," Gemma shot back.

"And I'm . . . I'm what?" he said, his back still to her. "Doing just fine?"

"Anthony . . ."

"Who were you talking to?"

His voice echoed off the glass. A lump swelled in Gemma's throat. Anthony never spoke like this to her. Even in their worst fights, Gemma's voice would rise but Anthony's never would. She loved this about him.

"Heinz," she said, embarrassed at how soft her voice was.

"Ah."

"What?"

Anthony turned to face her, crossing his arms and leaning his body against the glass. "I just find it ridiculous that you left me while our son is *in surgery*, to come make a call to your boss."

Gemma's eyes widened. "*He* called *me*!"

Anthony stared at her for a few seconds more before uncrossing his arms and walking toward the door. "But you answered."

Gemma shifted her weight. "He was checking on me."

"And what did you say?" he asked in a harsh tone as he put his hand on the door.

"I told him about the accident. What the surgeon said. That he's in surgery right now, but we're optimistic."

"Did you tell him how it happened?"

Gemma didn't know if he was asking this to punish her, or to protect her. All she could manage in return was "I told him I was thinking about cutting my maternity leave short."

"Are you serious right now?"

"I don't know, it was just something I was thinking."

"Since when?" he asked, his voice raised. "When the hell have you had time to think about returning to work?"

"I haven't been thinking about it!" she yelled, her voice rising to match his. "The idea just came to me while I was talking to him. I haven't made any decision. Calm down."

"Don't tell me to calm down, Gemma. My son is in surgery."

"*Your* son?" her eyes narrowed. "He's my son too."

"Then act like it," he said coolly over his shoulder as he walked out of the room, the heavy glass door's hinges sighing in disgust as they contracted.

——

Calvin's surgeon entered the room to find four adults not talking. Probably a typical day in the pediatric wing, but the air was so heavy that Gemma felt bad for him. Irene was creating the only noise in the room with the clicking of her knitting needles. She always carried knitting with her, though Mary and Gemma often joked that they had never seen a finished product. Jack was staring at his fingers, which were clasped in front of him on his lap. Anthony was standing, leaning against the wall, his gaze oscillating between the ceiling and his feet. And Gemma was sitting on the hard bench, looking from her mother to her father to her husband, over and over. She was grateful for a break in the monotony, even though that break could bring bad news.

But when the surgeon caught Gemma's eyes, he smiled. And Gemma immediately knew.

"My baby is okay?" she asked, phrasing it as a question though she knew the answer in her bones.

"Your baby is okay," he said.

Jack nodded and cleared his throat. Irene tossed aside her needles and stood. Anthony hoisted his body away from the wall and clapped once. And Gemma ran to the surgeon and threw her arms around him. He patted Gemma's back awkwardly with one hand.

"Okay, okay," Anthony said, while Gemma refused to let go of the doctor. "Tell us everything."

Gemma released her arms and backed away from the surgeon, who removed his glasses to speak.

"As I suspected, the X-ray and the CT scan were a little misleading. Meaning they looked worse than what it was. There weren't breaks in three bones as we originally thought, rather just a break in one, and the other two were fractured. This is very good news for a few reasons."

Gemma's heart was beating with such relief, such gratitude, that she found it hard to breathe.

"It means we had to repair less, so we were able to use less metal wire. And based on its location, your son shouldn't need a second surgery."

Irene started to cry. Gemma was always amazed at how much her mother could cry when she was happy. Gemma only knew tears of sadness, shame, and anger.

"The other reason it's good is because when these bones break, they're more likely to pierce the eye or have a shard break off and damage an ocular nerve. Because that wasn't the case here, your son's eye shouldn't suffer short- or long-term damage."

"What about the bruising?" Anthony asked.

"We're always happy to see bruising and protruding, because that means it's not happening inside, like in the brain. His bruising is just like any you would experience if you walked into a coffee table or got hit by a baseball. It's just more pronounced because he's so small."

"So now what?" Gemma asked, wanting to see her baby, wanting to leave the hospital immediately. Wanting to get some food. Wanting to take a shower. Wanting to get back to Eddie.

"Well, he's waking up in recovery. Mom, I'm going to take you back there to be with him while he does." He looked at Anthony and said, "It's a small space so we only allow one person per patient. We will keep Calvin at least one more night for observation. But you should be out of here and home with your baby by the weekend."

Gemma saw Jack remove his glasses and wipe an eye with

the back of his hand. Irene's makeup had long since been rinsed from her face by the salty wash she couldn't seem to stop. And Anthony was smiling, just slightly, for the first time all day. Seeing everyone around her visibly relax, Gemma felt her own body unfurl into a puddle on the floor and then evaporate into the air.

"I'll have the nurse schedule two follow-up appointments. One for a week from now, just to check the surgical site. And the other for about twelve weeks out, which is when we will know for sure if he's fully in the clear." The surgeon reached out to shake Jack's hand, then Irene's, and then Anthony's. "Mom," he said, turning back to Gemma, "you're coming with me to see your baby."

She turned to her family and smiled. All returned her smile except Anthony, who nodded and turned to sit in the plastic chair. Her heart tensed. But the thought of seeing Calvin moved her body into action.

Once they were in the hallway and walking toward the recovery unit, she looked up at the surgeon, only then aware of how tall he was.

"Thank you so much," she said. "I don't even have words to express how grateful I am to you."

He didn't respond. Instead he kept his eyes straight ahead and walked alongside Gemma in silence for a few paces before stopping at the intersection of two hallways to face her.

"I'm a pediatric ophthalmologist," he said.

"Yes . . . I know," Gemma said in confusion.

"So, forgive me for swimming out of my lane here, but my medical opinion is that you need to make sure you take care of yourself."

She blinked at him in silence. Knowing he was right, but unable to respond.

"Okay," he said, resuming his stride. "Let's go see that beautiful boy of yours."

CHAPTER 11

Gemma was warned by the surgeon before they walked into the recovery room that Calvin would look worse than when she saw him last. Even that didn't prepare her. Calvin's left eye was covered with taped-down gauze. His left cheek looked more swollen than before. What little hair he had was matted down with what Gemma assumed was sweat but might have been antiseptic. He was wiggling around on the gurney—a larger version of his bassinet—and whimpering. She stared at him for a few moments before a nurse interrupted her, saying, "Go ahead and pick him up, Mama. He needs you."

Gemma whipped her head around to see the nurse, a mousey older woman with gray at her temples. "Of course!" Gemma's eyes lifted to the ceiling with a deprecating smile. "I was just admiring him." She was filled with shame. Not just for how bandaged her newborn son's face was, but for how she didn't instinctively reach for him when she saw him. *What the hell is wrong with you?* she asked herself as she gingerly lifted Calvin to her shoulder.

The nurse continued to watch her, which was probably just a means of checking on Calvin, but to Gemma it felt for all the world like the glare of judgment. Her hands shook as she gripped her infant. She looked to her left and then her right before spotting a large rocking chair. As she lowered herself into the chair, she was relieved to see that the nurse had disappeared.

"There we go," she said softly to Calvin, whose face was still twisted in discomfort, wrinkling his eye patch. "Mama's here," she whispered, which brought on a gentle rain of tears. She pushed the chair back and forth gently with her feet. And though the movement and the way in which she held Calvin—and even the voice in which she spoke to him—was identical to everything she had done with Bo, she felt like a fish trying to walk. Perhaps it was because Calvin was so disoriented, but she couldn't get her body and his in sync.

Suddenly the nurse reappeared beside her. "This helps soothe them," she said, handing Gemma a small bottle labeled with the formula company's name. As she reached up to take the bottle, she remembered something a friend had told her before she gave birth to Bo: "Whatever you do, don't ever use those bottles of formula they give you at the hospital. It's a global conspiracy of Big Formula to push that crap on you."

Gemma had laughed. "Big *Formula*?"

"I'm not joking," her friend had said.

Even the one thing that might bring her child comfort came layered with judgment. Gemma nodded a thank-you to the nurse and tickled the nipple to Calvin's lips before he opened automatically and began sucking. With his lips sealed around the nipple and the sound of liquid entering his throat, he let out a contented sigh. "Oh Calvin!" Gemma whispered. And she started to cry, yet again. This time she almost believed, just almost, that her tears were the kind her mother always cried.

———

Mary was waiting in the room when Gemma returned with a nurse pushing a very full and sleeping Calvin in the bassinet.

"There she is," Mary said in a way that made Gemma feel happy like a little kid.

She rushed to Mary's embrace, burying her face in the stiffness of Mary's hair, tears and snot leaking in equal measure.

"It's all okay," Mary whispered. "He's okay."

Anthony positioned himself in front of the bassinet, making it impossible for Irene or Jack to get to Calvin.

"What all did they say?" Anthony asked, causing Gemma and Mary to break their embrace.

"Who?" Gemma asked, wiping her tears with the bottom of her T-shirt.

"The doctor? The nurses? Anyone in the recovery unit?" he asked without looking away from Calvin.

"Oh," Gemma said sheepishly. "I was able to soothe him and give him a bottle. There are pain meds in the IV, so he should sleep most of the day."

Anthony looked up at Gemma, and for a split second he held an expression that she was used to—one of love and warmth and friendship. He opened his mouth to say something, but before he could, Jack cleared his throat, causing Anthony to blink and his face to fall back into its twist of worry.

Everyone turned to face Jack.

"How about I get everyone some lunch downstairs?" he suggested.

Anthony looked at Jack in disbelief before Mary spoke up. "Anthony, why don't you go down with Mom and Dad and get you and Gemma some lunch. I'll stay here with Gemma."

Anthony nodded in agreement. It always impressed Gemma how much Mary could command a room. A courtroom, her living room, this hypertense hospital room. Plus, Anthony loved Mary deeply, like she was his own sister, and was slow to push back on her about much of anything. The day of their wedding, Anthony had been quiet and somber given the fight he and Gemma had had the night before about Eddie. Mary didn't know it, but Gemma overheard her pull Anthony outside—just a few feet from the window in the bathroom where Gemma was having her hair done—and say to him, "You are marrying Gemma today. Anything that happened yesterday, or hell, the past thirty years, does not matter now." Gemma hadn't been able to hear Anthony's muffled response, but she had burst with gratitude when Mary concluded, "Atta boy. Go enjoy your day." Gemma hoped Mary's presence now would ease the tension as it had then.

Jack, Irene, and Anthony filed out of the room, closing the door behind them. As soon as it clicked, Mary turned to Gemma. "Okay, talk."

"First tell me about Bo."

Mary swatted a hand. "Bo's fine. We took him to Al's this morning for pancakes."

"Does he know what's going on?"

"In the broadest of strokes," Mary replied, miming painting in the air.

"And Eddie's still with him?"

Mary clucked her tongue. "No, we decided to leave him at the diner. We trust they will raise him well."

Gemma sighed and started laughing. "Okay, okay," she said, reclining on the bench. "Is Eddie going to be all right?"

"I'm headed back there in just a bit," Mary said, glancing at her phone. "I told him I wouldn't leave him with Bo longer than an hour."

Gemma sat up straighter, her eyes narrowing with the rage that was trickling over her body. "Because heaven for-fucking-bid he be forced to do anything to help."

"Gemma," Mary warned. "That's not what I meant."

"Please."

"Gemma, the guy doesn't have kids. He doesn't know what to do."

"*You* don't have kids!"

Mary grinned. "Ah, but I'm incomparable."

"Stop it."

"Okay, okay. It was my call, not Eddie's. I figured you wouldn't want Eddie with Bo too long."

"Yeah, because he might take my kid to a documentary. Or a wine tasting."

The women sat in silence, space quickly filling up between them. Finally, Mary reached out and put her hand on Gemma's leg. "Tell me what happened."

"Why is everyone obsessed with that question?" Gemma snapped, brushing her sister's hand off her leg and standing up.

"Fair enough," Mary said, her hands up. "I just didn't get the story from Eddie because he said he didn't know." She looked at Gemma, who was pacing silently. "But you're right, it doesn't matter what hap—"

"I dropped him."

Mary stared up at Gemma. "What?"

"Yep. I had him, I was walking with him, and he was asleep and I was dicking around on my phone and I didn't see the coffee table and I tripped over it and Calvin went flying."

"Huh."

"What?"

Mary shook her head. "Nothing."

But Gemma was certain she saw a look of disbelief flash across her sister's face.

"Yes, this is all my fault," Gemma pressed further. "And Anthony is furious with me and will likely never forgive me because every time he looks at our child, he'll remember what I did."

"Gemma, it's *Anthony*."

"I'm aware." She walked back to the bench and sat down

with her head in her hands. "Nothing matters to that man more than the kids. Not even me."

"Hey, Gemma," Mary whispered, leaning over and rubbing her back. "What do you need?"

Gemma sighed heavily. "I need to stop crying."

"What else?"

"I need sleep. Like *so* much sleep."

"What else?"

"To make time pass quickly so I can get us all back home where my beautifully effective pain meds are."

"Okay, I have an idea that covers all three."

"Oh?"

Mary jumped up and opened the drawer under the bench to find a pillow and a blanket.

"Wow," Gemma said. "How did you know those were down there?"

"Meh. Lucky guess."

Mary fluffed the pillow and laid it on one side of the bench. She patted it for Gemma, who rolled her eyes but couldn't fight how good a nap would feel. She crawled down the bench and put her head on the scratchy pillow. Mary covered her with the blue blanket. Then she dragged the plastic chair closer to the bench and sat down beside Gemma.

"Now, you can't cry if you're sleeping." She smiled slyly. "And nothing passes the time like dreaming."

If she said anything after that, Gemma didn't hear it. She was already asleep.

———

Eddie is yelling.

Gemma sees her mother through the open doors of an ambulance.

There is a pain in Gemma's shoulder.

Gemma's ice cream cone is melting down her hand.

The faint sound of a desperate scream: "What have I done?"

Gemma yelped herself awake. Anthony was asleep in the plastic chair beside Calvin's bassinet. She was drenched in sweat and felt sticky and wet all over. She reached around to touch underneath her and felt the wetness. *Please be sweat,* she thought as she pulled her hand up to examine the moisture. It was bright red.

"Dammit!" Gemma growled, throwing off the blanket and standing to assess the damage. A stippling of blood dotted the bench. When she twisted around to peer at her backside, she saw the massacre.

She looked to Anthony for help, but his head was leaned back against the wall, and he was snoring. Gemma crept into the bathroom to remove her sweats. She squirted a blob of antiseptic soap onto the pancake-sized stain and turned on the cold water. While it ran over the stain, she began to work on soaping up her thighs, removing her mesh underwear and pressing a wad of toilet paper between her legs while she cleaned. Only when she began to rinse the underwear did she realize she had no other clothing options. She stood, naked from the waist down, sticky from sweat, nearly twenty-four hours since her last meal, her knees pressed together to hold the wad of toilet paper in place, and her mind racing over the details of the dream she had just startled herself out of. Her heart began pounding so hard she thought it might wake Calvin. A deafening roar rang in her ears. She felt certain that she was going to throw up. Or pass out. But she kept scrubbing, her hands shaking so violently she couldn't keep the fabric between her slippery fingers.

A soft knock on the door, then Anthony's voice: "Gemma?"

"Go away."

"Gemma . . ."

"I don't need help. Go away." As she spoke, the last bit of

energy drained from her body. Feeling her legs give way, she grabbed hold of the sink before collapsing onto the floor in a mixture of sweat and soap and blood and tile.

———

Darkness.

Sticky melted ice cream.

Sparks flying.

Her mother's long fingers stroking her hair.

The flashing lights are blinding.

Gemma startled awake again, opening her eyes to a circle of faces looking down on her, her body lying yet again on the vinyl bench. Irene's face came into focus first. She was waving something in front of Gemma's face. A magazine. She was fanning her daughter. Jack looked at her sternly. The nurse, Tomás, looked alert but not particularly concerned. And then her eyes panned over to Anthony, who looked as if he had aged a decade in a matter of hours. Her eyebrows knitted in confusion. She weakly reached out for him, but he shook his head as if to minimize his anguish.

"Anthony," she mouthed, her hand still extended.

The eyes of the circle followed the path of Gemma's arm until it met Anthony's. The circle broke into a horseshoe, allowing Anthony to kneel beside his wife and embrace her. They held each other and cried.

"Okay," Tomás said to Irene. "Here's a hospital gown for her, and I found some more of those mesh underwear."

Gemma and Anthony broke apart enough for her to look down and see that she had been covered from the hips down by a white towel. She nodded at Tomás appreciatively. Tomás nodded back and winked. Then he turned on his heel, looked quickly at the machines surrounding Calvin's bassinet, and walked out of the room.

"Well, this has just been a day!" Irene exclaimed. "Gemma, want me to help you get dressed?"

Gemma looked at Anthony, who kissed her firmly on the forehead before rising to his feet. He held out his hand to help Gemma stand, but once on her feet, she immediately had to sit back down.

"How about you and I give them a few minutes," Jack said to Anthony, slapping his back lightly. Anthony looked at Gemma for confirmation, who nodded once. He turned and left the room with his father-in-law.

Irene unpackaged the mesh underwear and went into the bathroom to find the extra pad. "I'm going to bring you into the bathroom. You think you can make it?"

Gemma nodded and extended both her arms. Irene guided her slowly into the bathroom and eased her onto the toilet. She turned away as Gemma cleaned herself, yet again, and inserted the pad into the sling of the underwear.

"Okay," Gemma said.

Irene knelt down in front of her daughter. "Right leg," Irene said as she stretched open one leg of the mesh underwear. Gemma complied. "Left leg."

"Mom," Gemma said.

"Mm-hmm?" replied Irene as she lifted her daughter and pulled up her underwear.

"Where's Mary?"

Irene worked to get the hospital gown around Gemma, fiddling with the strings. "She went back to watch Bo." She offered her arm for Gemma to loop into and together they shuffled slowly out of the bathroom.

"Just wanted to help Eddie?" Gemma asked, embarrassed she was hurt that Mary had left.

"No, dear. She had to *relieve* Eddie."

Gemma stopped a few steps from the bench and faced her mother.

"What do you mean?"

"He and Kat had to meet Mark and Lori. They want to get to Indianapolis and check into their Airbnb in time for an early dinner."

Gemma blinked at her mother. "Eddie . . . *left*?"

"He couldn't miss the marathon, dear," Irene said, her earrings swaying as she spoke. "He's been training for months."

CHAPTER 12

Gemma had been in the pediatric wing for thirty-six hours when Calvin was finally discharged. In the time between Gemma's mother informing her that Eddie had left, and Anthony tucking Calvin into his car seat for the ride home, a lifetime had passed.

For starters, Gemma had finally eaten. A cold hamburger and a bag of chips. She also drained two bottles of water in one sitting. But even with all that food and drink, she felt empty. Irene and Jack ran back to Gemma's house to grab some clothes and pain meds. While they were gone, Gemma watched from her vinyl bench as Anthony gave Calvin a bottle. Nurses came in and out to check on the baby, constantly tinkering with his IV and pressing on buttons that Gemma started to suspect were just stickers. When Irene and Jack returned—also bringing Anthony's car—Gemma was thrilled to fully doctor her vagina the way the labor and delivery nurse had so thoroughly instructed her to do before she left the hospital five days earlier.

"A dress?" she remarked as she pulled a knit empire-waist sundress from the bag Irene handed her.

"It will make you feel better," Irene said with a wink. "More like a woman."

After Gemma doctored her stitches, changed into the stretchy striped dress, brushed her hair and pulled it into a topknot, and washed her face, she was disheartened to find that she felt no better. No more refreshed or energetic. No more together than she had been while changing her pad, yet again.

Irene and Jack sat in the hospital room talking until sundown, at which point they kissed Calvin, hugged Gemma and Anthony, and left to join Mary and Bo back at the house.

"We'll be there tomorrow when you get home!" Irene called over her shoulder.

And as the door closed softly behind her, Anthony and Gemma were left all alone in the now-dim hospital room, their son sleeping peacefully.

"How are you?" Anthony asked.

"Okay," Gemma said, staring at her shoes.

Anthony gestured toward all the tubes and cords attached to Calvin. "I wish I could hold the little guy."

Gemma looked at Calvin but could not find an ounce of desire to hold him. She was grateful for the tubes. Grateful for the mandate from Tomás not to hold him until they took out the IV. Grateful for the break, however short, in her responsibilities.

"Yeah," she muttered. "Me too."

And then, without much talking, the couple found their resting spots—Gemma on the bench and Anthony in the chair—to sleep for the night.

There was blood splatter.

The smell of ice cream.

Streetlights popping against a dark sky.

When she awoke to the sounds of nurses shuffling in and out to remove all those barriers to Calvin, Gemma wished she felt the five hours of sleep. But instead she felt exactly the same fatigue as when she drifted off. Her heart was racing from the dream.

And now here they were again, loading their newborn baby into the car outside the hospital. Though this time, they weren't giddy with laughter and love. They were quiet with worry. And tension. As Anthony put the car in reverse and backed out of their parking spot, Gemma couldn't quite identify her biggest feeling.

But it felt an awful lot like dread.

———

"Mama!" Bo yelled as he burst from behind the front door, down the sidewalk, and into Gemma's arms.

"My baby!" she yelped, feeling her stitches pull as she bent down to hoist him onto her hip. "Did you miss us?"

"Nope!" he exclaimed.

Gemma laughed. "Yeah, I wouldn't have either."

Her sister appeared in the doorway as Gemma reached for the handle of the glass door.

"Welcome home," Mary said, reaching to take Bo. "Don't stress, but Mom's been cleaning."

Gemma shrugged, which she knew would confuse Mary, but she didn't care.

"I'm so grateful for how the surgery went," Mary said.

Gemma nodded and pushed past her. Mary backed away from the door, allowing Anthony to enter with the car seat.

"There's the little beefcake," Mary cooed down at the baby.

"Hey, Mare," Anthony said as he handed her the car seat. They hugged over the handle before he went back to get more things from the car. Jack and Irene came around the corner from the living room, but before they could get a word out, Gemma silently passed between them and ascended the stairs.

She walked into her room, threw herself down on her bed, and proceeded to cry. Yet again.

A few minutes later, there was a faint tap on the door.

"Gem?" Mary said as she pushed it open. "Can I come in?"

Gemma rolled over on the bed, her back to Mary.

"Okay," Mary said, coming over to sit beside her. "You're pissed at me." Gemma was silent. "Care to tell me why?"

The women sat in silence as Gemma continued crying. After her breath began to steady, Mary began to rub Gemma's back with such affection that she finally rolled over and looked up at her.

"You let Eddie go," she said, tears streaming from her eyes down into her ears.

Mary moved a hand over to stroke her sister's hair.

"You left me at the hospital," Gemma continued. "Having a fucking physical and emotional breakdown, so that you could let Eddie *also* leave me."

Mary nodded. "It probably feels like that."

"But it isn't?" Gemma huffed. "You actually *did* stay at the hospital with me? And Eddie is, what? Downstairs helping Mom cook dinner?"

Mary continued to comb her fingers through Gemma's hair. "I was trying to be here for Bo."

"I know," Gemma whispered. She wiped her eyes with the back of her hands. "I just wish Eddie tried to be that too."

"Yeah," Mary said softly, clasping her hands in her lap.

"He didn't even text or call."

"My guess is he didn't want to interrupt you," Mary offered. "Maybe he was just giving you space to focus on Calvin."

Gemma stared up at her sister's profile for a full minute. "Mary?"

"Mm-hmm," she answered, turning her attention back to Gemma.

"I keep having a really bad nightmare."

"About?"

"About me. And Eddie. And whatever happened to him that day of his football tryouts."

Mary drew a sharp breath.

"I have such a faint memory of that day," Gemma said. "And in the hospital, I started having these flashes in my dreams. And I can't tell if those are based in reality or not."

Mary was quiet.

"I mean, I remember being at Eddie's tryouts. I remember the bleachers being hot under my legs. And I remember Eddie calling my name and me running toward him. And falling? Did I fall?"

"Yes, that's how you broke your collarbone . . . ," Mary said, trailing off.

"Right," Gemma said. "Right."

The women were quiet.

"It's just that I don't remember anything about my collarbone. I just fell? Outside the Baskin-Robbins?"

Mary nodded.

"But what did Eddie have to do with that?"

Mary shrugged.

"Why can't I remember that day?"

"You were five."

"And you were, what, fourteen?"

"Yep."

"What the fuck happened? Why the hell have you and I not talked about it?"

"We've talked about it plenty, Gem."

"What? When?"

"Over the years. Pretty much every time any of us go to see Eddie. Or Eddie texts. Or anything is mentioned about Eddie, you bring up that day."

"Well, excuse me." Gemma sat up. "I had no idea I was so relentless."

"That's not what I meant." Mary sighed. "I just meant, we *have* talked about it."

"Sort of." Gemma looked out the window, realizing they had, in fact, spoken of that day often. "We've talked about how different he was after that day. We've talked about that day being the start of his anger toward me. But we've never talked about what exactly happened."

"Ah." Mary nodded. "Well, that was a bad day for everyone."

"Huh?"

Mary sighed again. "Gem, this doesn't feel like a good time to get into it."

"Into what? Why do you get so weird when I bring it up?"

Mary stood and walked to the window. "I don't get weird. I get worn out!"

"Worn out by me asking about a day no one wants to ever talk about?"

"As I've said before, I wasn't there. I was staying the weekend at Beverly's. When her mom dropped me home Sunday, I saw Eddie's truck was gone but he was in his room. You were napping in your room. Dad was gone. And Mom just said—in a really casual way—'There was a little accident Friday and Gemma fell and broke her collarbone. Everything is okay, but Eddie's truck will need some work.' And then she asked me to help her fold laundry."

Gemma closed her eyes and shook her head. "That's what doesn't make sense. Did Eddie and Dad have a car accident the same day I fell?"

"I don't know. I guess."

Gemma's brows narrowed at her sister. "Mary. You understand that to me, none of this makes sense. Everyone is so fucking weird about that day, which I expect from Mom and Dad, but why are *you* being secretive about it?"

Mary walked back to the bed. "I'm not being secretive, Gemma. I honestly don't know what happened. And I never asked."

"Why not?"

"I knew not to ask any questions. And no one was talking."

"So our family was just walking around like quiet zombies? And you didn't step in with your usual line of probing questions?"

"I wasn't born a litigator, Gemma." Mary sighed. "I was only fourteen."

Gemma's eyes moved back and forth across the quilt on the bed, as if trying to see through the confusion.

"There was just a vibe." Mary shrugged. "A tension around it."

"And you never brought it up later? Or asked Eddie?"

"It's hard to explain."

"Can you try?"

"I dunno, Gem! I was a teenager with other problems on my mind. I accepted what Mom said. You seemed okay. You had a sling for a few weeks, but you seemed fine."

"And Eddie?"

Mary's lips pursed.

"Goddammit, Mary!"

"I don't know, Gemma!" Mary shot back. "I do not know what you need to hear, but it was a bad weekend for a lot of reasons."

"What does that mean?" Gemma asked, her voice lower.

There was a soft knock on the door. Anthony's head appeared, hovering in the opening. "Your parents have made us some dinner if you want to come down and get something to eat. They've got Bo eating now."

"Oh," Gemma said, distracted. "Thank you."

He opened the door wider, allowing his body to join his head in the doorway. "Thought you were going to take a nap."

Gemma ran her hands through her hair. "Oh, I was, but Mary and I got to talking and I'm just trying to make sense of something she was telling me."

"Oh?"

"Yeah, about that day after Eddie's football tryouts."

Anthony's smile transitioned into a stern glower so quickly that Mary's eyes widened.

"You are up here talking about Eddie?"

"I mean—" Gemma started, but he cut her off.

"We just got home from the hospital with our newborn baby, *who is recovering from surgery,* and you are up here talking about Eddie?"

Mary stood. "Anthony," she started.

He raised his hand to stop her. "I cannot believe how much air and time and worry that man takes up in this family. And yet when his newborn nephew lands in the ER, he runs off to be with his friends. Heaven forbid that guy give a crap about anyone but himself!"

"Anthony," Gemma said, tears welling up.

"No. No. I will not stand here and have another conversation about him."

He turned on his heel, walked out of the bedroom, and slammed the door behind him. The picture of the two of them on their honeymoon in the Smoky Mountains fell off its nail, slid down the wall, and shattered on the floor.

CHAPTER 13

Gemma tapped her leather loafer on the waiting room carpet. The room was cold. Waiting rooms always seemed unnecessarily cold. The silence was punctuated every few minutes by a phone ringing and the receptionist's soft voice. Fluorescent lighting flickered over Gemma's head, causing a strobe-like effect across the oversized black-and-white images that adorned every wall. Artsy, high-contrast shots of carefree mothers laughing with their babies. *What is so damn funny?* Gemma wondered. *Where are you ladies finding the joy?* She had been waiting for fifteen minutes and felt nervous, for reasons she couldn't explain.

"Gemma Sinclair?" a curly-haired nurse in blue scrubs called from the door she was propping open.

Gemma rose slowly, smiled faintly at the nurse, and picked up her purse.

"Having a good day?" the nurse asked so sweetly that Gemma felt an eye roll coming on.

"Yep," Gemma responded, catching the door as the nurse released it to walk down the hall. "You?"

"No complaints!" the nurse said with a smile as she

gestured for Gemma to step onto the scale in the hallway. Gemma never understood why they put the scale smack-dab in the middle of the traffic, right next to the nurses' station and at the intersection of all the patient rooms. She sighed as she stepped onto the scale, not even bothering to take off her shoes. The nurse noted the digital readout, which Gemma didn't look at, then motioned for Gemma to follow her.

"We'll be in room eight, just down the hall here," the nurse chirped, as if escorting Gemma to a private spa.

They walked into the room, and the nurse handed Gemma a gown and sheet.

"I know you know the drill." She winked. "But before I step out and get the doctor, is there anything specific you'd like to discuss with him today?"

"Nope," Gemma said, too quickly.

"Any problems caring for the stitches?"

"Nope."

"Are you still bleeding?"

"Nope. It stopped last week."

"It's always a relief when it does," the nurse said, making notes. "And are you nursing?"

"Nope."

"Okay, and any signs of postpartum depression?"

Gemma looked up at her. "No. Why?"

The nurse smiled. "Just a routine question. PPD usually shows up by the six-week follow-up."

"Well, I'm fine."

"Fair enough. Let me just get your blood pressure, and then I'll step out and let you get changed."

After the nurse pumped the cuff around Gemma's arm, released the pressure, and ripped the cuff off—the sound of the Velcro was deafening in Gemma's ear—the nurse walked out of the room and closed the door behind her.

Gemma slowly pulled her top off, folded it, and placed it on the chair in the corner of the room. Then she unbuttoned her jeans, pulled them from her feet, folded them, and placed them beside her shirt on the chair. She bent her arms around her back and mindlessly released the three tiny hooks on the back of her bra. She tried not to notice the fluid way her breasts fell when she slid the cups off. She folded the bra as best she could and placed it under her jeans. A slight, inaudible chuckle of air escaped her nose as she pulled down her underwear. It was a TikTok she'd seen a few nights earlier in which a woman at her gynecologist's office folded her underwear and stuffed it into the pocket of her folded pants, the words across the screen reading *Why do I hide my panties from the man who's about to have his arm up to the elbow in my cervix?* Though she realized the ridiculousness of hiding her underwear, she too obediently tucked her panties into the pocket of her jeans on the chair. *Hiding is what women do best,* Gemma thought.

She felt the chill of the room ripple across her naked body as she quickly grabbed for the gown, knowing it needed to be open in the front. When it was wrapped around her like a robe, she hoisted herself up onto the exam table, the butcher paper crinkling beneath her. She barely had time to pull the sheet across her lap before there was a perky knock at the door.

"Gemma?" Dr. Johnson asked as he slowly opened it.

"Yeah," Gemma said, putting her hair nervously behind her ears. "You can come in."

"Well, hello!" he said happily, extending his hand. "So good to see you!"

Dr. Johnson always reminded Gemma of Beaker from the Muppets. He was a thin man with a bulbous nose and hair that went in a dozen directions. He frowned as he looked around. "No baby?" he asked, his arms up—emoji-like—in an exaggerated shrug.

Gemma looked down. "Not today." Irene had jumped at the chance to sit with both boys.

"Well, next time maybe," the doctor said, turning his attention to her chart. "How is the little guy?"

"He's better," Gemma said.

The doctor paused, looking at his notes before looking up at Gemma. "Better than what?"

Gemma sighed. "I thought maybe you knew. Like maybe his chart was sent to you." Gemma shook her head, feeling foolish. Dr. Johnson was *her* doctor, not Calvin's pediatrician.

The doctor closed her file, leaned back against the counter to face Gemma, and crossed his arms. "What's going on?"

Gemma worked hard to keep her voice from shaking. "We had an accident. He fell on the edge of our brick fireplace and broke one of his orbital bones." The twist of the doctor's face made Gemma's throat lump up, but she continued. "So, at five days old he had to have surgery on his left eye." She couldn't look at the doctor. "The bruising is gone now, and the incision is healing well, so I don't think it will scar that badly."

"Who did the surgery?"

Gemma shut her eyes, trying to remember. "Gosh. He had a mustache. Tall guy."

"Shipman," the doctor stated. "Excellent."

Gemma nodded in recognition of the name.

"How did Calvin fall, exactly?"

How many times am I going to be asked this question? she wondered. The answer was coming so automatically at this point, she was starting to forget the truth, even though the image of Eddie's extended arm constantly flashed into her mind. "I dropped him. I was looking at my phone while holding him and tripped."

"Accidents happen," the doctor said with kindness. "Don't worry too much about this, Gemma. One nice thing about babies is they are built to survive their parents."

"Let's hope, for my sake, that's true."

"And they have the memory of a goldfish," the doctor said

with a wink.

"Yeah, unlike me. The memory of all that, every minute of it, will never go away."

"I'm sure." The doctor tilted his head and looked at Gemma for a bit before turning back to his notes. When the silence was long enough to pique Gemma's curiosity, she looked up at the doctor to see him still studying her chart.

"What?" she asked, finally breaking the silence.

"Is this weight right?" he asked, pointing to the chart.

Gemma shrugged. "I didn't see it when she weighed me."

"Do you weigh yourself at home?"

"No? Do you?"

"Well, no, but I'm not six weeks postpartum."

"You don't weigh yourself because you're a man."

The doctor smirked but kept flipping through the chart. "This says you've lost thirty-two pounds in six weeks."

Gemma's shoulders rose. "Calvin's head was most of that."

"You only gained about twenty-five with this pregnancy. I'm a little concerned you've lost this much this quickly."

"Well, that's the first time I've had a doctor say that to me."

"Are you eating well?"

Gemma thought back over the past six weeks. After Anthony blew up at her, and after pushing through a tight-smiled meal with the McAlisters that evening, she and Anthony had found themselves tangled in a fight louder than they had ever engaged in before. He was furious with her for what he saw as her focus on Eddie—and the McAlisters in general—instead of on Calvin, or Bo, or him. And she was angry for reasons that she couldn't easily articulate but that felt more than justified as they came screaming out of her mouth.

The fight swirled like a cyclone, out of their lips, around their bodies, up to the cracked ceiling in their bedroom, and out through the roof, where it swirled and swirled and swirled around the house until, eventually, the movement died down and Gemma was left with the storm's aftermath: her husband's closet half emptied into his suitcase and a door slammed behind him.

Since then, she had eaten, of course. She just couldn't remember a single bite.

"I think so?" Gemma said.

"And sleeping a full eight hours?"

"I have a newborn. Be reasonable."

"But you aren't nursing, so certainly your husband is doing some of the feedings?"

"I handle those. It's just easier," Gemma said, not explaining it was easier because Anthony was staying on the other side of town.

The doctor's expression before he began moving his pen across her chart again stirred something in her.

"But my husband handles pickup and drop-off at day care, dinners, bath, and bedtime," she added, suddenly feeling defensive of Anthony, who, despite not sleeping at home, was over constantly to be with the kids.

Dr. Johnson's eyebrows rose. "Wow."

"Let's not celebrate in a man what we simply expect of a woman."

"Point taken."

"But to your question, sleep is hard."

"I'm wondering about writing you a prescription for some sleep aids."

Gemma shrugged. "I'll try it." But she knew that with sleep came the nightmares about Eddie—her subconscious desperate to dig up any memory that could help fill in the day of his football tryouts—so it felt easier to stay awake.

The doctor studied Gemma for a moment before pulling out the rolling stool that was tucked under the counter, moving it close to the exam table, and sitting down. He faced her.

"Gemma?"

Gemma kept looking at her feet. "Yes?"

"How often would you say you cry a day?"

Gemma looked up at the ceiling to both count tiles and avoid crying in that moment. "I've gotten it down to two. Sometimes three."

"What do you mean when you say, 'Gotten it down'?"

She attempted to smile. "I was crying so much, and I think it was irritating everyone, so I decided I would just cry once in the morning—in the bathroom—and once after everyone goes to sleep. But, you know, a random midday cry shows up sometimes."

"I see," he said. "And how about Calvin? How are you feeling about the baby?"

Gemma's eyebrows furrowed, but she said nothing.

"Do you feel close to him?"

"I'm literally with him around the clock."

"But do you *feel* close to him? Emotionally."

She stared at the doctor, trying to decide if she was brutally offended or if she felt seen for the first time since Calvin was born.

"I love him," she stammered, chin quivering. Even saying those words felt false. Her heart just didn't want to talk to her head.

"Of course you do," the doctor whispered. "And I know you are a wonderful mother."

Upon hearing the word *mother*, Gemma began crying with such unexpected force that she couldn't breathe. Dr. Johnson stood up, grabbed a box of tissues, handed it to her, and then put his arm around her. He was quiet while she sobbed. When she finally found her breath, she looked up at him with such desperation she felt shame.

"I'm going back to work Monday," she said, in as strong a voice as she could muster.

"Is there any chance you can take some more time?"

"Don't want to," she said, her eyes falling to the floor.

"Gemma," the doctor began.

"I'm fine. I'm just tired, and having all that stuff happen with Calvin just made it a rough start. But things are leveling out."

"I'm going to prescribe you a low dose of Lexapro along with the sleeping pills," he said, pulling a small pad from the pocket of his white coat. "Let's have you back here in three weeks to see if we need to increase the dosage on the antidepressant. Sometimes it takes a bit to get the dosage right."

Gemma didn't speak. She simply nodded once. The doctor patted her shoulder, opened the exam room door, and called for the nurse. Once the nurse was in the room, the doctor and Gemma began the routine the two of them had gone through together for more than a decade, motions every woman knows all too well.

She placed her feet in the stirrups.

He lifted the sheet over her knees and motioned with a wave of his fingers.

She slid down the table.

He placed his fingers on the site of her stitches.

She winced.

He motioned for the nurse to hand him the speculum.

She inhaled deeply.

He inserted it and widened her.

She felt the pressure of his hands maneuver within her.

He extracted the mechanism and handed her a tissue.

She wiped herself.

He said all looked good and that she was clear to resume sex when she was ready.

She bristled at the very idea.

He handed her the two prescriptions.

She thanked him.

He walked out of the room.

She got dressed.

Back in the lobby, the receptionist tried to make her next appointment for three weeks later, as the doctor's notes instructed. "How's the twenty-sixth at nine fifteen?"

"I'm not sure what my schedule will be that day," Gemma said, waving a hand. "I'll call tomorrow and schedule it then."

The receptionist, seemingly unaware she was being lied to, nodded and smiled. "Talk to you tomorrow, then," she said as Gemma turned to leave.

On her way out, Gemma balled up the prescriptions in her fist and pushed them into the swinging lid of the metal trash can sitting just to the left of the door.

<h1 style="text-align:center">CHAPTER 14</h1>

Gemma watched her reflection dab concealer under her left eye. "Why even ask me that?"

"Because you scheduled twelve weeks of maternity," Mary replied, her mouth full of foamy paste. "It's only been six. So it's fair to ask if you're sure you want to go back already." She spit into the sink.

"Okay," Gemma said, leaning away to avoid splash back. "And I suppose a better mother would want to stay home all day tending to her baby."

"Gemma . . ."

"Well, then what?" Gemma set the pot of concealer on the porcelain sink and turned to face her sister. "What would you like me to do?"

"I want you to feel you got enough time with Calvin."

"Not today, Mary."

"Okay, okay," she said, her hands up in defense.

"And for the last time, can you please use the other bathroom?"

"I'll stay here as long as you need, but I am *not* using the kid's bathroom to get ready."

"You can't share a bathroom with a five-year-old boy?"

"I won't share a bathroom—or a life—with any man of any age."

"A woman, then?" Gemma looked over at her with a wink.

"I wish. God, how much easier would all of life be if we were attracted to women?"

Gemma laughed. "Well, before you moved in, I would have said infinitely easier. But dear god, Anthony is far easier to share a bathroom with than you are."

In truth, Gemma had loved having Mary stay with her the past few weeks. She found it comforting. Even if she did feel cramped for counter space in the bathroom.

"No man makes anything easier," Mary said, spraying down her hair.

"You know I'm a licensed therapist. I can help you with your rage."

Silence hung between them.

Mary cleared her throat. "Are you sure you want to drop off Bo and Calvin? Because I can be a few minutes late today."

"Yes, I'm sure. I'm happy to do it."

"It just feels like a lot for you to do the drop-offs by yourself."

"My first session isn't until nine," Gemma said, her mouth open wide as she cautiously swept mascara on her lashes. "And I'm a capable mother."

"I'm not saying you aren't."

The sisters stood beside each other, poking and prodding at various parts of their faces and hair in silence.

"I need to go back to work," Gemma resumed, keeping her eyes on the mirror. "To feel normal again. I need to get out of this house."

"I get that," Mary said, turning to face her. "But in your line of work, you can't do your job if *you* are not okay. You're the one who always says that."

"I *am* okay."

"Your OB felt you were ready to go back to work?"

"I don't need Dr. Johnson's permission to live my life."

"I just mean, he checked you out and thinks you are okay to go back to work this soon?"

"All he can assess is if my vagina is healed. He can't determine if a grown-ass woman is ready to sit in a room with patients and listen. My ears are not in my twat."

Mary's mouth sprang open and her head flew back in laughter, a reaction Gemma relished whenever she could evoke it in her sister.

——

Gemma's heart raced as she inserted the key. When she turned the knob and pushed open her office door, a smile spread across her face. She hung her coat on the rack and walked around to sit at her desk, a large mid-century stunner. She had found it on Facebook Marketplace and made Anthony drive her all the way to the east side of St. Louis to buy it from a woman who was clearing out her deceased mother's house. She rubbed her hands across the desk and breathed in deeply. She had spent three weeks refinishing it in their garage, and she loved how smooth the surface was after her Olympic-level feat of sanding.

She spun her chair around to face the wall of windows that looked down on the square. People walked in every direction, headed to start their days, or meet a friend for coffee, or just take a lazy day to shop. *It was oddly painless to drop off Calvin,* she thought. She had gingerly handed him to one of the teachers, placed his bag on the floor beside all the cubbies, waved to the rest of the staff milling around the room, and walked out feeling lighter. *I hugged Bo and kissed him. But did I kiss Calvin? Did I even say goodbye?* Gemma got so lost in the pattern of heads zipping in and out of storefronts that she didn't hear the soft knock at her door. The clearing of a throat brought her back to her office, and she turned to see Dr. Heinz standing in the doorway, smiling at her.

"Well hello, Boss." Gemma smiled back brightly.

Dr. Heinz was in his standard attire: a T-shirt—Rolling Stones, no less—jeans, and gray Converse. He was two decades older than her, but he still dressed like he was in college. His sartorial choices, overly relaxed though they might be, were remarkably effective at relaxing patients. The clothes, mixed with his soft build and balding head, made him ridiculously approachable. But it secretly bothered Gemma. Only a man could get away with such a lax approach to professional attire. She stood, adjusted her suit jacket, and walked toward him with her hand extended.

"Don't call me that," he said with a grin as he shook her hand.

She motioned toward one of the deep leather chairs in front of her prized desk. "Come, sit."

He took a seat, crossed his left ankle onto his right thigh, and clasped his hands on top of his head, leaning back slightly. That was his default posture, and the sight of it calmed Gemma.

"Ready to jump back in?" he asked.

"Like you wouldn't believe."

"How's Calvin?"

"Wonderful!" she said in a voice she knew wasn't authentic.

Dr. Heinz's face twisted for a split second before he asked, "Eye is all okay?"

Gemma nodded. "We had the follow-up appointment with the surgeon and the incision is fine. But we won't know until our next appointment, in a couple of months, if we are out of the woods with his vision."

Dr. Heinz shook his head. "What an ordeal."

"Yeah. It's just so surreal."

"Where are you on processing it all?"

Gemma swatted a hand. "Totally good."

"And Anthony?"

"Back at work."

"No, I mean how has he processed everything that happened?"

Gemma shrugged as she felt a lump rising in her throat. "He's fine. We're all fine. Even Bo didn't skip a beat. It all just feels like a blip on the radar." She mindlessly shuffled papers around on her desk to keep the tears at bay.

"Well, who's on your calendar today?" he asked.

Gemma sighed with relief that he had moved on to work. She opened her laptop and pulled up her calendar. "Just one today. Betty Johansen."

"Nothing like hitting the ground running."

Betty wasn't exactly Gemma's easiest patient. In fact, she had been a patient of their colleague Dr. Hamilton before becoming so enraged during a session that she demanded a referral. Gemma liked the challenge of referrals—especially angry ones. And while Betty was no picnic, Gemma felt proud of the inroads she had made with her during the past six months.

"Think she missed me?" Gemma teased.

"Well, she only came to one session with me while you were on leave."

Gemma clucked her tongue. "So she's all pent up and ready to spew?"

"I put the notes from that session on the portal. You should have access."

"I'll take a look."

"You sure you're up for her today?"

"Absolutely. I think we are making progress on the issues she has with her son."

"You're one of the best." He unclasped his hands, dropped his left foot to the floor, and stood. "It's why I hired you."

"Thanks, Boss." She gave him a flippant salute as he turned to go.

He stopped in the open doorway and turned back to look at her. "Gemma?"

"Mm-hmm?" she said, staring at her computer screen.

"We've treated enough postpartum depression in this practice that you, above all people, would know the symptoms."

She looked up at him. "What is wrong with everyone? I'm fine!"

He nodded once. "I figured." And out the door he went.

Gemma let out a sigh and refocused her attention on the notes about Betty. She needed to prepare for their session, which, according to her watch, was less than a half hour away. Gemma didn't often get the luxury of this much prep time—she usually had ten minutes or less between sessions—but Candice, their office manager, had purposefully booked a slower week to help Gemma reacclimate.

She liked how Dr. Heinz did his clinical notes. How Candice was able to read them for transcription was beyond her, but he always organized them into four sections: Agenda, Temperament, Assessment, and Strategy. This was different from the DAP method—data, assessment, plan—Gemma had learned in grad school, but she preferred his approach. She longed to someday provide the useful insights in her own notes that he did in his.

Her eyes scanned over *Agenda. Patient insistent on talking through her anger at her son.* Gemma nodded. Every session with Betty had been about how angry she was with her son. Gemma knew her task was to let Betty process those feelings, though she really wanted her to discuss her feelings about herself. But Betty loved to blame. She had a son with a substance abuse disorder who kept stealing from her, so she had every right to her anger, even though Gemma knew that, in this case, anger was masking sadness—an emotion Betty seemed unwilling to acknowledge.

Her eyes moved down to *Temperament*. *Patient unusually calm. The anger is presenting in words, but the audio and visuals don't align.* Gemma's eyebrows rose. Dr. Heinz was an expert at catching inconsistencies between what a person said and how they said it. But Betty was usually so angry her voice could be heard by Gemma's colleagues on either side of her office. Seeing Betty described as "calm" made Gemma wrinkle her forehead in confusion. She wondered if the change was a reaction to Dr. Heinz or if something had shifted for her patient.

Under *Assessment*, Gemma read Dr. Heinz's brief note: *Repressed anger at her mother.* Gemma's eyes immediately began to sting with tears. She grabbed the box of tissues. As she dabbed her eyes and blew her nose in front of the window, she glanced down again at the popcorn of people below. Her tears were a constant source of annoyance. A spontaneous bodily function as unavoidable now as sneezing. They came at unexpected times, like when she was folding towels. But they wouldn't come at expected times, like when she and Anthony fought the night he left. She had grown accustomed to the sudden arrival of her tears, but she hadn't expected them at work. She had foolishly thought they would only appear in the privacy of her home. But now here she was, sitting at her desk in a wool pantsuit and heels in the middle of her office—not at home on the couch in one of Anthony's blood-drive T-shirts—discovering the tears were much more capricious than she had given them credit for.

Yet these tears were different, she noticed. They weren't just an involuntary reflex; she felt a tightness in her chest. Dr. Heinz had seen something in Betty she hadn't. Maybe she never would have. In six months of weekly sessions, Gemma had never heard Betty even mention her mother. "Bullshit,"

Gemma muttered to herself. Yes, she decided, she was mad at Dr. Heinz.

Just then, her phone vibrated on the desk. It was Anthony.

How were drop-offs?

She sighed so loudly she wondered if the patients in the waiting room would hear her. She balled up her tissue and threw it in the wastebasket under her desk, then picked up the phone.

Great. But headed into a session.

Okay. Good luck today.

Gemma stared at the screen for a second before responding.

Thanks.

She had twenty-two unread messages. She clicked to see what she had missed: it was a group text with her mother and sister. Gemma clenched her jaw. Irene and Mary were what Gemma had diagnosed to Anthony as Group Text Abusers. "I'm working to get it in the *DSM*," she said to him one night when they were trying to watch a movie and the dinging of her phone was incessant. By the time they finally paused it—Anthony throwing up his hands in annoyance—she had missed a forty-message exchange about the last episode of *Downton Abbey*. Now, with her session minutes away, Gemma skimmed the current barrage of messages to get a sense of what they were discussing. Irene and Jack wanted to come see the boys and would bring dinner over tonight, and Mary had agreed to come as well, all before Gemma had known this was a possibility, discussed it with Anthony, or attempted to clean her house. She shook her head in disbelief at the string of presumptions and quickly typed her response.

Sounds good! See you tonight!

Then she locked the phone and threw it in her desk drawer as the light next to her door flashed green. Betty was waiting.

Gemma inhaled deeply, blew out the imaginary candles, smoothed her jacket, and walked to the door. She opened it wide to see Betty in the waiting room, flipping through an old copy of *TIME*. She called Betty's name and greeted her with a smile, never having had a chance to read the last line of Dr. Heinz's notes, just under *Strategy*.

Encourage her to face her own childhood.

CHAPTER 15

Gemma assumed Betty had been a cheerleader in high school, or at least very popular with teenage boys. She was leggy with big breasts, and though she was in her late fifties, from a distance she didn't look a day over forty. Her hair was full of buttery highlights, her nails immaculately polished. She almost always wore tight capris and strappy sandals. She was the kind of woman whose looks intimidated Gemma. Just like her mother.

"So." Betty gestured at Gemma. "You had your baby."

"Yes. A boy."

Betty sat back on the couch. "Good luck with that."

Gemma kept her face neutral. "Betty, can you imagine how I might experience a statement like that?"

Betty looked out the window. "I'm just saying, sons are tough."

"Is your son on your mind today, Betty?"

"Meh."

"You'd rather talk about my sons?"

Betty laughed. "Danny called yesterday evening asking to stay the night."

"And how did you respond?"

"I told him yes."

"Then what happened?"

"He came over. He was high, but he was calm."

"Did you talk?"

Betty paused. "Yes. Which upset my daughter."

Gemma tried to hide her surprise. She glanced down at her notes. Her mind raced back over the past six months but came up empty. "Have you mentioned your daughter before?"

Betty looked up at Gemma and shrugged slightly. "I'm in therapy about my relationship with my son."

"Sure, but she's part of that relationship."

Betty narrowed her eyes. "How?"

Gemma felt her chest tighten but stayed calm. "Well, when we think about our relationships with individuals within our family, we need to understand how the family unit works together."

"I don't agree with that."

"Tell me why."

Betty looked down at her hands. "Because my relationship with Danny is complicated. Difficult. He's an addict. I don't struggle with Sidney in the same way."

"But you *do* struggle with Sidney?"

Betty threw up her hands and let out a huff. "No! Sid and I are fine. She's fine. She isn't relevant here!"

Gemma swallowed hard. Her heartbeat was quickening. She was trained to stay on a topic that a patient resisted. But she could feel herself getting emotional. She worked to slow her breathing. "Tell me about her."

Betty's dangling gold earrings glinted in the sunlight as she turned her head toward the window again. "What's there to say?"

Gemma worked to control the shakiness in her voice. "How about what she's like?"

Betty stared at her for a long beat before rolling her eyes and sighing. "She's twenty-three."

"And?"

"She and Danny don't get along."

Gemma felt her stomach tightening. "What does Sidney like to do for fun?"

"I think it's because they are so similar."

"What is Sidney like?" Gemma asked, her voice the slightest bit louder than before.

"Like, if Sidney would just be a little more . . . I dunno, chill around Danny, I think they could really be close. . . ."

Gemma broke in. "May I make an observation?"

"Isn't that what I pay you for?"

Gemma took a deep breath before replying. "When I ask about Sidney, you talk about Danny."

"Talking about Danny *is* what I'm paying you for," Betty said.

Gemma felt her hand begin to tremor, so she decided to change tactics. "Take me back to last night. Why was Sidney upset you were talking to Danny?"

"Beats the hell out of me!" Betty's voice trilled as she brought her fingers up to her long, lean neck.

"You can't think of a single reason she might be upset?"

"Look," Betty said, quieter. "Sidney can be a little . . ." She trailed off and looked out the window before finishing with the help of her miming fingers: "High-maintenance." She turned her gaze from the window to look straight at Gemma. "You know the kind."

Gemma's face flushed. "Let's pretend I don't. Explain it to me."

Betty rolled her eyes. "She's a bit needy."

"What does she need?" Gemma asked, her hand continuing to shake in her lap.

"Oh, who knows?" Betty swatted her hand in defeat, leaning back on the couch and crossing her legs. "She's always bursting into tears about something."

Gemma bit the edge of her tongue. "How long has she done that?"

"Always. She's always been a crier. Could be anything. Not *feeling heard* is one I hear her whine about a lot."

Gemma felt a lump quickly rising and worked to swallow it over and over. "Betty, was Sidney trying to talk to you about something when Danny came over last night?"

Betty shrugged. "She was talking. I don't know if it was *about* anything."

"Why does it need to be about something?" Gemma asked, her voice raised just enough it jerked Betty's eyes to meet hers.

"Because whatever it is, it's just more blame about what an awful mom I am."

Gemma adjusted her posture and inhaled deeply. "Has she said that to you before? That you are an awful mom?"

"Not in those words."

"What has she said?"

"I don't know!" Betty spoke so forcefully that Gemma dropped her pen. "Look, my daughter is a great kid. Good grades in school, taking classes at the community college, and has never touched so much as a drop of alcohol."

"Which means what?"

"It means I don't need to focus on her. Danny is the one who needs me. Sidney is fine."

Before she could stop them, tears spilled out of Gemma's eyes.

"Maybe I'm not fine!" Gemma's voice cracked as it ascended, before she threw her notebook on the table beside her chair and stood up. "And I'm doing everything in the world you want me to do, but you insist that only your son deserves your focus!"

Betty's eyes darted from side to side in confusion. "Wait, what?"

Gemma jabbed a finger toward the long, lean neck of the woman sitting in front of her. "I'm tired of feeling so isolated," she spit. "He doesn't live anywhere near here, we never see him, and yet he gets more of your focus than I do. And I live in the same damn town as you!"

"I know you do," Betty said slowly. "What are you even talking about? Isolated from what?"

"Of course you don't know what I'm talking about! You never do!"

Betty slowly reached for her purse and brought it tight to her chest. "Okay, I don't know what's going on here, but you don't seem right."

"Of course you don't think I seem right. All you ever do is judge. You know what? Fuck *you*!" The words blasted out of Gemma's mouth, slapped Betty across the face, then made their way under the door of Gemma's office, across the waiting room, and into the ears of Candice, who immediately left her post behind reception to find Dr. Heinz.

The women were staring breathlessly at each other when the door flung open.

"This woman seems possessed," Betty exclaimed, pointing at Gemma.

"All right, all right," Dr. Heinz said calmly but sternly. "Betty, let's have you step into the waiting room for just a moment while I speak with Dr. Sinclair."

Betty stalked over to Dr. Heinz and jabbed a painted fingernail in his face. "You better call your lawyer." She stormed past the waiting patients and past Candice and pushed so hard on the office door, Gemma thought it would break.

Dr. Heinz turned to Gemma and motioned for her to step back so he could enter her office, then closed the door firmly. He gestured for Gemma to sit on the couch with him. "Let's take a seat."

Gemma shook as she walked to the couch. The moment she lowered herself onto the soft leather, she began crying violently, her body trembling. Dr. Heinz sat quietly beside Gemma while her body convulsed. After a few minutes, she regained her composure, reached for the tissues on the coffee table, blew her nose, and leaned back into the couch, not able to look at Dr. Heinz, who watched her silently.

"I don't know what happened," Gemma finally managed to say.

"I have a theory," Dr. Heinz said, leaning back beside her.

Gemma turned her head to meet his gaze. She was surprised that he didn't look angry. "I'm listening."

"You and Betty talked about her son," Dr. Heinz said matter-of-factly. "And it stirred something in you."

Gemma pressed a wad of tissues to her nose and nodded.

"And your emotions overcame you and you did a little projecting."

Gemma covered her face with her hands. "Like a twenty-something straight out of grad school."

"We all do it. No matter how long we've been at this. When did you first feel the emotions in your body?"

"When she started talking about her son."

"Mmm."

Gemma looked at him. "What?"

"She's talked about nothing but her son for the six months she's worked with you."

"Yeah, Boss. I get it. I'm projecting because I feel insecure about my relationship with my son."

"Mmm," he said again, his head tilted.

Gemma sighed in frustration. "What?"

"Think back on the conversation with Betty. Again, when did you first feel the emotions in your body?"

Gemma closed her eyes and went back through the conversation in reverse order, as if rewinding a scene in a show her children had interrupted, to ensure she didn't miss anything. She watched her conversation with Betty back up to when she first felt the tightening in her chest. Her eyes popped open.

"Whatcha got?" Dr. Heinz asked.

Gemma frowned and her eyes narrowed.

"Guessing it wasn't when she was talking about her son."

"No," Gemma said, sitting up on the couch. She turned her head back to look at Dr. Heinz. "It was when she mentioned her daughter. Danny's sister."

"Ah," Dr. Heinz said.

"I must just be tired."

Dr. Heinz sat back for a moment longer before pulling his body upright to mirror Gemma's. He inhaled and exhaled slowly. They sat quietly next to one another, both looking ahead.

"Gemma," he finally said.

"Yeah?"

"You're not ready to be back at work just yet."

She lowered her head. "Don't do this."

"Don't do what?"

"Be one more guy saying I'm incapable. Or need more rest."

He looked over at her. "I haven't said any of that."

"You're thinking it."

"You don't know what I'm thinking."

"Then just tell me," she said softly, shaking her head and still refusing to meet his gaze.

Dr. Heinz inhaled. "I can't have you back at work right now."

"Dammit, Heinz. I made a mistake today. Have I ever made one before? Jesus, cut me some slack!"

"You didn't make a mistake."

"Right, my boss had to run into my office to break up a fight because I was doing the exact right thing."

"You didn't make a mistake," he said again, firmer. "You displayed a need."

"Jesus Christ."

"You have some unresolved issues you need to address before you can return to work."

"Ah. The postpartum depression talk again."

"No," he said. "I'm talking about your unresolved issues with Eddie."

At the mention of Eddie's name, Gemma shot up from the couch. "What the hell?"

"Have you spoken to Eddie since the night Calvin was injured?"

Gemma winced at the memory. "No." She began pacing near the windows. "I mean, he was on a group text with my parents and Mary about his marathon. He sent pictures and his times and stuff."

"But have you talked with him one-on-one? Has he texted *just* you?"

Gemma bit at a fingernail. "No. But that's not unusual."

"Have your parents spoken to him? Has Mary?"

"I don't know."

"Right," he said, slapping his knees and standing up from the deep couch.

"So what? What do you want me to do?"

"I'm going to refer you to a colleague. I have an old classmate who moved here recently, and I think she'd be a good fit for you. I suggest you work with her to face your issues with Eddie and your family."

"My family?" Gemma said, putting her hands up in

defense. "If I have any issues—and I'm not convinced I do—they are just with Eddie."

"Right. Like Betty's issues are just with Danny?"

Gemma stared at him for a few seconds before responding. "I'm not going to talk to anyone about this. I know I shouldn't have let my emotions get to me today, and I'll be better tomorrow. But I'm not seeing anyone about this."

"Yes you are," he said, his face neutral.

"No I'm not," Gemma said, her voice rising slightly.

Dr. Heinz sighed and walked to the door. With his hand on the knob, he turned back to face Gemma, the full width of her office between them.

"Gemma, I'm the boss, as you love to remind me. And I'm saying this to you as my employee: Please don't return to work until you address this issue. However long that takes. Candice will set up your first appointment and reschedule your upcoming patients."

———

"Mama!" Bo hollered, running toward Gemma as she came in the front door.

"Bo-Bo!" Gemma exclaimed, dropping her work bag and purse to the floor to embrace him. "Did you have a good day?"

"Yes! I got to see Calvin in the baby room!"

"How fun!" Gemma said, setting Bo back on the ground.

"Hey there," Anthony called from the living room. "You're home early."

"Yeah." Gemma rolled her eyes in frustration. "But you are too?"

Movement caught Gemma's eye, and she turned to see Anthony walking toward her with Calvin in the crook of his arm.

"There's my baby," she said, bending forward to kiss the top of his head.

"How was the first day back?" Anthony asked.

"Um, good," she said distractedly, hanging her purse on the hooks by the door. She carried her work bag over to the buffet in the dining room. She moved a pile of magazines, a couple of dirty bottles, and several of Bo's cars to make room for it. She leaned against the door frame as she lifted one foot, reached her hand down, and slipped off a heel. Then she did the other. She removed her suit jacket and laid it on top of her bag before pulling her shirttail out of her pants. When she turned around, she found Anthony and the boys positioned directly behind her.

"What?" Gemma asked.

"Well," Anthony said, smiling slightly. "We, me and Bo, kind of have a surprise for you."

Gemma's chest expanded at the sight of Anthony's smile. To hear him say he had something for her. Though they had seen each other every day since he stormed out of the house, she hadn't felt close to him for weeks. Until this moment.

Anthony handed Calvin to Gemma, who carried him into the living room and sat down on the couch. Bo and Anthony followed her into the room, smiling at her as they perched themselves on the edge of the coffee table, now elaborately embellished in foam padding.

"So, what's the surprise?" she asked, hoping her voice didn't sound as needy as it felt.

Anthony rubbed his hands together and smiled again. "I picked the boys up early so we could go to Rick's to get your favorite seafood pasta. To celebrate your first day back at work."

Gemma's eyebrows rose in excitement and then relaxed immediately into a pained look.

"What? What's wrong?" Anthony asked as Bo jumped

down from the coffee table and ran into the sunroom to get his bucket of cars. Gemma turned her head to make sure Bo was out of earshot.

"My parents are coming over tonight and bringing dinner for me and Mary."

"Since when?" Anthony asked, his face suddenly serious.

"They texted this afternoon."

He sighed. "Okay."

"I didn't know you'd planned something. Why would I even think you would with what's going on with us?"

Anthony rubbed his temples. "I took off work early . . ."

"Yeah, I get that," Gemma said. "I'm not trying to ruin anything. I just didn't know you were going to do this."

"I wanted us to do something together. I wanted to try and work things out. Turn down the volume on all this tension. I want us to be . . . *us*."

"I love that. I want that too."

"I feel like I haven't unclenched since we took Calvin to the hospital. I'm finally starting to feel a little bit normal again."

"Lucky you."

Anthony ran his hands through his hair, and Gemma could tell he was working to choose his words carefully. "This has been really hard on all of us," he finally said.

"Yeah. Okay. I get it," she said, shifting Calvin from her arms to lengthwise on her lap. He looked up at her, his incision still a deep pink. "I fucked up. I'm sorry."

"Gem, I'm really trying here."

"Am I that much work?"

Anthony sighed and stood up from the coffee table. He walked to the window and looked out.

"I'm having a really hard time finding my way back to you," he said.

"I'm not trying to be difficult. But can you cut me some slack?" She felt the silence as he waited for her to provide a reason for the request. "I had a pretty tough day back at work."

"Did something go wrong?"

Gemma looked over at him. His body was still facing the window, but his head had turned to her expectantly. She knew Anthony was trying his best to help things run smoothly despite their physical separation. And despite how angry he had been at the hospital, he had never let it show around the kids. The last thing she wanted was to put any more distance between them than the miles there already were each night.

"No," she said quietly, before forcing a smile and adding, "Not at all. I'm just tired."

Anthony walked back over to the couch and sat on the coffee table in front of her. She could hear the sound of Bo's metal cars slamming into one another from the next room. She looked down at Calvin, whose eyes were heavy. Anthony put his legs on either side of Gemma's, bent down and kissed Calvin's head, and rested his hands over hers.

"I'm sorry," she said, tears welling up.

"Whoa, hey, it's okay."

Gemma pulled her left hand out from under Anthony's and wiped her tears. "I would like us to be okay."

"We will be."

Gemma continued crying.

"I should have told you my plan for tonight," he said.

Gemma shook her head. "No, it was a lovely surprise."

"Look, the pasta reheats well," he said with a wink. "You know that better than anyone."

"But what about my family?"

He winced. "What time are they coming?"

CHAPTER 16

The pain in her shoulder.

The outline of her dad in the distance.

A man in uniform.

The clear words: "Level three concussion."

The chime of the doorbell startled Gemma awake. She instinctively reached for Calvin, and when she discovered her lap was empty, she bolted upright in panic.

"It's okay," Anthony said. "I have him."

Gemma had her hands on her chest, breathing hard. "I didn't realize I had fallen asleep."

"Your family is here."

"Okay, okay," Gemma said, rubbing her eyes and fighting hard to swim out from under the weight of her dream. She inched her way to the front door and pulled it open.

"Where's that baby?" Irene exclaimed with a smile. Then her eyes narrowed on Gemma. "You okay?"

"Yeah, I was just napping on the couch." Gemma opened the door wider. "Come on in."

Irene reached around Gemma with a quick hug before

pushing into the living room. "Hello, Anthony!" She patted his arm before demanding with a laugh, "Give me that baby!"

Anthony stood slowly with the stirring baby and passed him to her. "He's going to be ready for a bottle, so I'll go make one."

Gemma waited at the door for Mary and Jack to make their way up the sidewalk. Mary had pulled in just behind her parents, and they were talking while walking very slowly toward the house.

"Geez. I thought you'd never make it to the door," Gemma said as they finally reached the porch.

Mary seemed confused, then arranged her face into a smile. "Hey there, Gem," she said, warming as she pulled her sister into a hug. "Where's Bo-Bo?"

"In the sunroom, with his cars." Gemma stepped aside to allow Mary to slip past her in search of her beloved nephew.

"Hi, Dad," Gemma said, happy to see her father standing on the porch, this time in a straw hat that she thought made him look older than usual.

He nodded once and held out his fist for a bump. "Gem."

She smiled, wrapping her arms around his neck. "You can take a hug."

As they made their way into the living room, Irene looked up from Calvin. "Gemma, you'll need to go out to my car and get the groceries."

"Groceries?"

"Yes, I'm making dinner!"

"Right." She looked at Anthony, who was still holding Calvin's bottle. "I guess I thought you were bringing something you had already made."

Irene waved a hand casually. "Oh, I ran out of time. But I brought steaks for your dad to grill, and I'll bake potatoes and make a salad."

She watched Anthony's eyebrows rise before falling. It was clearly going to be a longer night than Gemma had anticipated. She could tell Anthony wasn't pleased, and in truth neither was she.

"Okay," Gemma said. "But we will need to call it an early night. For bedtimes and all."

Irene looked at Gemma blankly before glancing down at her watch. "How early?"

Gemma looked to Anthony for an assist, but he wasn't looking at her. "I mean, I guess by eight or so."

Irene looked at Jack. "Okay then, Jack, you better start the grill. We'll need to hurry."

"You don't have to rush," Gemma said to Jack. "I just want to make sure the kids get the sleep they need."

"Of course, of course," Irene said, handing the baby to Mary, who was sitting with Bo on the couch. "I'll get going on the sides."

"No, no," Gemma said. "You came to see the kids. I just thought you were bringing something quick. We can do whatever you want." She watched out of the corner of her eye to see if Anthony reacted. He was as still as a stone.

"Well," Irene sighed. "We could just order pizza. . . ."

"No, no. I know you don't care for pizza."

"Yes, but I know you probably don't have anything for us to eat here."

Gemma looked at her and was quiet.

"Oh, Gemma, come on." Irene swatted her hand. "I just meant because there are so many of us. You wouldn't have enough in your fridge to feed us all."

In that moment, Gemma was overcome with an intense desire to leave the house. Or to kick her family out of it. To do whatever would put her as far away from them as possible. She had never felt this way, but she feared she might scream if she didn't move her body. She put up a finger and said, "Excuse me for just a minute," then walked out the front door, closing it behind her.

Even with a solid oak door between her and her family, she didn't feel any better. She looked to the left and then to the right. Her neighbor to the right was on his hands and knees, mulching his flower beds. Mr. Ruiz could be so chatty since his wife passed away. Every Monday morning when Gemma was on bed rest, he brought her a dozen eggs from the three chickens he kept in his backyard. Gemma had loved his visits, partly because she was lonely and bored, but also because Mr. Ruiz was such a kind and funny man. But right now she couldn't stomach the thought of having to talk to him. So she walked down the steps, down the front walk, and down the driveway, and turned left. She kept going until she came to an intersection in the center of their quiet, tree-lined neighborhood. Pausing at the stop sign, she still felt anxious. At the corner was the large white house Gemma and Anthony had always talked about wanting to renovate. She looked up at the second-story windows and wondered, for the hundredth time, how big the bedrooms were. The last time she had talked to Anthony about that house, she was just a few months pregnant with Calvin. She often commented on the big oak banister she could see through the windows and how big the back yard looked through the fence, so Gemma had said to Anthony one night in bed, "Just go knock on the door and ask to buy it."

"With what money?"

"Minor detail."

It had been a happy moment, joking and dreaming about their future as a family of four. In this wild dream of theirs, they walked right up to the door, knocked on it, shook hands with the owners, and made an offer. The owners were so charmed by Anthony and Gemma that they agreed to sell them the house on the spot and well below market value. And, of course, once she and Anthony were inside their new home, they realized it had already been renovated exactly to their tastes.

Gemma shook her head at the memory, her chest tightened in mourning for that time in bed with Anthony, and she quickly began to move her body again, walking straight through that intersection until she came to the next one. She stopped to watch a jogger who ran by their house every morning. *Those perky breasts,* Gemma thought. *That tight stomach.* Gemma's legs began moving again in an attempt to walk her out of the shame and jealousy. She kept walking. And walking. And walking, until she was five stop signs away from her house, at which point she sat down on a grassy slope in the middle of an intersection, brought her knees up to her chest, bent her head down on her knees, and cried. *Pull it together, Gemma,* she thought. *Pull it together.*

Her phone had been buzzing incessantly, but she wasn't ready to face the screen of worry just yet. As her body began to calm, she stretched out her legs and looked up at the sky. She extended her body backward and flattened out on the ground to better observe the clouds. After a few more minutes, she pulled her phone from her pocket and brought it to her face. The screen was full. Anthony had started the barrage.

Where did you go?

You okay?

Then Mary chimed in.

Gemma? Where are you?

Then Irene.

Are you outside?

We can just order pizza!

And on and on.

Your Dad is asking where the charcoal is. I'm not sure we have any??

Is that place around the corner any good? Mary and I are wondering about sandwiches from there.

Gemma. Please respond. Where are you?

I'm coming to find you.

Heads up. Mary has gone out front to find you.

Mary's on her way to find you. Do you have any charcoal?

Gemma rolled her head to the right to see a sideways Mary walking toward her.

"What's going on?" she hollered, her blond bob not even blowing in the breeze.

Without moving a muscle, Gemma watched her sister approach.

"Jesus, Gemma," Mary said as she reached her. Her chest was heaving slightly, which let Gemma know she had run most of the way. "You okay?" she asked, hands on her hips.

Gemma turned her head back to the clouds.

Mary lowered herself to the ground and sat cross-legged beside her sister. "You gotta talk to me."

Gemma didn't take her eyes off the clouds. "Don't know what to say."

"Gemma," Mary said in a softer tone. "I'm worried about you."

Gemma kept her eyes on the sky. The women sat next to each other in silence as a silver Civic rolled up to the stop sign. The driver—a middle-aged man—looked at them quizzically, then slowly drove on.

Gemma finally spoke. "Have you talked to Eddie?"

Mary sighed. "Not recently."

"When?"

"I dunno, Gem. Two weeks ago?"

Gemma's eyes looked to her sister. "You talked to him two weeks ago?"

Mary shrugged. "Yeah?"

"Is that the first time you've talked to him since he was here?"

Mary shook her head. "No. What's this about?"

"Did he ask about Calvin?"

"Gemma, I don't remember everything we talk about."

"You'd remember if Eddie had asked about my newborn son, who was in the hospital having surgery when he left to run a marathon."

"Okay." Mary put her hands up. "No. He didn't ask about Calvin. He hasn't."

Gemma's eyes filled with tears. "Or Bo?"

Mary hung her head. "Or Bo."

"Have Mom and Dad talked to him?"

"I assume so."

"Wow."

"Is this what's bothering you? Eddie?"

Gemma stood up and brushed grass clippings from her legs and back. "I'm not bothered by a thing, Mary. Not a goddamn thing." She walked back toward the house, Mary following a few steps behind her.

———

Gemma had experienced a few clairvoyant moments in her life.

Once was when she and Anthony were on their first road trip together, just a few months into dating. He was driving, she was navigating. A feeling came over her that they were about to collide with something. "Anthony!" she yelled, grabbing his arm. When she looked around, there wasn't a car for miles—nothing but the open Indiana highway. But not ten minutes later, Anthony was fiddling with the radio and looked up just in time to slam on the breaks and avoid careening into the back of a slowed semi. After the car jerked to a stop, they looked at each other and simultaneously mouthed, "Whoa."

Gemma had the same kind of feeling now as she walked

back up the driveway of their home, Mary a cautious ten feet behind her. She knew in her gut what awaited her on the other side of the door. And yet there was a small part of her that was still surprised when she opened the door, stepped inside, and smelled what she knew she would smell.

"Gemma?" Irene called from the kitchen before coming around the corner. "All okay? Sweetie, where did you go? We didn't mean to upset you."

"What is that cooking?" Gemma asked, but she already knew. She had known even before she passed through the final intersection and saw Mr. Ruiz's khaki-covered rear end poking up from his petunias.

"Well, I heard your concern about bedtimes, and you were right, steaks would take too long."

"What is that cooking?" Gemma repeated, her jaw clenching.

Irene looked at Gemma, confused. "I found a full pan of pasta in the fridge. I've got that warming and I'm just making the salad. Dinner will be ready in ten minutes!"

As Irene turned back to the kitchen, Gemma walked into the living room to find Anthony sitting on the couch, propping a bottle in Calvin's mouth, a glare affixed to his face.

"I'm so sorry," she whispered.

He continued to look at her without changing his intense expression.

She glanced out the window to see Bo and Jack playing catch in the yard. She turned back to Anthony with tears in her eyes. If he saw them, he didn't say anything. He returned his attention to the baby.

Gemma stood for a few moments in the living room, hoping to see a break in the clouds of Anthony's face, but when she was met with nothing but a storm, she walked back into the kitchen to find Mary and her mother whispering. They jerked out of their secretive stance when they realized Gemma was standing there.

"Hi, sweetie!" Irene said, too loudly. "Ready to eat?"

Gemma crossed her arms. "What were you talking about?"

"Nothing, nothing. Mary was just telling me about some work stuff."

Gemma looked back and forth between her mother and sister. "What work stuff was that, Mare?"

"Gemma," Mary said quietly.

"You two are ridiculous."

"Gemma!" Irene said, somehow both angry and pleading at the same time.

"What the hell were you whispering about?"

Irene's shoulder went up slightly. "I was just asking Mary where you went."

"Didn't think to ask me?"

"You weren't in here."

"Ah, okay." Gemma nodded. "You asked Mary out of convenience. Because she was in the room."

"Why, yes."

"Mom, that is such utter bullshit."

"Gemma Elise McAlister!"

"It's Gemma *Sinclair*, actually."

Irene's voice dropped to a soothing tone. "Honey, I was worried about you. We aren't in here telling secrets. I was just checking on you."

"So no secrets in here?"

"Oh Gem, of course not." Irene stepped forward and put an arm around her daughter, who stiffened at her touch.

"Great," Gemma said. "Then tell me what happened that day after Eddie's football tryouts."

Irene broke her arm's seal around her daughter and looked at her. "What?"

"I want to know what happened that day."

Irene looked at Mary, whose eyes moved to the floor.

"Gemma, where is this coming from?"

"From my childhood, Mom."

Irene shifted on her feet. "Sweetie, I don't even know what you're talking about."

"Oh?"

"That was thirty years ago."

"So you don't know what I'm talking about, but you know when it was?"

"I remember how hard it was those first few months after having a baby," Irene said, softening her voice.

"Don't blame this on Calvin."

Irene stepped back. "Blame what?"

"You tell me," Gemma pressed.

"Gemma, you're tired."

"No, I'm curious."

"About Eddie's tryouts?"

"No, what happened after that."

Irene's eyes shifted to Mary. Then back to Gemma. Her arms dropped to her side. "Gemma, your father and I did the right thing. I firmly believe that."

As Gemma opened her mouth to respond, she heard Bo's voice growing louder behind her.

"Gamma!" he said, running toward Irene and wrapping his arms around her legs.

Gemma turned to see her father trailing Bo with a smile on his face.

Jack laughed, patting Gemma on the back. "Kid has an arm on him."

Irene patted Bo's back until he unhooked from her and ran into the living room in search of Anthony.

Alone in the small kitchen, with the aroma of marinara and clams permeating from the oven, the four adults stood facing each other. Jack looked quizzically around the circle, suddenly aware there was tension. When no one spoke, he cleared his throat and clapped his hands once.

"Mary, Gemma, let's set the table."

And with that, Irene turned back to the salad, Mary opened a cabinet and began handing Gemma drinking glasses, and Jack opened the drawer next to the dishwasher and took out the silverware.

Within five minutes, the McAlisters and the Sinclairs were sitting around the table, sharing Gemma's favorite meal. Calvin was sleeping peacefully in the pack and play Anthony had moved beside his chair. Anthony had one hand on Calvin's stomach while the other held his fork. Mary and Jack talked about her latest case. Irene plucked clams out of Bo's helping. Gemma desperately wanted to eat the pasta—she hadn't gotten any of the pan Dr. Heinz sent over after Calvin's birth—but she had lost her appetite. Though an accommodating smile was affixed to her face, her mind was twisting around her mother's words: "Your father and I did the right thing."

CHAPTER 17

Gemma hated waiting rooms. She even hated the one at her own office, despite the fact that she had helped Dr. Heinz with the design. It didn't matter what art was hung, or which chairs were picked out, or even how current the magazines were, waiting rooms were temples to the worst part of human existence: waiting. And with most waiting came the additional worry of what lay beyond the waiting room door. A test to be run. A lump to be found. A new medication to try. The mind could just swirl and swirl with panic and worry—about scenarios that wouldn't come to be. But that's what happens in a waiting room. The body is forced to sit in limbo, but the mind wastes no time; it jumps immediately into action, working hard to solve the problems it imagines are on their way.

Gemma hadn't heard from Anthony since he left the house the previous night, immediately after the McAlisters departed. But she hadn't reached out to him either. Whatever small crack in the wall between them she had felt yesterday, before her family arrived, had been properly plastered up, watertight.

As her body sat still and her mind worked furiously in the waiting room of the colleague Dr. Heinz had referred her to—Dr. Piper Fox—Gemma began to wonder if Anthony would even come over tonight. And if he did, would she tell him how her morning had gone—how Bo had a meltdown so terrible she could barely get him into the day care center? His screaming had caused Calvin distress, and together the Sinclair brothers cried with all their might as Gemma wrangled them into the facility, her elbows and hands full of car seats and bags and shoes and blankets and bottles. When she got back to the car, she burst into tears and sobbed the entire crosstown drive to Dr. Fox's office.

Of course, if Anthony did come over tonight and she told him all this, she would also have to explain why she had cried all the way to Dr. Fox's office rather than to her own. She would have to fess up to the fact that she had lost her damn mind with a patient and been punished by Dr. Heinz with mandatory therapy until she could get her act together. As she sat there thinking over how that conversation would go, how Anthony would react, she decided it was best that he just believe she was getting up every day and going to work. As soon as she was able to get a handle on her emotions, she would return to work having spared Anthony more of her bullshit. Yes, that would be the plan. Her jaw tightened as her hands gripped the arms of the waiting room chair.

"Gemma Sinclair," a wispy dark-haired woman with small round glasses said to her through an open door into the waiting room.

Gemma stood and nodded as she made her way to her. The woman was wearing a gray cable-knit sweater with a high collar, jeans, and hot-pink Nike Dunks. She smiled widely at Gemma, showing her perfectly straight white teeth, and held out her hand. She appeared to be at least a decade older than Gemma.

"Gemma, pleasure," she said, gesturing into her office.

Gemma stepped cautiously into an extraordinarily plain

room. Not a piece of decoration in the place. The walls were beige, same as the couch. There was a leather chair that was worn and cracked, and a metal desk like you'd see in a government office. There wasn't even a plant, let alone a book, in the entire room. A single window looked out on a small green space adjacent to the building. *This is who Heinz recommends?* Gemma thought as she took a seat.

Dr. Fox sat down in the leather chair without a pen or notebook; folded her legs crisscross style, like she was an elementary school kid playing duck, duck, goose; and rested her wrists on her knees. Gemma expected her to begin with a brief explanation of her process. Or to go over her background. Or to ask how she was feeling today. Instead, she just looked at Gemma, her head ever so slightly cocked to one side.

After what felt like an excruciatingly long silence, Gemma finally spoke. "I don't really need to be here."

"Oh?"

"I mean . . . I know I'm not bouncing back after this baby like I did with my first. But I'm okay."

"Ah."

"All right, okay. I get what you're doing. You understand I'm a psychologist too, right?" Gemma knew that, when in session, the less the therapist said, the more the patient would say. That tactic was one of the harder ones for Gemma to utilize. Mostly because she had a nervous tendency to fill silences, a habit born of growing up with an aloof brother and functionally mute father.

"What am I doing?" Dr. Fox asked.

"You're being quiet so I'll talk."

Dr. Fox didn't respond.

"I'd prefer you not do that," Gemma said.

"What would you prefer I do?"

"I don't know."

"If *you* don't know, how would I?"

"Jesus." Gemma rubbed the side of her neck with her left hand. *What about this woman did Heinz believe was a good fit for me?* she wondered. Dr. Fox remained silent. Gemma sighed before continuing. "What did Dr. Heinz tell you about me?"

Dr. Fox shrugged. "Not much."

"I'll bet."

"What are you worried he said?"

Gemma shook her head once. "I'm not *worried*."

"So why did you ask?"

"Because I can only assume what he said about me."

"What might he have said?"

"Perhaps that I flipped out with a patient, and that I'm probably suffering from postpartum depression, and that I'm not a good mother, and that I'm ruining my marriage, and that I have issues with my family."

Dr. Fox raised her eyebrows, but her voice remained neutral. "That's a lot for Dr. Heinz to say about you."

Gemma shrugged with her palms out as if her argument were proven.

"Tell me," Dr. Fox said. "What else might Dr. Heinz have said to me?"

Gemma thought back to her coffee with Dr. Heinz at the academic conference where they met, when he offered her a job after a few cups at a small table outside the Starbucks in the hotel lobby. He had had such high hopes for her, and she had felt so proud that he singled her out after her paper presentation and asked her to join his practice on the spot. She had wondered over the years if he ever regretted that. If he should have taken one of the other presenters from that session to coffee instead of her. If he should have offered anyone else the job.

"He could have told you I was a terrible hire."

"What else?"

"That I constantly focus on the wrong things in life."

"Like what?"

Gemma blinked back tears. "I dunno."

"What if I told you that when Dr. Heinz called me, he complimented you."

Gemma snorted a sarcastic laugh.

"Can you imagine what that compliment was?"

Gemma studied Dr. Fox's face. She had kind, round brown eyes. If it weren't for the crow's feet and the few thin streaks of gray running through her shoulder-length black hair, she could have been mistaken for a college student. She couldn't pinpoint what about Dr. Fox felt almost magnetic. Was it that she reminded Gemma of someone, or that she was like no one Gemma had ever met before? Her mind worked to figure out what it was about this woman, in her dreary office, that simultaneously comforted her and put her on edge.

Gemma inhaled. "I never call in sick."

"Is that all he would compliment you on?"

Gemma shrugged, a tear sliding slowly down her cheek. "Yes."

Dr. Fox watched her a moment before speaking. "Well, Gemma. The truth is, I haven't spoken to Dr. Heinz about you."

Gemma's eyes narrowed. "But he referred me to you."

"True, but he and I didn't go out for drinks and discuss you late into the night. I simply got a call from your office manager, who gave me your name and set up the appointment."

Gemma blinked at her.

"I didn't know a thing about you when we shook hands."

"Oh."

"But now I know a lot."

Gemma swallowed hard. A wave of embarrassment flooded her body, flushing her face with warmth. Dr. Heinz had been a supportive boss for years. *Do I really believe he thinks so little of me?* she wondered. "Yeah. I'm clearly paranoid."

"You're clearly hurting."

Additional tears forced their way up and out of Gemma's

eyelids and down her cheek. "I think I might be having a mental breakdown."

"After giving birth? That's mighty inconvenient."

Gemma's eyes shot up to meet Dr. Fox's. A smile poked out from Gemma's lips. "Yes, highly inconvenient."

Silence hung between them for a beat.

"I'm here because I had an emotional outburst with a patient," Gemma admitted.

"What did that look like?"

"It looked like me yelling 'Fuck you' in the middle of our office."

"Ah. Yes. We've all done that one."

Gemma laughed once, then put her hand over her mouth, feeling the wetness of her cheeks in her palms. "What?"

Dr. Fox smiled. "Well, I didn't tell a patient that *exactly*. I think what I actually said was 'Fuck *off*.' But essentially the same thing."

Gemma smiled. "Holy shit."

"The patient was so agitated during a session that he picked up a decorative boat I had on a table and threw it at the wall."

"Damn."

"That boat was a gift from my wife, and I just lost it when I saw it shatter."

"Well, yeah."

Dr. Fox gestured around the sparse room. "Which is why I no longer decorate my office."

"Your wife was unwilling to buy you another boat?" Gemma asked.

"She passed away."

"Oh god. I'm so sorry."

"And she hasn't bought me much of anything since."

Gemma's jaw dropped. She watched Dr. Fox's perfect teeth slowly appear as the curtains of her lips drew up in a wide grin.

This curious, tiny woman was making a morbid joke in the middle of a therapy session. Gemma was enthralled.

"That's dark."

Dr. Fox's smile faded but the twinkle in her eyes remained. "My wife died eight years ago."

"I'm really sorry to hear that."

"She had been gone six months when my patient picked up the boat and threw it."

"Ah."

"Point is, Gemma," she said, sitting up slightly, "if we don't handle our trauma, our trauma will handle us."

"Right." Gemma nodded. "Right." Her gaze lifted to the ceiling. "But I haven't experienced any trauma."

"Oh?"

"Not like you. Not a death."

"And death is the only trauma?"

"Well, no . . ."

"Oh." Dr. Fox uncrossed her legs, pushed back in her chair, and clapped her hands once. "You're *that* person."

Gemma looked at her in confusion. "What person?"

"That *one* person who hasn't experienced any trauma in her life. I've always wanted to meet you."

"Okay, okay," Gemma said, putting her hands up. She took a large breath and rubbed the tops of her thighs slowly before continuing. "My son, Calvin—my six-week-old—had an accident when he was five days old and had to have surgery on his eye."

"That's a lot."

"He, um, he fell on the fireplace. We have one of those fireplaces with like a, um . . ." Gemma gestured with her hands close to the floor. "That have a ledge. Like a hearth. And you can sit on it."

Dr. Fox nodded.

"And, well, he fell onto the corner of the fireplace, which is really sharp. And my mother had been nagging me to put those bumpers on it. You know, those padded strips that stick to sharp corners of tables and stuff."

Again, Dr. Fox nodded.

"And the ironic thing is, we were about to put them on the day Calvin fell." Gemma looked out the window. "We were *just* about to put those on. Dad and I had gone down to the basement to get them."

"What stopped you?"

"Eddie showed up," Gemma said, still staring out the window. "Eddie and Kat," she clarified.

"Who are they?"

"My brother and his wife. My brother was in town visiting."

"To see the baby," Dr. Fox suggested.

"No, actually. I mean, sort of. He was running a marathon up in Indianapolis. He stayed with me before heading to it."

"What is your relationship like with Eddie?"

"Strained."

"But he was in town and staying with you."

Gemma lowered her head. "I thought it might be a chance for us to spend some quality time together. Bonding opportunity, I suppose."

Gemma stared at her hands as she thought back to the day Eddie arrived. How nervous and excited she had been. The effort she had put into cleaning the house, preparing the guest room, planning the food, fetching the beer and coffee. It was all supposed to set the stage for something that never came to be.

"You had some pressure on this stay," Dr. Fox said.

"You sound like my mother."

"How so?"

"She always blames me for my strained relationship with Eddie."

"How does she do that?"

"By giving me advice on how to act around him. Telling me to be more relaxed. Reminding me not to ask too much of him."

"Does your mother always protect Eddie?"

Gemma looked up in confusion. "How is that protecting him?"

"It sounds like she's trying to manage his reactions by managing your interactions with him."

Gemma's eyes darted back and forth across the floor in thought. "Yeah. She does do that."

"When your mom is trying to control everything, what is the rest of your family doing?"

Gemma took a long breath in. "Well, Mary—my sister— feels like she's in the middle. I mean, she technically is, as the middle child. She walks a tightrope between us. She kind of clams up when I try to talk about Eddie. I think she's trying to be Switzerland."

"Anyone else?"

"My dad. He's quiet. He's always quiet."

"Why is he quiet?"

Who the hell knows? Gemma thought. She rummaged around in her memories for a few moments before landing on one she hadn't thought about in years. She was very young, she and her dad were headed somewhere together, he was buckling her into the back seat, and he clipped a piece of her skin in the buckle. She let out a cry, but he didn't look at her. He didn't even act like she was crying. Instead, he closed her car door, got into the front seat, put the car in reverse, and headed off to wherever they were going. Gemma recalled working hard to quiet her tears to match her father's silence. She was confused in the moment and felt at fault for her hand getting pinched. Moments later, her father was upbeat again, narrating to Gemma, as parents do when their kids are young. And though her father's earlier reticence didn't make sense to Gemma at the time, it began a pattern: she never wanted her distress to silence her father again.

Gemma shrugged. "I can't answer that. He just always seems silent. He's a very powerful attorney, so Anthony jokes that my dad uses up all of his words in court."

"Who's Anthony?"

"My husband."

"What is he like when Eddie is around?"

Gemma shook her head dramatically. "He is *not* a fan."

"Are you?"

"Am I what?"

"A fan?"

"Of Eddie? He's my *brother.*"

"By that logic, Eddie is a fan of yours."

Gemma's eyes went hot. "I don't believe that's true."

"So how do you really feel about Eddie?"

"I don't know." Her voice rose slightly. "How the hell am I supposed to answer that?"

"Sounds like you haven't given it much thought."

"No, actually, I've thought about Eddie way too much. That's certainly Anthony's opinion."

"But *how* do you think about him?"

Gemma's mind went back to Mary confessing that she and Eddie had talked recently. And that he hadn't asked about Calvin. Gemma had taken this as evidence that Eddie was mad at her.

Gemma shrugged. "I think about what I could do differently so I don't annoy him."

"But you don't spend any time thinking about *your* opinion of *him*," Dr. Fox stated.

Gemma gazed at her, at a loss for words. They sat looking at each other for a moment until Dr. Fox tucked her hair behind her ear thoughtfully and asked, "How did Calvin get hurt?"

"Like I said, he fell on the corner of the fireplace."

"The same day Eddie arrived, right?"

"Right." Gemma looked away.

"How does an infant 'fall'?"

Gemma's chin quivered. She bit her lip. She tried to answer but the tears interrupted her. She held her chin up—her gaze still out the window—as the tears fell in a steady stream. "Um, Eddie, um." She choked on her tears before swallowing hard and continuing. "Eddie was holding him."

Out of the corner of her eye she saw Dr. Fox slowly lean forward.

"And Eddie fell asleep in the chair beside the fireplace." Her tears were dropping at such a rate that she could feel them hitting her forearms. But she kept her head up and her eyes on the tree just outside the window. "His arm relaxed, and Calvin rolled out and onto the fireplace."

Dr. Fox let the silence settle on the two of them. Gemma continued to cry, bringing up her hand to wipe away the wetness, but she couldn't look back at her.

"Then what happened?"

Gemma inhaled, trying to slow her tears. "I was, um, I was on my fucking phone. On the couch. And I heard this awful thump mixed with this . . . this . . ." Gemma brought her hands up to her face and paused. "Bloodcurdling scream."

Dr. Fox remained motionless.

"And I looked up and saw Eddie with his arm outstretched. And on the floor was my baby. My gorgeous baby lying on the floor, face down."

"Then what?" Dr. Fox asked gently.

"I started screaming for Anthony. And I leapt up and over the coffee table and scooped Calvin up. And I couldn't bear to look at my baby. Oh god, I couldn't even look at him." She turned back to Dr. Fox, expecting to see disgust on her face. Instead she saw true compassion. "And I thrust him at Anthony just as he got down the stairs. I didn't even look at Calvin's face. I was just looking at Eddie."

"What was he doing?"

Gemma's body shook with exhaustion. "Sleeping."

"Through the screaming?"

Gemma balled a fist over her mouth. "I thought he was dead."

"Because he wasn't moving."

Gemma nodded. "I mean, I don't know if I truly thought he was dead, but that thought flashed through me because he wasn't moving. His chin down on his chest. Still through the screams." She swallowed hard at the prospect of Eddie's death. The mere thought of it made her feel such shame, such regret.

"What did you do?"

"I called 911, of course. But then I shook Eddie awake."

"What was his reaction when he woke up?"

Gemma's forehead wrinkled in thought, her tears abating momentarily. "Defensive? Annoyed?"

"Concerned?"

Gemma felt something shift in her head. "No, not concerned. He didn't even ask if Calvin was okay."

"How is Calvin?"

Gemma grabbed a tissue from the box on the end table beside the couch. "Better now. We went to the hospital that night and stayed a couple of days, and he had surgery. The doctor is optimistic he won't have long-term problems with his eye. We got lucky."

"Have you and Eddie talked about the incident?"

Gemma shook her head.

"Has he reached out to you with an apology?"

"He doesn't know it was his fault."

Dr. Fox's eyebrows rose. "How does he not know?"

Gemma shrugged. "He was asleep."

"Right . . . ," Dr. Fox said, her eyes narrowing. "But certainly your parents, or your sister, or Anthony, told him what happened."

Gemma shook her head. "They don't know it was his fault."

"Not even your husband?"

"Especially not him."

"Gemma, why don't they know?"

"Because I told them it was my fault."

"What made you do that?"

Her question was obvious, but Gemma's answer wasn't. She still couldn't believe she had so easily lied to her husband, and then had kept the lie going with him and everyone else. What did the lie do for her? What did it get her? What was she avoiding? Deep down, she knew.

"Because I was protecting Eddie." Saying this, and admitting how true it felt, surprised her.

"Eddie must be quite fragile if he needs all this protecting."

"It's not that simple."

"Maybe it is."

Gemma looked at Dr. Fox and saw a knowing expression on her face as she relaxed again in her chair, placed her elbow on the arm rest, and dropped her chin into the palm of her hand.

"I have a lot of questions, Gemma," she said. "But one stands out the most right now."

Gemma motioned with her hand for Dr. Fox to say it.

"What is everyone protecting Eddie from?"

CHAPTER 18

Gemma drummed her fingers on the table as her eyes darted around the busy restaurant. Her mom wasn't late; Gemma was early. Perhaps she had arrived when she did out of nervous energy. Perhaps it was because she didn't have much filling her days right now. She'd been pretending to go to the office every day for the past two weeks so as not to arouse suspicion from Mary or Anthony, but instead had been doing a variety of other time-killing activities, like shopping, going for walks, and of course having her twice-weekly sessions with Dr. Fox. After their third session, during which they had explored how hard it was for Gemma to talk with Irene without feeling dismissed—or worse, judged—Dr. Fox encouraged her to talk one-on-one with her mother. She called her a few days later and invited her to lunch. The excitement in her mom's voice had filled her with shame.

Now her eyes were hot with tears, but she blinked them back when she saw Irene step up to the hostess stand. Gemma raised her hand and wiggled her fingers until her mother's face illuminated with recognition. As Irene swept toward her,

Gemma's heart quickened. Dr. Fox's words came back to her: "What is everyone protecting Eddie from?"

Gemma stood to embrace her mother. "Hey, Mom."

"My girl!" Irene was wearing a cream-colored turtleneck, matching slacks, and a pair of large earrings made of gold wires twisted into the abstract outline of honeybees. They were from her mother's newest collection. "It's good to see you in clothes and makeup!"

Gemma sucked in air through her teeth as she put her arms around her mother. Their hugs were never very long or particularly comforting. Irene flitted around too much for a truly warm embrace. "Your mother is like a hummingbird," Anthony once said. "She'd take that as a compliment because they weigh so little," Gemma had responded.

Not only did Irene move around a lot, but she also attracted a lot of attention everywhere she went. Her tall, lanky body swam gracefully through rooms, and her outfits, accented with her custom-made jewelry, caught the eye of most any woman in her vicinity. Irene's magnetism worked on her youngest daughter too. Gemma often felt like a moth to her mother's glow, even though the flame sometimes burned her.

Irene settled herself facing Gemma and waved the waiter over. "I'd love a champagne! And a hot tea. A glass of ice water and some extra lemon slices on a plate. Gemma?"

Gemma looked up apologetically at the waiter. "Just water, thanks."

As the waiter walked away, Gemma felt her chest tighten. "Mom?"

"Mm-hmm," Irene said absently, scanning the menu.

Gemma reached over and touched her mother's arm, forcing Irene's gaze to meet her own. "Before we order, can we talk?"

Irene dramatically snapped the menu shut, placed it on the table, and folded her hands over it. "Of course! I must tell you about my upcoming trunk show in Chicago!"

Gemma smiled. "I heard about that from Mary. I'm so proud of you."

Irene swatted a hand, showing her long, thin fingers tipped with lacquered red nails and a large sapphire ring on her pointer, a piece she had made herself years ago. "They have me showcasing with some young designer at the show. Some plump girl with pink hair who casts her gemstones in enamel. Can you believe that? Enamel? It's the new trend. It will be gone in a few years, I promise." She rolled her eyes and shook her head.

Gemma took a deep breath. "Actually, Mom, I wanted to talk about something specific."

"Oh. Okay. Are you all right? How's Calvin? And Bo? Goodness, that boy is full of energy."

"They're fine, Mom."

"And Anthony?"

Gemma's eyes fell to the table. In an effort to not dismiss or downplay, to show up with her mother in a way she wished her mother would show up with her, she said, "Well, in truth, he's very mad at me."

"Anthony? At *you*?"

"Yes. Very."

"Oh, I don't believe that for a minute. The man worships you."

"No," Gemma said forcefully. "He's very mad at me. He's actually not been sleeping at . . . at home."

Irene's eyes widened. "What? Since when?"

Gemma looked up at the ceiling to think. "Oh, gosh. Six weeks. Maybe eight."

"Anthony hasn't been sleeping at home for *two months*!?" Irene's voice rose to a pitch that prompted some inquiring looks from adjacent tables.

Gemma glanced around the room, embarrassed. "I didn't think it would last this long. But it's become the routine. He comes over in the morning to help get the kids to day care, and then he's over after work to have dinner with us and put the kids to bed. But then right after that, he leaves."

"Where the heck does he go?"

Gemma winced. "His friend David's house. Well, his apartment."

"So, what? He's sleeping on a futon?"

Gemma shrugged, her lips pursed. "Mary's been staying with me most nights and every weekend, so I have some help."

"She didn't tell me this! Why does no one tell me anything?!"

"I asked her not to." Gemma gave her mother a pointed look. "I didn't want to deal with the questions."

"Gemma, what's going on?"

"Mom . . ."

"You must have *some* idea."

"He won't really speak to me right now. At least not about us."

"He's ignoring you? That doesn't sound like him."

Over Irene's shoulder, Gemma watched the waiter approach their table with a tray full of glasses and what appeared to be three lemons' worth of slices on a small plate.

"What sounds good today, ladies?" he asked.

Irene's bejeweled hand rose. "Actually, we are going to need a minute."

"Certainly," he said. "I'll check on you in a bit."

Gemma smiled at him with her lips tight and nodded her thanks.

"Have you just *asked* him what he's feeling or thinking?" Irene resumed.

"It's not that easy."

"It's absolutely that easy. You walk up to him and say, 'What the heck, Anthony?'"

Gemma sighed. "Mom, I'm the one who pushed him away."

"Even if that's true, like hell are you going to be ignored because of it."

Gemma felt a lightening in her chest. Her mother's defense of her was a welcome, if not unexpected, turn. But then she remembered back to that night, and how Irene had rooted around in her fridge, extracting the pan of pasta Anthony had sweetly procured for their special night, all while Gemma was having a full-on panic attack at the base of a stop sign five blocks away.

"Mom, I don't need to ask him. I'm pretty sure I know what he's thinking."

"Oh? What?"

Gemma bit her lip. "That I put our family over him."

"Whose family? Yours?"

"The McAlister family."

Irene swatted Gemma's hand lightly. "Oh, hardly."

"Mom."

"He's got a problem with us? That's silly." Irene sat back and crossed her arms.

"He doesn't have a problem with *you*, exactly. It's with me. And how I interact with you all."

"I don't understand."

"I think he feels like I don't prioritize him as much as I do you and Dad and Mary."

Irene rolled her eyes. "Oh, come on."

"And Eddie."

Irene looked at Gemma a beat, her eyes narrowing. "He's never liked Eddie."

"Can you blame him?"

"Of course I can. What's Eddie ever done? He's harmless."

"No, Mom, he's not."

"He never even sees Eddie. How could he be that big of a problem?"

"Mom."

"What?"

"Anthony's issue is with how Eddie treats me. And how I act when Eddie is around."

Irene picked up the menu and began skimming. "You do get weird, dear."

"Because I'm always afraid Eddie is mad at me! And I don't know what I've done!"

Irene sighed but kept her eyes on the menu. "Gemma, I don't know what you're upset about, but I am not to blame for Anthony not sleeping in your home. That was your call."

Gemma shook her head and closed her eyes tightly. "That's not what I'm saying."

"Then what are you saying?" Irene asked distractedly, still skimming.

"I'm trying to have an honest conversation with you about the dynamics in our family. Can you at least look at me?"

Irene set the menu back down. "Okay, I'm listening."

Gemma paused and wiped her eyes. "It really hurt that Eddie . . ."

"That Eddie what?"

"That he left while I was at the hospital with Calvin."

"Well, he had the marathon, sweetie. You know that."

A tear rolled down Gemma's cheek and she caught it at her chin. "How in the world does that matter?"

Irene pursed her lips. "He stayed and helped with Bo."

Gemma knew she shouldn't be surprised by her mother's reaction. Irene always did this. Ever since Gemma was little, Irene had brushed aside Gemma's hurt over Eddie's icy be-havior toward her, even excusing Eddie's absence at Gemma's high school graduation. She'd walked around the party at their house, telling guests—most of whom were clients of Jack's—that Eddie was so busy at work he simply couldn't break away. Though this was absolutely Irene's pattern, Gemma still felt something akin to shock that it was playing out in front of her yet again.

"Are you seriously giving him a pass?" she asked.

"It's not a pass, Gemma. He had plans. He did what he could before he had to go."

"He didn't even call to check on Calvin. He *still* hasn't."

Irene leaned back in her chair and craned her neck in search of the waiter. "You know how he is."

"Mom, why do we treat Eddie like this?"

"Like what?"

"Like he's exempt!"

Irene's eyes became slits and she leaned in. "Gemma, let's not do this," she whispered tersely. "Not here." She leaned back, rearranged her face into a pleasant expression, and smiled out into the room—for whom, Gemma didn't know. "I thought this was going to be a fun girls' lunch. Come on, your hair is fixed and everything! But now you're upset, and if you cry your mascara will run."

Gemma's stomach twisted. The all-too-familiar feeling of spinning out against her family's indifference gripped her like a vise. She was always made to feel crazy, irrational even, for asking questions about Eddie. Every member of her family would either swat a dismissive hand, laugh off a question, or grow quiet and unresponsive. As a result, Gemma was made to feel annoyingly intrusive.

"And you can't possibly understand why I'm upset?" Gemma's voice was soft.

"I get that it's about Anthony and Eddie, but . . ."

"But what?"

"But sweetie, that has nothing to do with me. I can't control where your husband sleeps or how your brother acts."

"No, you just try to control me."

Irene laughed nervously, her long fingers splayed across her chest. "Where is *this* coming from?"

"From my fucking childhood," Gemma hissed.

"Gemma Elise," her mother whispered sternly. "Watch how you talk to me."

"Mom, I am trying so hard to be heard right now."

"Oh, I hear you just fine."

Gemma crossed her arms. "Tell me why you choose Eddie over me. Tell me why you favor him. Why you always take his side. Why you make me feel like a crazy person every time he's around, thinking I'm going to say or do the wrong thing. Tell me why my brother's peace of mind is more important than mine."

Irene stared at her daughter as tears rimmed her eyes. "Do you honestly believe all of that?"

"With every cell in my body."

"I don't know what to say."

"An explanation would be a great start."

Irene sighed and reached across the table to touch her daughter's crossed arm. "Gemma, I didn't know you felt this way. But Eddie is just, well, he just has to be handled differently."

"Handled?"

"That's not quite what I mean. I just mean, we've always needed to treat Eddie differently."

"Oh? You've *needed* to?"

"Gemma."

"Mom, what is going on?"

Irene brought the napkin from her lap up to the corner of her eye. Gemma worked to breathe through her pounding heart, an automatic reaction any time she saw her mother upset. *I'm not making her cry,* she reminded herself. *The situation is making her cry, and I did not create this situation. I'm trying to fix it.*

"It's complicated. It's hard to explain, and hard to understand."

"Try me."

"Have you ever talked to your father about this?"

Gemma tilted her head to the side. "About Eddie? No."

"Well, maybe you should talk to him instead of me."

"Why?"

Irene shook her head and continued wiping her eyes. She was quiet for a full minute. "Gemma," she finally said.

"What?"

"All of this is making me anxious for Thanksgiving."

Gemma shook her head, confused. "What?"

"Eddie and Kat want to go to Brazil during Christmas, so I've invited them to spend Thanksgiving with us, and they haven't said either way what they are doing, but if they come, I don't want it to be . . . awkward."

"In this moment, right now, you're worried about how I'll act at *Thanksgiving*?"

Irene paused and looked at Gemma. "I just don't want you—*it*, I don't want *it*—to be weird if Eddie does come. I want to enjoy the holiday."

Gemma blinked at her mother in disbelief. Out of the corner of her eye she saw the waiter approaching their table again with a wide smile.

"Have I given you lovely ladies enough time?"

Gemma pushed her chair back and stood up, throwing her napkin on the table. "Actually, nothing for me today. I seem to have lost my appetite." She grabbed her purse, slammed her chair up under the table, and marched to the door, her mother and the waiter watching her in stunned silence.

———

"God!" Gemma yelled as she slammed her fists on the steering wheel in the parking lot. She had managed to start the car, despite how shaky her hands were. She put the car in reverse with unnecessary force. As she backed up, she heard her phone buzz. Before she shifted into drive, she glanced at the screen staring up at her from the passenger seat.

Gemma, please come back.

I'm sorry, let's just talk.

I'm going to order something for you. Take your time and then come back in when you're ready.

I love you.

Every ding, every word, made Gemma angrier. She threw the car into drive and sped out of the parking lot. Her body was shaking and her chest was tight. Her face felt flushed. Her head was pounding. Her appointment with Dr. Fox was scheduled for one thirty. But now that she had cut her lunch with her mother short, Gemma had over an hour to kill before her session. She didn't know where she was going, she just knew she couldn't be anywhere close to the moment she was in. She pressed her foot harder on the pedal and roared down the street.

As she drove, she started feeling worse. She was so exhausted. Even though Calvin was sleeping long stretches now, she still wasn't sleeping well. The night before, after tossing in bed alone for four hours, she had finally fallen asleep but awoke two hours later having sweated through the sheets so badly that she had to change them. She then skipped breakfast, even though she had time to eat; Anthony took the boys to day care.

She felt her stomach lurch. This time she didn't think it was her anxiety; she knew it was hunger.

She pulled off the road and into a McDonald's drive-through. The idea of fries sent a tingle of joy up her spine. As she ordered, her mouth began to fill with saliva. She was hungrier than she realized. She ate a hamburger in six massive bites. She wasn't even sure she chewed the fries, but she reveled in their salty, hot deliciousness. After inhaling her meal, she crumpled the bag, threw it on the passenger-side floor-board, rolled her windows down, and reclined her seat. With her belly full and her eyes closed, she replayed the conversation with her mother. "Gemma, let's not do this. Not here," Irene had said. Gemma shook her head at the image of her mother, with her straight posture and long, lean neck, trying to shush Gemma. *And then she defended Eddie.* Gemma squeezed her eyes tighter.

Their talk at lunch took Gemma back in time to the Indiana University's first home game in the fall of 1998. Irene and Jack had bought four season tickets. Eddie was a sophomore and had been redshirted his freshman year, so it was the first home game in which he was eligible to play. When Eddie wasn't put in the game, Gemma felt her parents' tension as they all watched from the stands. Jack went really quiet, not even yelling at the referees. Irene rubbed her hands together nervously. Mary was chewing gum. Gemma remembered watching her sister blow a big bubble and feeling weird that Mary was being so casual while her parents were so intense. Mary seemed to be in another place altogether. Chewing, blowing, and popping, over and over, while Jack grew quieter and Irene started to shake.

Even as a nine-year-old, Gemma knew her parents were not in the mood for questions. But she wasn't able to help herself. She tugged on her dad's shirt, and he looked down at her, frowning.

"Is it going to be okay if Eddie doesn't play today?"

Jack stared down at her. "Hush."

Gemma felt hurt and confused. "Why can't I talk?"

"Gemma," Irene said from the other side of Jack. "Be quiet."

Gemma looked over at Mary just as a bubble popped on her nose. Mary looked back at Gemma and shrugged. As soon as the game was over, Gemma jumped up to leave.

"We are going to wait for Eddie outside the locker rooms," Irene said. Gemma was disappointed. The game had been long and boring, and she needed to go to the bathroom. But Irene insisted. After they made their way down the bleachers and around the corner to line up at the locker rooms, Irene pulled Gemma aside and knelt down in front of her so their eyes were level.

"Now Gemma," Irene said. "You are not to say anything to Eddie."

Gemma swallowed hard and stayed quiet. Her father's deep "Hush" still rang in her ears.

"Well, you can say hi," Irene clarified with a slight smile. "But you are not to say anything to him about not getting in the game today."

"Can I tell him about my piano recital?" Gemma asked so quietly Irene barely heard her.

Irene shook her head.

"But I want him to come."

"Gemma, Eddie has a lot going on with school and the team. Let's just focus on him today. You will have plenty of recitals," Irene had said.

Gemma's eyes popped open at the blare of a car horn nearby. She had revisited that moment outside the locker rooms many times over the years. She had even told her college roommate that story. But only now did the realization hit her: Eddie never came to a single one of her piano recitals. However, her family did not miss a single one of Eddie's games until he was permanently benched following his third concussion. As her mind wandered around the memory, and the hurt it evoked, her phone buzzed once more. She brought the phone to her face. It was her mom again.

Don't do this to me.

Gemma threw off her seat belt, threw open the car door, and threw up every delicious fry.

CHAPTER 19

"I'm feeling awful today," Gemma said as she settled into the beige couch in Dr. Fox's office. She noticed a striped blue throw pillow beside her. *This wasn't here last time, was it?* she wondered.

"Describe it," Dr. Fox said.

"I threw up earlier. But I'm not sick."

"Did something happen?"

"My mother happened."

Dr. Fox let out a laugh. "Ah."

"I did as we discussed and tried to confront her about Eddie," Gemma said.

"How did that go?"

"I walked out of our lunch together. I didn't even order."

"What happened?"

"I tried to talk to her about Eddie and my feelings, but she literally made it all about how Eddie is coming in for Thanksgiving."

"How did she do that?"

"She wanted to make sure I wouldn't be weird and whiny when he's here."

"What were you trying to say about your brother?"

"I was trying to tell her how hurt I am that Eddie left to go to the marathon—without a word—while Calvin was in the hospital."

"What did she say?"

"She made excuses and said Eddie deserves special treatment."

"Were those her words?"

Gemma looked up at her. "I didn't have a court reporter there."

Dr. Fox smiled. "I'm just curious what she said. Not what you heard."

Gemma immediately felt embarrassed. One of the more common occurrences with patients—or with any person on the street, frankly—was that they would express an opinion and pass it off as fact. They would insert their interpretation and intentions on anything that was said or done to them. The work of therapy was, in part, to separate facts from feelings. Once the facts were known, the feelings could be explored. Despite Gemma's deep familiarity with and thorough training in this, she knew she had just done the same thing. She sighed with recognition.

"At first, she said that 'Eddie has to be handled differently.'"

Dr. Fox raised her eyebrows but said nothing.

"But when I pressed her on that, she corrected herself and said, 'We've always needed to treat Eddie differently.'"

"How did you interpret that?"

"That Eddie gets a pass on all human decency."

"And what part of that bothers you?"

"Well, it sucks that he gets preferential treatment."

"Do you think Eddie sees it that way?"

"Oh, for sure. He gets to float through life without a worry in the world, and he can fuck up and be inconsiderate and people will just make it all okay for him."

"Do *you* want to be able to fuck up and be inconsiderate and have it not matter?"

"Well, no," Gemma conceded.

"Then what are you envious of?"

Gemma looked down at her hands, which still stung from repeatedly beating the steering wheel. She didn't know what came over her in the car. She had beaten that steering wheel with such rage. *What if someone saw me doing that?* she wondered for the first time. A wave of shame washed over her as she imagined how she would have looked to someone glancing over. Out of the corner of her eye she noticed Dr. Fox uncross her legs and sit forward in her chair.

"I don't know," Gemma finally said.

"Then what were you wanting to happen when you talked to your mom today?"

"I wanted her to take responsibility."

"For Eddie?"

"For how Eddie acts—what he gets away with—yes."

"Mmm."

"What?"

"It sounds like you're displacing your anger."

Gemma's right eyebrow rose. "Oh?"

"You sound really angry at Eddie."

"I am!"

"But you wanted your mother to apologize on his behalf?"

"Because she tries to control and manage how we interact with Eddie."

"And you don't want her to do that?"

"Obviously not!"

"And yet you approached her hoping she would control or manage an interaction with Eddie."

"No," Gemma said loudly. Then she exhaled. "No . . . ," she said more softly.

Dr. Fox sat quietly while Gemma ruminated. Gemma

couldn't deny what Dr. Fox was suggesting. Some part of Gemma had wanted her mother to apologize for Eddie. Even though it was Eddie who should apologize.

She looked at Dr. Fox with sadness in her eyes. "But if I'm really just mad at Eddie, then why do I feel so mad at my mother?"

"Because you *are* mad at your mother."

"But you just said I can't be mad at her about Eddie."

"I said your anger at Eddie needs to be directed at Eddie."

"But then why am I mad at my mom?"

"You tell me."

Gemma leaned over sideways until she was lying on the couch. When she felt the scratchy upholstery on her face, she instinctively reached out for the blue striped pillow and tucked it under her cheek. "I don't know anymore."

"I'll bet you do."

Gemma had this feeling a lot, but it was hard to explain—and even harder to catch what made it surface. It was as if she were in middle school and had walked into the girls' locker room after PE and knew she'd been talked about although nothing was being said. While her family acted for all the world like they were open and honest, she couldn't shake the feeling that they were hiding something from her. Irene was the prime suspect. "I feel my mother is lying to me," she finally said. "Or not telling me something."

"Did you tell her that?"

"No."

"I wonder why."

Gemma closed her eyes for a few seconds.

"I wonder if you're avoiding something very painful," Dr. Fox said.

"How so?"

"Well, for starters, you're avoiding telling Eddie how mad you are at him for going to the marathon. Beyond that, you're avoiding telling your mother what you're really mad at her about—feeling deprived of some vital information. You also physically avoided her by walking out of a restaurant in the middle of a conversation."

Gemma pushed her body back up to a seated position, her hand resting on the pillow. "You certainly had all that locked and loaded."

Dr. Fox paused, smiling slightly. "Point is, you're doing an awful lot of avoiding."

Gemma sighed, ran her fingers through her hair a few times, and leaned back into the couch, pulling the pillow onto her lap. "I'm also avoiding my husband."

"How so?"

Gemma swallowed, unable to look at Dr. Fox. "Anthony hasn't been, um . . . sleeping at our house. He kind of moved out? I mean, he's at the house every day, he just leaves when it's time to sleep."

"You've avoided telling me this, yes?"

Gemma shrugged. "I felt—I *feel*—ashamed."

"And have you talked to Anthony about it?"

"What do you think?"

Dr. Fox smiled sadly. "Gemma, your path to getting better, to getting back into this seat"—she pointed at her chair—"is confronting your trauma."

"I *am*. I told you all about what *really* happened to Calvin. I'm here talking about my damn trauma. How is that *not* confronting it?"

"Not that trauma, Gemma."

Gemma looked at her, confused. "Then what?"

"Remember last week when you told me about your recurring dream? The one about your brother's football tryouts?"

Gemma shrugged. "Of course. But a broken collarbone is hardly trauma."

"Gemma, you and I are trained in this. You know that

trauma can't be measured on an objective scale. It's about how it impacts the individual."

"Maybe I'm exaggerating the importance of that day."

"I don't think it's about that day, exactly. I think it's about how that day was handled. How everyone reacted to it."

Gemma inhaled sharply.

"Something land with you in that?"

Gemma nodded slowly. "Feels like every moment after that has been built around whatever happened that day. Like some Princess and the Pea bullshit."

Dr. Fox smiled. "Then why not confront your family about that day? Find the pea, so to speak."

Gemma studied Dr. Fox's face. No matter how many times she tried, she had never been able to fully articulate to anyone—especially Anthony—the palpable feeling that kept her from digging in too much about that day. Something that had never been explicitly said but had been deeply felt every day since.

"Because no one will let me ask them about it," she finally said.

"How many times have you tried?"

Gemma shrugged. "A few."

"And *how* did you try?"

Gemma let out a laugh. "Usually with anger and almost always with tears. Is there any other way?"

Dr. Fox smiled.

Gemma put up her hands. "I know, I know, confronting *in* anger is another avoidance tactic."

"Well, *someone* paid attention in grad school," Dr. Fox said with a wink.

"But I honestly don't know any other way to do it."

"What questions do you have about that day?"

"I have *all* the questions."

"Such as?"

"Such as what the hell even happened. I know just bits and pieces. And even the stuff I know, I'm not even sure if I really *know* it. I can't tell what is truth and what is just my dreams over the years, embedded in my brain as reality."

"And what has been an obstacle to understanding the reality before?"

Gemma shrugged, her hand curled around the corners of the pillow. "My parents are tough to confront. They are really good at keeping people at a distance. I mean, they are warm and loving, but there's a wall. Like, they have this ability to keep people from asking them questions. I don't know how to describe it."

Dr. Fox sat up straighter. "I do."

"Oh?"

"Yeah, it's called avoidance."

Gemma smiled. "Well, see? I come by it naturally."

"A more accurate assessment is that this behavior, this avoidance, is all you've ever had modeled for you."

Gemma swallowed hard, increasing her grip on the pillow. What Dr. Fox was saying was so heavy with truth, Gemma felt herself sinking under the weight of it. "I don't think I ever realized my parents are avoiders," she said softly. She felt her eyes become wet. The observation was shifting something in her mind, like the turning of a kaleidoscope. "For so long I've felt like they were denying me something." She turned her eyes toward the window. "But it's that they were avoiding something." She wiped away a tear. The feeling of responsibility, with all its crushing weight, was lifting slightly from her chest. "It wasn't about me," she whispered. "It's about them."

Dr. Fox sat with her in silence for a minute before responding, "Good."

Gemma turned her eyes to her and smiled weakly.

"So," Dr. Fox said slowly. "What do you really want to know about that day?"

"I just want to know the facts. What happened when."

"Sounds like you need to go on a fact-finding mission."

"It does indeed."

"Focus on facts, not feelings."

Gemma nodded. "Is there any way I can gather these facts without having to actually confront anyone in my family?"

"You can no longer avoid them," Dr. Fox said with a wide smile. "But might I also make a suggestion?"

Gemma nodded again.

"Perhaps rethink who you should confront."

CHAPTER 20

Gemma worked to get the USB cable into the slot on the back of the seat. The man in front of her, with sweat beading on his bald spot, kept adjusting his position, making the chair shake just enough that guiding in the metal prong was difficult. She closed her eyes for a moment so as not to scream in frustration. Once the man settled, she tried to push the head of the cable in, realized that was the wrong way, flipped it over, realized *that* was actually the wrong way, and flipped it back again, at which point it slid effortlessly into place.

She moved her hands over and under themselves along the cable, like it was the rope in gym class, until she found the end, which she jammed into the bottom of her phone, illuminating the lock-screen photo of her boys. She inhaled. *Forty-five more minutes,* she thought, pulling her jacket around her and leaning back into its hood. She watched the flight attendant walk toward a woman a few rows ahead who had pressed the service light. She wondered what that woman wanted, and if the flight attendant could provide it.

If I pressed the button, what would I ask for? she thought. *A Bloody Mary, sure, but then what? Perhaps for the weight on my chest—most likely repressed anger—to be instantly dissipated? Could the flight attendant fetch that for me?*

Gemma smiled slightly when she saw the woman had just wanted a cup of water. *There is something so lovely about getting exactly what you need right when you need it.*

Her body shook with nerves. She hadn't thought through any of this fully, yet here she was, on a 2:00 p.m. flight with nothing more than a change of underwear, a pair of extra pants, her toothbrush, and a notebook she always carried, all shoved into an old backpack from grad school.

Of course, there was only so much impulsivity allowed for a mother. She had called Mary as she was leaving Dr. Fox's office, asking her to pick up Bo and Calvin and manage them for the night and the next morning because she had something to take care of out of town.

"Like what?" Mary asked in a neutral tone.

"Just something," Gemma responded.

"You're going to be gone overnight?" Mary probed. "Where are you staying?"

"I'll explain later."

"What about your patients?"

"I don't have any until Thursday," Gemma lied, her irritation growing. "Can you handle the boys for one night?"

"I can handle anything and everything that anyone could ever ask of me," Mary said with a tone only Gemma would have detected as humor. "But in exchange, I want to know what's going on."

Gemma rolled her eyes. "Mary, I'll tell you what I can when I can. I just can't right now. Take the kids, and I'll be back in time to pick them up from day care tomorrow." With that, she hung up the phone.

More avoiding, Gemma had thought at the time, and she thought it again now as she folded her body tighter into the space between her seat and the window. She stared at the hard plastic of the shade, noticing the various dents and smudges from hundreds of hands over thousands of flights, working to focus her brain on what she was after. As if she could force herself to have as easy a request as the woman a few rows ahead who simply needed to quench her thirst.

Maybe it would be easier to think about all of this like a new patient case file, thought Gemma. She uncrossed her arms, sat up, and reached under Bald Spot's seat for the notebook in her bag. She lowered the tray table and drew three lines across the page. She labeled each section using the DAP method for patient notes she had learned in her training: Data, Assessment, Plan. She began writing out everything she remembered from the day of Eddie's football tryouts.

Data, she thought. *What are the facts I know?*

Data

Dad took me to Eddie's tryouts.

It was a hot day.

Dad was worried about me sitting still so I took a book—Where's Waldo?

Gemma squeezed her eyes shut. She could still see the beach scene, her favorite part of the book, and its array of colors from thousands of characters who cluttered the pages, obscuring that one bespectacled man. *Where was Dad?* she wondered. As much as she had thought back on that day, she could not remember where her father was.

The bleachers burned the back of my legs.

Eddie yelled at me.

Gemma shook her head. This didn't make sense. *Eddie wasn't mad at me, was he? He was, what, yelling up at me? From the field?*

I was in Baskin-Robbins.

Was the ice cream after tryouts? How did I get from tryouts to Baskin-Robbins?

I was inside when I heard Eddie yelling.
What was he yelling? Why was he yelling?
I fell outside Baskin-Robbins and started screaming.

Gemma looked up from her notebook. She could never work out how she had actually fallen. And every time she'd ever asked her mother, Irene would simply say, "You tripped, dear. And what a trip it was!"

An ambulance came.
I was in the back of the ambulance.
Mom was with me.
I saw Eddie through the sparks.

Were there for sure sparks? What was making those? Was Eddie hurt? Did I have a concussion?

There was a lot of commotion.

Was that all for me? Gemma shook her head. She couldn't capture the memory. She wasn't even clear it *was* a memory. Maybe just a sloppily glued-together story from fragments over the years. As she scanned back over the data, she could make only one true claim: *Eddie had football tryouts the same day I broke my collarbone.*

Okay, what's the assessment? Gemma asked herself as she looked back over the data section. With a patient, she'd always think about what wasn't said. What she didn't hear. What was still confusing or unclear. Patients often omitted a key moment in time, or didn't mention a child—as was the case with Betty—and that omission was just as important as what was said. Her pen touched down and wrote,

Assessment
The link between these two experiences is unclear.

Her breath caught in her throat. Thinking back to the session with Dr. Fox, when she expressed anger at her mother for what felt like leaving out crucial information, she suddenly realized that she'd spent her entire life chasing after fuzzy

memories of an event everyone around her should clearly remember. *Why have I acted like this is just something I forgot?*
she wondered.

*There has been an effort—perhaps orchestrated—to keep
whatever happened that day quiet.*

*I've been gaslit into thinking I was unreasonable to ask for
details about that day.*

She looked at the final section of the page and tapped the
tip of her pen on it lightly.

Plan

This is *my plan. Whatever* this *is,* she thought as she looked
up and out into the cabin of the plane. The knitted scarf in the
lap of the woman beside her was growing with each click of
the needles. Bald Spot seemed to have calmed himself. *This is
the plan.*

Under the word *Plan*, she simply wrote, *This.*

She read the word. *This.* It meant nothing and everything.
She had made it onto the plane. She was taking action. She was
running toward something, not away. That was as far as she
had it in her to think through. But right now, in the moment,
she didn't know any more than she had when she boarded the
plane. She didn't understand any more about what happened
the day of Eddie's football tryouts.

*I was at tryouts with Dad, who disappeared for some rea-
son. Then, after the sun had set, I was at Baskin-Robbins, where
I ran outside and fell, breaking my collarbone. The ambulance
came, and I went to the hospital. Everyone in the family knew
about this. They were all there. Weren't they? So why the hell
have I spent my entire life feeling like the memory was only
mine to keep?*

Simple enough, Gemma thought as she leaned back into
the hood of her jacket again. *Simple enough that it tore our
family apart.* She closed her eyes. This plan, whatever *this* was,
suddenly felt like the most foolish thing she'd ever done. Left

her therapist's office, called her sister to arrange for the kids, rushed home to stuff a few things into a backpack, and driven straight to the airport. And for what? What had made so much sense to her while talking to Dr. Fox that she ended up, less than three hours later, in this seat next to a woman who was knitting and behind a sweaty man who was now snoring? Had she just been so overcome with the idea of understanding her past that she fled, yet again, from her present?

Gemma closed her eyes as a feeling of angst washed over her. And without knowing it, she fell asleep in a fit of frustration.

She is in a hospital bed.

Her mother sits on the bed, at her side.

The room is cold.

Gemma is covered with blankets, but still she shakes.

Her mother gently strokes Gemma's head.

The rings are gone from her mother's fingers.

Gemma can feel the true warmth of her mother's hand.

The room is empty.

No Dad, no Mary, no Eddie.

"Ladies and gentlemen." Gemma jerked awake with an audible gasp. "We have now begun our descent into Boston. Please put your tray tables up and secure your seat belts as we prepare for landing."

Gemma was breathing hard as she fumbled to put away her notebook, which was still open on the tray table. Her fingers shook as she locked the tray back into place. Her arms twitched as she crossed them tightly around herself while the plane touched down with force. And she inhaled sharply as she lifted the window shade to discover it was raining hard against an already-dark sky.

When she emerged from the plane, something began forming inside of her. A tightness deep within her chest that seemed to grow in size and pain with each pounding step she took. *Why wasn't Eddie in the hospital when I broke my collar-bone? Why wasn't he at the hospital when Calvin was injured? Where the fuck did he go when people he loved were hurting?*

The anger pulsed through her as she ran, hunched over, toward her Uber. The anger raged within her as the driver wove through the slick streets, Faneuil Hall Marketplace blurred through the rain-streaked window. The anger vibrated along her insides as the car pulled up to the rowhouse on Dorchester Street, a house she mailed holiday cards to each year but had never visited. And her anger exploded into a yell as she slammed the car door and stood outside in the pouring rain.

"Eddie!" she screamed. She climbed the steps to the door. Though she knew she couldn't be heard over the downpour, she couldn't stop the anger escaping her. "EDDIE!" She gripped her fist tightly and began beating on the door, screaming his name to the rhythm of her pounding.

Just as she was losing her voice, her face drenched in tears and rain, the door flung open and there stood her brother, a look of confusion on his face. But before he could step forward, before he could even part his lips to say her name, his eyes grew wide at the sight of what came flying toward him through the sheets of water: Gemma's raw and vengeful fist.

CHAPTER 21

Gemma gasped at the sound her knuckles made when they collided with Eddie's face. He screamed out in what could have been pain but sounded more like sorrow. His hand flew to his left eye, and he bent forward in the doorway. Gemma stood in the rain, her fist frozen in the air.

Kat appeared behind Eddie and, without speaking, bent herself around him to check the damage. She patted his back a few times until he stood. With her other arm, Kat hurriedly waved Gemma into the house. Kat worked Gemma's backpack off and slid her soaked coat down her arms, placing it in an expanding puddle of rainwater on the entryway floor. She put her palms on Eddie's back and gently pushed him toward the kitchen as she looked back at Gemma and nodded for her to follow them.

Gemma marveled at the cleanliness of the house as they wove through the living room and around the dining area. She noticed a record player perched on a credenza, with a Sufjan Stevens album cover laid beside the spinning disc. *Of course they listen to him,* she thought. *And of course they listen to him on vinyl.* A pang of jealousy washed over her as she thought about the last time she and Anthony went to a concert to-gether. Or listened to anything that wasn't Kidz Bop. Or had the luxury of a room free of toy clutter.

In the kitchen, Kat opened the freezer drawer and extracted an ice pack, wrapped it in a dish towel, and pressed it gently to Eddie's eye. He winced and replaced her hand with his. Kat then grabbed a paper towel, ran it under warm water, and handed it to Gemma, who patted the blood from her knuckles.

"Well," Eddie said, the first word spoken since Gemma was screaming his name in the rain, "to what do we owe the pleasure?"

One side of Gemma's mouth lifted slightly. She looked at Eddie, her earlier anger dissipating as quickly as the bump under his ice pack was growing.

"Do you want something to eat?" Kat asked, her expression warm but her tone neutral.

Gemma shook her head. She couldn't speak. She felt panic rising up, and her body began shaking—tremors at first, but rapidly escalating to uncontrollable convulsions.

Eddie's face flooded with concern. "Gemma?"

"Come sit down," Kat said, stepping around the kitchen island to grab Gemma by the elbow. She walked her swiftly to the couch and lowered her down, then grabbed a blanket from the back of an armchair and wrapped it around her. "A hot shower might help," Kat said, her tone softening.

Gemma smiled weakly as she watched Eddie rewrap the ice pack and walk toward her. He sat down in the chair beside her and put a hand on her knee. "We made some garbure. Would you like some? Might warm you up."

Gemma looked at Eddie with her brows furrowed. "What is that?"

"It's a French stew," Kat said tightly.

Gemma let out a laugh. "On a Tuesday night? Jesus. Have you two never heard of sandwiches? Or mac and cheese?"

Kat and Eddie looked at each other, but neither spoke.

"You are truly the most pretentious son of a bitch on the planet."

Eddie lifted his hand from Gemma's leg. His expression grew dark. "Maybe you should punch me again."

Gemma swallowed hard, her eyes cast downward.

The three of them sat silently in the room. The tick of an antique clock on the bookshelf sounded as loud as a drum. Gemma noticed the wall above the shelf was neatly adorned with matching gold frames. In each one was a picture of Eddie and Kat against a different backdrop. The Taj Mahal, a snow-covered mountain, somewhere in Greece. Eddie was smiling wide in every picture. It sent a pang through Gemma's chest to see him so happy.

Eddie broke the silence. "Why are you here?"

Gemma looked at him, then at Kat, and back again, her eyes rimmed with red. "Calvin" was all she could croak out.

Kat's face twisted. "Is he okay?"

Gemma looked over at Eddie, who seemed equally interested in her answer. "That night when Calvin fell on the fireplace . . ." Her voice cracked.

He adjusted the ice pack. "Yeah?"

Gemma swallowed hard. "You had fallen asleep with Calvin in your arms. And well, your arm relaxed and Calvin . . ." Gemma brought a hand to her face to wipe a tear. She didn't know if she could say the words. She looked at Kat, who only looked back in confusion.

"My arm what? Huh?" Eddie said.

"You dropped Calvin," Gemma said, her voice loud enough to make Kat and Eddie lean back just slightly in surprise.

Eddie brought the ice pack slowly from his eye and stared

at Gemma. She watched as his expression morphed from confusion, to anger, to undeniable shame.

"Fuck," he whispered.

Gemma looked at Kat, whose mouth hung slightly open as her eyes trailed back and forth between Gemma and Eddie.

After what felt to Gemma like an eternity, Eddie finally spoke. "I deserved that punch."

"No," Gemma said quietly. "You didn't. You didn't even know what happened . . . no one does. And I was fine with that. It's just when I saw you, for the first time since . . . I just lost it."

"Wait, what?"

"I'm sorry. I shouldn't have punched you."

"What do you mean, no one knows?"

Even though the truth was that Eddie was to blame, Gemma still felt guilty for having lied about it. No matter how many times she tried to rationalize what she'd done, she couldn't understand it herself. *So how could any of them?* she had reasoned.

Gemma met Eddie's eyes and held them. "I told everyone—Mom, Dad, Mary, even Anthony—that it was my fault. That I dropped Calvin. They still think that's what happened."

Eddie looked at her in obvious disbelief. "Why didn't you just fucking tell me in the moment that I did it?" he growled.

Kat put her hand on her husband's arm. "Eddie . . ."

Gemma's thoughts felt stuck behind a wall in her brain. "I don't know. I think I just wanted to keep the peace. Make it easier for everyone."

"How did lying make it easier?" Eddie asked.

Gemma's shoulders rose slowly. "I didn't want one more thing, one more trip to the hospital, to come between us."

"What does that even mean?" Eddie asked.

"I don't actually know, Eddie," Gemma said firmly. "There is a weirdness that exists between us, and I don't know why, and I don't know how to fix it." She paused, collecting her thoughts and mustering her courage. "That's why I'm here."

Eddie looked at Kat, then back at Gemma. "I'm not following."

Kat stood, her lips pulled downward in a frown. "I think I'm going to give you two some time to talk alone."

Eddie nodded but didn't break eye contact with Gemma. Gemma smiled softly up at Kat and nodded once. As Kat left the room, Gemma let out a sigh and leaned back into the couch.

"All right," Eddie said, the ice pack resting in his hands. "Let me have it."

CHAPTER 22

Gemma felt herself fidgeting with her hair. Eddie was quiet and still. In the beginning, their conversation was slow and awkward. Thunder rumbled as the rain beat against the window. Finally Gemma let out a sigh and explained that she was feeling really uncomfortable, which seemed to unlock something in Eddie, who acknowledged he was too. Then he admitted that Kat had actually encouraged him to go to Bloomington because she felt something was off with the family and that he needed to address it. He confessed he didn't really know what she meant, but he had agreed to give the trip some thought, though it never came to be. Gemma felt her heart quicken for Kat, realizing she may have misread her all this time.

They started talking about Calvin, and Eddie struggled to understand how the accident happened. It occurred to Gemma that, while the memory of that night replayed in her head on a near-constant loop, it had been perceived differently by her brother. She recounted his coming home late and falling asleep in her chair. He shook his head in disbelief when she told him again how Calvin had slipped from his arms. But when she described how he hadn't woken up with Calvin's screams—and then *wouldn't* wake up despite Gemma's shaking—something in his face betrayed recognition.

He explained that this happened frequently, that Kat often had to yell in his face to wake him. Once, during a road trip together early in their dating, Eddie had started to doze off behind the wheel, and Kat hadn't been able to get him to wake up fully. It scared her so badly she insisted they turn around and go home. Kat forced him to see a doctor, because that wasn't the first time he had dozed off behind the wheel, nor was it the first time someone had struggled to wake him up.

A specialist diagnosed Eddie with chronic traumatic encephalopathy—CTE—caused by the repeated concussions he endured playing football in high school and college. He told Gemma that he still suffered several symptoms of varying severity, including recurring headaches and periodic blurred vision, and that when he was removed from the university's football team, it was the most relieved he had ever felt. Moving to Boston and working in an office had felt like a second shot at life, even though he still had some lingering effects of CTE, the most prominent being bouts of excessive and deep sleep. And while the symptoms were manageable, they were often induced by periods of high stress.

"It's why I like working at Spectify," he said. "The culture there is such that I can work from home when I feel foggy or I'm worried about driving. But also, I just love the work. Coding is all about precision, and always knowing what's supposed to happen next. It's comforting in a weird way."

Gemma's gut twisted in pain. *How did I not see this?* she wondered. Her dissertation had been on the effects of head injuries resulting from falls—particularly among the elderly—and in some circles, at least when she was in graduate school, she was becoming known as an expert on the topic. She told Eddie she felt ashamed for not seeing the symptoms in her own brother. He sighed and shrugged, saying that it was hardest to see things like that up close. And besides, he added, he had kept it hidden from the family and his friends. Only Kat, and his boss, knew.

Their conversation wove in and out of their childhoods, the pets they had, the creepy neighbor who always seemed to be hitting on their mother, and how hard it had been to mow the massive front lawn of their parents' house. At the mention of Jack and Irene, they both grew quiet.

Eddie looked pained. "I suppose we need to talk about that day, huh?"

"I wouldn't be here if we didn't," Gemma said.

"Right."

"I have very few memories of that day," Gemma started. "But I've been seeing a therapist and have discovered that that day set in motion a family dynamic that hasn't been serving me well lately."

Eddie's eyes widened. "Who talks like that?"

Gemma laughed. "Therapists."

"You have no memories, huh?"

"Very few. But extremely regular recurring dreams about it. Well, nightmares, really."

He sat forward, placing the ice pack on the coffee table. "I'm sure."

"I actually confronted Mom and Mary about it and demanded to know what happened that day."

"Damn," Eddie said, impressed. "I can't imagine that was an easy conversation."

"Of course not." Gemma gave a half smile. "Mary was tight-lipped. And Mom basically said, 'Go ask your father.'"

"And did you?"

"No. I came here."

Eddie looked down at his hands. "Right. Well, Dad and I have never talked about it. Or Mom either."

She nodded. "I figured."

Eddie sighed and leaned back in his chair. Gemma worried the window was closing again between them. Her hands felt cold, and she had a lump in her throat. Just as she opened her mouth to say something to force the conversation forward, he began to speak.

"I didn't feel right when I came out of the locker room."

Gemma nodded but said nothing. She knew she had to use her therapy skills in the moment. She was not his sister right then. She was an objective observer of a situation she hoped to understand more fully.

"I remember it being really hot, even that late in the afternoon," he continued. "And when I looked up at you in the bleachers, I remember being really worried you were wearing shorts, because those metal bleachers get hot."

Gemma's eyes began to sting, but she kept her expression as neutral as possible.

"I dunno, it was a weird thing for me to notice. But it made me mad that Dad dragged you there and made you sit in the hot sun. And then he left you to go shmooze with the other parents."

Gemma felt warmth within her chest, hearing about Eddie's concern for her.

"Anyway, I knew I was going to make the team. I was the tallest, fastest player. Even better than the seniors. So when Dad showed up, I dunno, it didn't really feel like support."

"What did it feel like?"

He sat for a minute, staring at the coffee table. "Doubt, I guess."

"How so?"

"I've tried to explain this to Kat before, and the only analogy I can come up with is, let's say you ask someone to do a simple favor for you. Like, maybe you ask someone to go lock your car doors. And the person—who is fully capable of doing such a simple thing—agrees. But then you ask them two minutes later if they did it. And they feel weird, because now, instead of feeling like a competent person you can trust with a favor, they feel questioned. Doubted. Which makes them question themselves, doubt themselves. They get up to go lock the doors *now*, because you've pestered them. And then you say, 'I'll go with you to lock the doors,' because you don't trust they will actually do it. You never really did."

"Dad being at the football tryouts was like him going with you to lock the doors?"

"Yeah, I know it's not a great explanation. But it was like, 'I'm going to make the team.' There had been no doubt. But he still had to come watch tryouts. Like he didn't trust me." Eddie looked at Gemma. "It's a weak analogy, I know, but it's the only way I can think to describe how it felt that he came to watch my tryouts."

"You know what I think is the most telling part of that analogy?"

"What?"

"That you compared trying out for the varsity football team with doing a favor."

Gemma watched as every muscle in Eddie's face relaxed. She had seen that dozens of times in her work—that moment when you said something to a patient that they had never considered, but that resonated so deeply within them that their body relaxed into a fuller understanding of themselves.

He scratched his dark beard. "Damn, Gem."

She sat in silence. She knew better than to talk right now.

"It was just so fucking important to him that I was on that team. That I was a football player."

"Did he say that to you? That it was important to him that you were on the team?"

Eddie nodded. "Absolutely." Then he paused and looked up at the ceiling. "Well, I don't know if he said those exact words. But I knew."

"How?"

Eddie was still looking at the ceiling. Gemma could tell he was tearing up. "Shit. I dunno. I guess maybe he implied it? It was like one of those things that, maybe he never actually said it, but I heard it loud and clear."

"I get that."

He lowered his eyes from the ceiling to meet hers. "You do?"

"Yeah, of course." She smiled. "I think a majority of the dynamics between people, especially in families, are unspoken. The family is a unit, but every person in the unit perceives events, emotions, and behaviors in their own way."

Eddie looked at Gemma a long time. "I remember him screaming at me to wake up in my truck," he finally said.

Gemma swallowed hard but kept quiet.

"I remember coming out of the locker rooms and wanting to take you somewhere, like as a reward for sitting through those fucking tryouts. It was getting dark, and it was well past dinnertime, but even so, I remember thinking that taking you to get ice cream was the thing to do."

"Baskin-Robbins," Gemma said under her breath.

Eddie nodded. "So what do you remember?"

Gemma took a big breath in. "I remember running out of the store with my ice cream. I remember the ambulance. And I remember being in the hospital and Mom stroking my hair. Without her rings on."

"That's it?"

"Every time I've ever asked about it, Mom always says I just tripped. I guess over that curb close to the door? I dunno. That's all I've got."

"Well, I'll tell you what I remember." Eddie sighed. "But it's not everything. And it's not great."

Gemma listened intently as Eddie explained how he had started feeling funny after they ordered the ice cream, so he canceled his own order, paid for Gemma's, and told her he needed to go sit down, said he would meet her in his truck. As he got to the truck, he felt worse, his head clouding over. He sat in the truck and felt a wave of nausea creep up but thought it would pass. He stuck his head out the truck window and called for Gemma to hurry, because he knew he needed to get home. As soon as she got her cone, Gemma came running out of the store, but by that point he was so confused that he thought she was in the truck. He put the truck in reverse and backed out, hitting Gemma with his bumper and knocking her to the ground.

Gemma let out a gasp as her hand flew to her mouth.

Eddie's chin quivered. "I ran you over."

Tears welled in Gemma's eyes as she watched her brother work to hold in his own.

"I didn't even know it. I don't remember any of that. But I ran you over and sped out of the parking lot and then immediately crashed into an electrical box beside the Baskin-Robbins. It was like a big transformer. Crashed into it and hit my head on the steering wheel. When I came to, Dad was screaming at me to wake up, and it was so dark outside, and there were sparks flying in front of my windshield. The ambulance was there, and you were in the back of it, and before they took you away, I threw up and then blacked out again."

Gemma exhaled. "Holy shit."

Eddie nodded. "They took you to the hospital, and you stayed there with Mom overnight."

"That I remember."

"And I went home with Dad."

"Did you not need to get checked out?"

"The EMTs did. I had a concussion, a level three actually. But Dad refused to take me to the hospital."

"Wait, what? Why?"

Eddie shrugged. "Beats me. The rest of that time is blurry. I just remember the EMT saying I had a concussion and Dad saying there was no need to go to the hospital. Next thing I knew, we were back home. I don't know how or when my truck got taken to the shop. I don't even remember the ride home with Dad. You came home from the hospital the next morning, and Mary came home from . . ." Eddie's face twisted. "Where had Mary been?"

"Spending the night at Beverly's."

"Right, that's right. She got home later that day or something. I don't really remember even talking to Mary. Maybe I did? I'm not sure. But that's what happened," he said, rubbing his palms together. "At least what I can remember."

From there, Eddie explained, it had been like a weird dream. Irene and Jack did such an expert job of pretending nothing had happened—likely not even telling Mary much about it—that Eddie quickly started to question whether or not it actually had. And he could never fully understand why their father wouldn't take him to the hospital, but he had buried that question, along with all his others, deep down. Gemma had shown no lingering effects from her injuries, but he still hadn't been able to bear looking at her after the wreck. He never drove again when Gemma was in the car, a fact she hadn't realized until he said it. It had been easier to ignore her altogether, he explained, than spend time with her and risk hurting her again.

His hurtful behavior was rooted in love, Gemma thought, tears dripping down her cheeks.

He explained that he had spent a long time hating Jack for everything—for caring about football, for taking Gemma to the tryouts, for not knowing his son had a concussion before the crash, and then for not taking his son to the hospital after the crash when Jack knew he had one. For all of it. And yet despite all that hate, Eddie had also wanted Jack to look at him. To talk to him. To acknowledge him. To forgive him. But Jack hadn't seemed able to look at Eddie—to truly *see* him—unless he was on the field. So Eddie played. And played. And played. Until the day he played too hard for the last time.

Then came the relief.

But also, the distance. Between himself and Jack. Between himself and everyone, especially Gemma. And every time Kat brought up that distance to Eddie, he shut her down. She wanted to address something—fix something—that he was unwilling to admit was there.

Eddie ran his fingers through his hair. "So that's all I know."

"You got a concussion at the tryouts . . . ," Gemma said slowly.

"Yeah, but I didn't know it. The coach checked me out." He shook his head. "Of course, it was the same genius who also let underage boys drink on school property."

"What do you mean?"

"Oh, the coach always had beer for us in the locker room. As a 'reward' for playing well."

Gemma's nose scrunched in disgust.

"I wasn't drinking that day though," Eddie quickly added. "I mean, I certainly did lots of other times. But not that day. I never would have driven you if I had been. Or if I'd known I had a concussion. I would never intentionally put you in harm's way."

Gemma nodded, smiling through her tears. Eddie gave her a half smile and looked down. They sat there in silence, Gemma's tears continuing to seep down her cheeks. She didn't dare move a muscle to wipe her face, for fear any movement might end their conversation.

"Gemma." Eddie looked up to meet her gaze, his eyes wet. "I'm sorry."

"I'm sorry too."

"For what?" he asked so earnestly her chest ached.

"For the decisions that were made on your behalf that day."

Eddie brought the palm of his free hand up to his uninjured eye.

"Fuck, Gemma," Eddie said through his tears. "You do this shit for a living?"

Gemma laughed as she wiped her cheeks. "I know, right?"

Eddie let out a laugh before his face settled back into a serious expression. "I'm so sorry about hurting Calvin."

"I know you are," she said. "But you're apologizing for the wrong thing."

"What do you mean?"

"What you should apologize for is leaving for the marathon without checking on me. For leaving when I was hurting. For not being there for me."

Eddie nodded a few times.

Gemma held her breath to find her courage. "It hurt like hell that you left without checking on me or Calvin."

"I can see now how that was a dick move on my part. I guess I just don't know what to do in those situations."

"Maybe it's genetic. Mom and Dad truly don't know what to do in those situations either."

Eddie let out a sad laugh. "Still, I should have come to see Calvin in the hospital."

Gemma nodded in agreement. "And Dad should have taken you to the hospital."

"Yeah." Eddie clucked his tongue. "Yeah."

Gemma shook her head. "What the fuck was that about?"

Eddie took a few deep, slow breaths. "I always took it to mean that Mom and Dad chose you over me. You got to go to the hospital. I didn't."

Gemma blinked back more tears. "That's kind of funny to hear because my whole life it's felt like they chose you."

"How?"

Gemma shrugged. "I can't explain it. Just always felt like

you were the most important thing to them. They always seem so worried about you. So desperate for information on how you are. So protective of you. So on guard against anything that might upset you."

"My guess is that's their guilt talking."

Gemma's eyebrows shot up.

Eddie smirked. "Would your colleagues be impressed with my insight?"

"Oh, my colleagues would have a field day with you."

Eddie's head tilted back with laughter, and it broke open something in Gemma. She felt light pouring in, like sunbeams refracting behind a cloud and spreading rays across her chest.

Eddie rested his chin in his hand. "It's been thirty years," he finally said. "At this point, what's there to do?"

"Absolutely nothing."

He looked at her, eyebrows knitted. "Oh? Why was I expecting more?"

Gemma shook her head. "We can't change the past. We just have to be mindful of how it shows up in the present."

"Meaning?"

"Well, this whole mess," she said, pointing between them, "has made me so conflict averse. Mom and Dad have made it impossible to question anything that happened that day, impossible to have or express any feelings about it because *they* seem to get upset, so I just learned to not rock the boat. Not upset anyone. And now, when my emotions are high, or there's conflict, I have no clue what to do so I just . . . I just want to run away. I mean, I literally do sometimes."

Eddie's eyes went wide, betraying his surprise. Then his expression slowly changed into recognition. "Well, what about me?" he asked, his palm on his chest. "I ran away, to run a marathon."

Gemma clasped her hand over her mouth to suppress a laugh. "Yeah, that's next level."

The side of Eddie's mouth drew upward.

"Look," she said, more seriously. "What happened back then to you and me, the decisions Mom and Dad made, *fucking sucked*."

He nodded.

"And it's created a weird dynamic among all of us. A lot of things unspoken."

"Yeah, that's true."

"And that sucks. But now that we see what's happening, the question is, What are we gonna do about it?"

He tilted his head to the side with a half smile. "Stay exactly the same?"

"Close."

"All right, what then?"

"To be fair, I'm not quite sure. But I do know it will need to be different from what we've done up to now."

"Worth a shot," Eddie said as he grabbed the ice pack and lifted it to his eye.

CHAPTER 23

Gemma watched Calvin's eyelids flutter as she rocked him back and forth. The scar under his eye had already faded to a medium pink. She closed her eyes to summon the feeling in her chest, that feeling she had felt for Bo the second she saw him emerge from her body, but that she hadn't yet felt for Calvin. *What is wrong with me?* she wondered.

Gemma opened her eyes to see that Calvin had finally drifted off to sleep. "I love you so much," she said. And she did. She knew she did. *So why can't I feel it?* She stood carefully, stepped toward the crib, and gently lowered Calvin onto the mattress, sliding her arm out from under him—a technique perfected by expert mothers everywhere. She ran her thumb across his cheek. He was a gorgeous baby. Gentle. Quiet. Perfect in every way, save the mark under his eye—a reminder to Gemma of all that had happened. Of that awful night, and his harrowing scream.

A tiny voice interrupted her thoughts. "Can I have some spaghetti?"

Gemma raised her head to see Bo standing in the doorway

of the nursery. She laughed. "Spaghetti? Sweetie, it's bedtime. You had dinner already, remember?"

Bo shrugged. "I like spaghetti."

"I get it. I do too," she said as she bent to pick him up. "How about we get you a glass of milk and then get into bed, okay?"

Bo nodded. Her chest warmed as he nestled into her.

"Where's Auntie Em?" she asked.

"Washing the dishes," he said.

She lowered him back to the floor. "Okay, go get your jammies on, and I'll get you some milk."

"Okay, potato!" Bo said as he ran into the hallway.

Gemma looked back to check on Calvin, whose eyes flickered rapidly behind his closed lids with the promise of a deep sleep, and walked downstairs into the kitchen to find Mary, a dish towel over her shoulder, loading plates into the dishwasher. Gemma went to her and hugged her.

"What's this for?" Mary asked, hugging with her wrists to keep her soapy hands off Gemma's clothes.

"I just really appreciate all you've done for me the last few weeks," Gemma said, unable to let go of her sister.

"It's nothing."

"It's everything."

"Well, I'm still owed something."

Gemma released her embrace. "Like what? Money? Jewels? One of the kids?"

"I want to know where you went last night."

Gemma's eyes squeezed shut. "I *just* got home . . ."

"Hours ago. I let you eat dinner. I let you have time with the kids. Now I want to know where the hell you went and what you were doing."

Gemma leaned against the kitchen counter and let out a massive exhale. "I went to see Eddie."

"What?!" Mary exclaimed with obvious feigned surprise.

Gemma crossed her arms. "Okay, so if you knew, why did you ask? Also, *how* did you know?"

"You honestly think you can disappear for a night and I'll just let it go? That I won't try to figure out where you're going? Jesus, Gem, what if you had gotten hurt, or stuck somewhere, or had a medical emergency? Or if one of the kids had? I needed to know what was going on."

Gemma swallowed hard, realizing how foolish it had been to just bolt without telling the person watching her children where she was going. "Did Eddie tell you?"

"No."

"Did you tell Anthony?"

"Nope. Said you were working late."

"Thank you."

"You bet."

"How did you find out?"

"The iPad."

"Huh?"

"I was playing a game on it with Bo and a text from American Airlines popped up with your gate change."

"Geez, Mare." Gemma laughed. "You're acting like you're some kind of Hercule Poirot."

"Who?"

"The detective from the Agatha Christie novels? Read a book."

Mary flicked soapy water at Gemma's face.

"I'm just saying, don't act like you're some sleuth when all you did was passively read a text message not meant for you."

Mary shrugged with a smile as she placed a mug in the top rack of the dishwasher.

Gemma reached into the cabinet to get a cup, then went to the fridge for milk. As she poured, she began thinking back to her night with Eddie. After they talked, he'd shown her to the guest room, where she was able to take a long, hot shower and collapse into the nicest sheets her skin had ever touched. *Double income and no kids certainly has its perks,* she thought as she drifted to sleep. When Gemma awoke the next morning, Kat had already left for work. Gemma ate breakfast with Eddie—overnight oats he'd made—and then she called for an Uber to the airport for her ten o'clock flight. She and Eddie didn't talk about anything more of consequence. Just Boston weather, his latest coding project, and a funny story about the first time she tried to cut Bo's hair. As she left, he hugged her and said, "Hope the holidays are good for you and Tony."

She pulled away from him. "Aren't you coming back for Thanksgiving?"

Eddie gave her a surprised look. "No? Hadn't planned on it."

Gemma nodded. "Okay then." She walked down the front steps of his house, and as she opened the door to her Uber, she looked back at him and called out, "His name is Anthony. Not Tony!" And with a smile, she got into the car and shut the door.

Mary's closing of the dishwasher brought Gemma back to the moment. "I'm going to run this up to Bo and tuck him in," Gemma said.

"Oh no you don't," Mary said.

"What?"

"I want to know what happened with Eddie."

"Oh, for sure. There's just so much to tell you. Just give me a minute."

"Give me a hint."

Gemma held up a hand. "Okay. Fine. I now finally know everything that happened the day of tryouts."

"What do you mean, *everything*?" Mary asked, an edge in her voice.

"Well, for starters, I know how I broke my collarbone."

"And?"

"Eddie backed into me with his truck."

"Wait. Are you serious?"

"Yeah. He had a concussion from football practice but didn't know it. Backed into me and then slammed into a transformer beside the Baskin-Robbins parking lot."

Something flashed in Mary's eyes, but Gemma didn't know what. "Let me take this up to Bo, and then I'll tell you everything."

Upstairs, she handed Bo the milk, watched him gulp it down, and then curled up beside him in his bed. "I love everything about you, Bo."

"I know," he said.

"You are kind, and smart, and I'm so lucky to know you."

"You are."

Gemma laughed. "You ready to get some sleep?"

"Mama, why does Mary stay here and Daddy doesn't?"

Gemma swallowed. "You know, that's a great question. And one that doesn't have a good answer."

"Every question has an answer."

"You're right," she said, brushing hair off his forehead. "I guess my answer is that Mom and Dad need to sort some things out."

"And then he'll sleep here?"

"That's the idea," Gemma said, aware she hadn't given this much thought, which only further proved Anthony's point.

"I like Aunt Mary being here."

"Me too. But I know you miss your dad."

"Don't you?"

"Very much," Gemma said with sadness as she dropped one more kiss on top of Bo's head. "Now, you get some sleep, okay?"

"Okay!" Bo said, lying still so Gemma could tuck in the blankets around him just the way he liked.

After looking in on a sleeping Calvin one more time, Gemma made her way back downstairs. She felt the familiar tightness in her chest. Another loose thread in her life—her husband. And she hadn't given it a moment's thought. She'd been so consumed with Calvin, and her issues at work, and her parents, and her conversation with Eddie, that she hadn't put together a single thought about how to resolve the stalemate with Anthony. With that realization, she began to worry that this said something about how she felt toward him. Why couldn't she get herself to feel the right feelings for her family—she couldn't bond with Calvin, she didn't think of her estranged husband—or for her own life? It felt like she was in a cloud, a fog, desperate for clear air.

"Hey, Mary," she said as her foot hit the bottom step. "Do you think Anthony and I—" But as she turned the corner into the living room, she saw Mary on the couch, crying.

"Mary?" she said, rushing to sit beside her. "What's going on?"

Gemma could count on two fingers the times she'd seen Mary cry, and this was one of them. Mary's crying now was a display of just how buttoned up she was. Even her tears seemed to fall in polite and quiet lines down her face. She looked less like she was crying and more like she was leaking. As if something in her had broken, a small mechanism finally faltering.

"Did I say something wrong?" Gemma asked, thinking back over the conversation in the kitchen ten minutes earlier. "Something about Eddie?"

Mary looked at her with red-tinged eyes. "Gemma."

"Yes, what? What is it?"

Mary took a deep breath and let it out slowly. "The day of Eddie's football tryouts, I was staying the night at Beverly's."

"Yes, I know."

Mary's fists were balled in her lap. "We were watching a movie in their upstairs rec room."

"Okay . . ."

"Do you remember Beverly's brother?"

Gemma shrugged. "Vaguely?"

"His name is Todd. He was two grades older than us. On the football team."

Gemma's forehead wrinkled. "Was he at tryouts that day?"

Mary wiped her cheek with the back of her hand. "Yeah, he was. When he got home, he came up to the rec room to watch the movie with us. It was *Empire Records*. Bev and I had watched it a dozen times. I was excited he wanted to watch with us on their big couch under all these blankets. The older brother of your best friend . . . just something about it."

"I get it."

"Anyway, we were about a half hour into the movie and suddenly the power went out. Bev's parents were out—god, I don't even know where they'd gone—so she jumped up and said she'd go get flashlights and candles downstairs in the kitchen. It was so unbelievably dark in the house. In the room."

Gemma felt an uncomfortable wave wash over her, as if she were watching a scary movie and knew something was about to jump out.

"She'd only been gone for a minute and all of a sudden I felt something on the waistband of my jeans."

Gemma's hand flew to her mouth.

"And we had all these blankets on us, and it was so dark, and it wasn't exactly registering to me it was Todd's hand. He was kind of tugging at them. Really aggressively. And he was so big, so much bigger than me, so I just looked over at him, sort of stunned, but I couldn't see him. It was too dark to see two inches in front of my face. I was just kind of paralyzed by shock and also, just the weight of him."

"Mary . . ."

"But even though I couldn't see his face, I could just feel he was . . . determined."

"Jesus."

"And he got the button of my jeans undone and the zipper down and put his hand down in—" Mary let out a sob.

"Oh my god, Mary."

"And then Beverly came back into the room with flashlights and candles and was fussing with them while his hand was still down my pants, hidden by the blankets. He was so rough. It hurt."

"Asshole," Gemma gasped.

"Somehow I managed to wriggle away from him and jumped up to help Beverly with the candles. And he just kept lying there. I told Beverly I wasn't feeling super great and that maybe I needed to go home. But her parents were gone, so I went down to the kitchen to call Mom. The phone rang and rang. And you know, we didn't have cell phones then, but Mom had a pager. So I sent her a page. And I waited by Bev's kitchen phone for a long time, but then Bev came down and wondered where I was. I had no choice but to go back upstairs with her and Todd. We had finished the movie when Mom finally called. I said I needed to come home. I told her that the power had gone out at Beverly's and I wasn't feeling well and I was scared. She said—" Mary inhaled deeply. "She said I needed to stay there because I had made a commitment to Beverly. That I had promised to sleep over."

"Did you tell her what happened?"

Mary shook her head. "She was at the hospital with you. I didn't know that at the time, of course, but I pieced it together later."

Gemma's nostrils flared as hot air escaped. "Even so, Dad could have come to get you."

Mary shrugged. "That wasn't offered."

"Oh Mary. I am so sorry."

"I didn't sleep at all that night. I stayed stretched out next to Beverly with my eyes on the door. Todd's room was next door, and I was sure he was coming for me."

"But he didn't, right?"

Mary shook her head. "No, but I've kept my eye on doors ever since."

Gemma thought back to Mary's time in high school and college, and never hearing of her going on dates or even going to parties. Even now, at forty-four, Mary's iciness toward men hadn't thawed. A pang of sorrow hit Gemma at the realization of why Mary was the way she was—a feeling so heavy that she let out a low moan. "Mary, I don't even know what to say. I'm so sorry you went through that. And that I didn't know all these years. And Mom and Dad? You never told them?"

Mary shook her head again. "When Bev's dad dropped me off the next day, I found out you'd broken your collarbone. But they didn't tell me about Eddie's accident until days later, when I asked where his truck was."

"I guess we now know why they were secretive about that."

Mary nodded. "And it made sense why Mom couldn't come get me. She was dealing with you at the hospital and Dad was handling Eddie. And then everyone seemed distracted and distant when I got home, and there just wasn't . . . there just wasn't room for me."

Gemma took Mary's hand. "I always have room for you."

Mary smiled sadly.

"I now get why you act so uncomfortable when I talk about the day of football tryouts."

"I've never told anyone anything about that night. Until now."

Gemma felt such love for her sister. "Thank you for sharing with me."

The sisters sat in silence on the couch, holding hands and sniffing back tears.

"Mary?" Gemma finally said.

"Mm-hmm?"

"Why *did* you share this with me?"

Mary looked at her silently.

"I mean, why now?"

"Because you've been trying to solve the mystery of your collarbone for decades. And in doing so, you solved a mystery of mine."

"Oh? What's that?"

"I've thought back on that night at Beverly's countless times. For years I blamed myself for being in that position—under a blanket with a sophomore who had beer on his breath and testosterone running through him like wildfire."

"You have to know that absolutely none of what happened was your fault!"

"Sure, *now*. But I was fourteen at the time. And without talking to anyone about it, I didn't know how to make sense of it. The only person I could blame was myself."

"Which you don't anymore, right?"

"No, no. I dropped that around my college years. Too many reports and issues with girls I was in class with. It became very clear who was at fault in every scenario like mine. I think men always get portrayed as these plotting, planning, strategizing predators, hunting women. And I think they *can* be. But from what I've seen—from what I experienced—more often than not, men are just taking advantage any time they can. I mean, maybe *some* men are plotting. But a lot of them are just crimes of opportunity. They see something they want, and if the opportunity presents itself, they grab it."

"Right, so if Beverly hadn't left the room—"

"No. If the power hadn't gone out."

"Oh, right."

"It was the weirdest thing to have the power go out in the middle of a summer night. No storm, no wind. And it wasn't just Bev's house, it was the whole block."

"A freak thing."

"That's what I always thought. But of course, now I know it wasn't a freak thing."

Gemma's eyebrows furrowed.

"Do you remember where Bev's house was?"

Gemma shook her head.

"Right behind Baskin-Robbins."

CHAPTER 24

Gemma sat on Dr. Fox's couch with her arms and legs crossed. She hadn't said a word since entering the office seven minutes earlier. If this made Dr. Fox uncomfortable, Gemma couldn't tell. Dr. Fox sat in her standard pose—legs crisscrossed in her chair, elbows on her knees, chin in her hands—looking at Gemma as if she were an engrossing documentary.

"I confronted Eddie," Gemma finally said.

"Would you like to talk about it?"

"Not really."

"Okay," Dr. Fox said. "We can just sit here."

"Good."

Gemma tapped her foot on the beige carpet. She chewed on the inside of her mouth. As her eyes scanned the room, she noticed a decorative bronze clock on Dr. Fox's desk.

"First a throw pillow and now a clock," she said. "What gives?"

Dr. Fox glanced at the clock on her desk. When her face turned back to Gemma, it was wearing a smile. "Oh, that. Funny story. My therapist encouraged me to decorate my office. So I bought that, and it doesn't even work."

"*Your* therapist?" Gemma asked.

Dr. Fox smirked playfully. "You think you're the only one with problems?"

Gemma shrugged, her mood not lifting.

Dr. Fox smiled. "We're all on a journey."

Despite the anger at Dr. Fox that Gemma had carried into the room, she now looked at her with softness. She let a moment of silence pass before continuing. "I now know what happened that day," she said.

"The day of your brother's tryouts?"

Gemma sighed. "What other day would I be talking about?"

"You seem angry."

"I am."

"Would you like to talk about your anger?"

"No. I would not."

"Okay. We can just sit here."

"You really piss me off. You know that?"

"Oh?"

"Yes."

"How so?"

"Well, you asked me to confront all of this, and now I'm worse off than when I first met you."

"You are?"

"Yes."

"Where did I go wrong?" Dr. Fox asked calmly.

"You focused on the wrong thing."

"What did I focus on?"

"This shit from my past. This stuff with Eddie."

"And I should have focused on . . . ?"

"What's going on right now. My postpartum depression. My relationship with my husband. My issues at work. My generally fragile mental state."

"And all of that isn't connected to your past?"

"Nope."

"I see."

"Stop it."

"Stop what?"

"Sitting over there having your theories about what it all means. Drawing your conclusions. Thinking your thoughts."

"Okay. I'll sit here and not think, and you can sit there and not talk."

Gemma's palms slapped the couch beside her. "Dammit, Dr. Fox!"

Dr. Fox's methods reminded Gemma of a grad school classmate who always broke the rules somehow. He either ignored the parameters of an assignment, or brought in music to score his presentations, or wore mismatched sneakers. Gemma was always annoyed when he acted above the rules, but it made her blood boil when she realized how effective his eccentricities were. She wondered if Dr. Fox had made some high-achieving student in her class angry with all her unconventional behaviors.

"All right," Dr. Fox said, attempting to restart. "So, you talked to Eddie, who told you what happened that day, which I'm guessing was hard to hear."

"Brilliant, Holmes."

"I'm curious. When you found out what happened, did you feel differently about your current issues with Eddie?"

"Nope."

Dr. Fox tilted her head to the side. "Your anger is very obvious."

"Well, I am very angry."

"At whom?"

Gemma chewed on her lip. She didn't know. In the moment, she felt angry with Dr. Fox, but she couldn't figure out why. "I guess I'm mad at you because I don't feel any better."

"Better than what?"

"Better than when I was ordered to do this," Gemma said, gesturing back and forth between them.

"What would *better* have looked like?"

Gemma threw her arms up in irritation. "I don't know, but not this!" She was so tired of trying to explain herself. Tired of convincing others that her pain was real, that her emotions were strong. "I'm exhausted."

"Tell me more about that."

Gemma shrugged her shoulders. "Everywhere I look, everything I dig into, reveals more than I can handle."

"What would it look like for you to *handle* everything?"

"Not letting every detail I uncover completely destroy my life. I feel as if everything I've worked so hard to manage—my job, my marriage, my family—has completely unraveled. And the more I learn, the more frayed I feel."

"That's a bad feeling."

"Yeah," Gemma sighed. "I'm so overwhelmed."

"You just listed a lot of aspects of your life that feel chaotic. Which one is top of mind in this moment?"

Gemma inhaled slowly and closed her eyes. She was surprised at the image of the face she saw. "My dad."

"Oh? What about him?"

"I dunno. There is just so much to process around what all happened that day. And my dad's role in that still feels unclear to me. And even my mom, really. There's some stuff with Mary. Just the idea of telling you all that I learned the past few days makes me want to curl up in a ball on the floor and cry."

Dr. Fox allowed a few moments of silence to pass. Then she extended her arms, palms up. "How about this? Just tell me what *decisions* were made that day?"

Gemma swallowed hard as she thought through what she knew. "Well, Dad made the decision not to take Eddie to the hospital when he crashed his truck because of a concussion he got at tryouts."

Dr. Fox's eyebrows lifted for a split second before settling into a neutral expression.

"And my mom made the decision not to let my sister come home from a sleepover after she was almost—" Gemma inhaled sharply. "After she was attacked by her friend's brother. Oh, and on top of all that, my parents decided not to tell me that I broke my collarbone because Eddie backed into me with his truck."

Dr. Fox took a deep breath and then tucked her hair behind each ear. "So, when you were really young, your father and your mother made decisions during a difficult situation that impacted everyone in the family, without consulting anyone in the family."

Gemma's eyes searched the carpet. "Yeah, and they got away with it."

"Got away with what?"

"Accountability."

"You don't think your parents have had to face consequences for their decisions?"

Gemma shrugged. "I guess. But not as severe as the ones Eddie and Mary and I have."

"How do you know that's true?"

Gemma met Dr. Fox's eyes for a moment, then looked down. They sat there, patient and therapist, in a silence full of pain.

"Gemma," Dr. Fox said, "do you have any regrets as a parent?"

Gemma's eyes narrowed. "Of course."

"Tell me one."

"Um, okay, how about the fact that I let my son, my newborn baby, get injured in his first week of life!" Gemma's voice rose in anger and cracked in her throat.

"How much does that regret hurt?"

"It's been unmanageable," Gemma gasped out through a sob. "Obviously, I cannot seem to manage."

"And how long have you had that feeling?"

Gemma looked at Dr. Fox in confusion. "Since it happened. Two months ago."

"Right," Dr. Fox said quietly. "Now can you imagine carrying that feeling for the next thirty years?"

Gemma hung her head, overcome with defeat. Tears dripped straight from her eyes to her knees, peppering the denim with dark spots. "That's so much pressure."

Dr. Fox sat quietly, not responding.

"It's all too much pressure."

"Meaning?" Dr. Fox asked gently.

"The pressure of every decision I make haunting my kids for their entire lives. And my decisions haven't been great. Not only did my kid get hurt, but I lied to my entire family about it. I exploded at a patient. I've likely ruined my marriage. And then I abandoned my kids to get on a plane just to talk to Eddie, and out of nowhere I turned violent." She looked up at Dr. Fox. "I didn't even tell you yet, but I punched my brother in the face."

Dr. Fox's expression remained neutral. "Why do you think all of this has happened?"

"Because I'm pathetic!"

"Gemma."

"I am! I'm falling apart under the weight of everything. From the pressure of being a mother. How is it *this* hard? *Why* is it this hard? I sometimes think about all the things it takes to be a mother, the daily tasks, and frankly it all sounds so easy. Trite, even. Bathe the kids, feed the kids, play with the kids, and yet I can't find the energy for any of it. As if any one of those is such an overwhelmingly difficult task that the very thought of it makes me tired. I'm so overwhelmed that I'm bored, and I'm bored by how constantly overwhelmed I am. Why does every movement I make as a daughter, wife, and mother feel so scrutinized, and yet I feel absolutely invisible?

I have disappeared from my own life. Just try to make fucking friends at this age or find a pair of jeans that fit a body that is no longer familiar to you while also being surrounded by strangers who smile at your baby as you walk by but won't even meet your eyes. I am nothing anymore. I'm nowhere to be found. And add unrelenting shame to that because of how self-centered that sounds. Who the fuck am I to complain about this life I *decided* I wanted? I wanted to be married, and have a career, and kids, and now that I have all of that, I cannot seem to manage all of it. Or enjoy any of it. God, I'm choking with privilege, but I still have the breath to complain. I have no idea how to be there for my husband and kids while feeling the pull of my own family. How can I be a mom when I still feel so much like a daughter? I've got to keep everyone's feelings in mind with every decision I make. And even trying to explain what it feels like to be doing constant emotional labor is like, I dunno, like waking up and trying to explain a fading dream that was so vivid the night before. So how? *How* can I possibly manage everything and everyone? Who do I prioritize? And why am I the one who has to make all the decisions? Because whether or not my kid is breastfed, or how long he uses a pacifier, or if he's sleeping well, or where he goes to school, or if I work or stay home, or what we have for dinner *every fucking night* seems to be on my shoulders. I mean, I can't even imagine what would happen if I just didn't lead the planning of a birthday party for my kids. Or didn't figure out Mother's Day plans for my mom while pretending to enjoy the day myself. Or wasn't always the one the day care teacher calls when Bo is sick? Why? When did I sign up to be fully responsible for absolutely every decision, but to have power over nothing?"

Gemma felt a mixture of relief and regret in her chest from expelling the air and the sorrow that came from all she said. She watched as Dr. Fox sat for a beat and then uncrossed her legs, stood up, walked over to the couch, and sat beside her.

Dr. Fox turned her body to face Gemma. Feeling strange at the closeness, Gemma turned her head toward her. "What are you doing?"

"I want to make sure you feel seen," Dr. Fox said.

Gemma scooted back a few inches on the couch. "This isn't what I meant."

"Should I sit on the other side of you?"

"What? No."

"Would more eye contact help?"

"What is happening?"

"I want you to feel my presence."

"Okay, well, it's felt. Go back to your seat."

Dr. Fox nodded, walked back to her chair, and sat down.

"I'm very confused about what just happened," Gemma said.

"After hearing all you had to say, I made a decision to come sit next to you. You didn't like it."

"That part I got. What I don't get is why."

Dr. Fox shrugged. "Why does that matter?"

"Because I'm confused."

"But what I did is done. Why does your confusion about it matter?"

"What?"

"I made a decision. The decision is done. The impact of my decision happened, and you didn't like it. But you still want to know what my intention was. Right?"

Gemma's forehead wrinkled into a maze of confusion.

"You made some decisions the night Calvin was hurt. The impact of those decisions has happened. So what do your intentions matter?"

"Because I never intended for my child to get hurt!" Gemma yelled out before covering her mouth with her hand.

Dr. Fox nodded. "So your intentions in those decisions do matter?"

"Yes, of course. Of course they matter. Even though what I did is done, I need it to be understood that I never intended for my child to get hurt. Or to hurt my husband, or Eddie or anyone."

"Okay, so when you say you feel you have to make all the decisions and yet feel you have no power, what does that mean? Where are you powerless? In the intentions of your decisions, or in their impact?"

Gemma sat for a minute before squeezing her eyes closed. "I suppose in the way my decisions will be perceived."

Dr. Fox nodded. "You want to have power over how everyone will interpret your decisions?"

A faint laugh escaped Gemma's nose. "Can I?"

A smile appeared on Dr. Fox's lips. "I wonder what judgments you are making about your parents' decisions. That day. Tryout day."

Gemma sighed deeply. "I just can't understand why they did what they did. My dad wouldn't take Eddie—who had a *concussion*—to the hospital. My mom wouldn't let Mary come home from her friend's house even though she was nearly . . ." Gemma shook her head. "They didn't tell me *how* I got hurt. I just don't get it."

"Can you imagine someone feeling that way about your decisions the day Calvin was dropped? And all your decisions since then?"

Gemma nodded sadly.

"And if someone were judging you for those decisions, what would you say to them? In defense of yourself?"

Gemma shrugged. "Decisions made in chaos are tough to explain."

"Mmm."

Gemma hugged her body, too overwhelmed. "I may not understand why my parents did what they did that day, but I have to assume it was like any decisions made in chaos."

"So you can empathize with your parents?"

"I think they made the wrong decisions."

Dr. Fox stretched out her arms and rested her palms on the top of her head. "And did you?"

"I mean, this may not make sense, but what I did didn't *feel* like decisions."

"What did it feel like?"

"Panic," Gemma said, a sigh so large accompanying the word that she felt like a deflating balloon. She closed her eyes and thought back over that night. About the decisions she made. Deciding to scroll on her phone rather than watch her son in her sleeping brother's arms. Deciding to lie about having dropped Calvin to save Eddie, herself, and her family pain. Deciding to let Anthony leave the night of their fight, and deciding it was okay for him to stay gone. Deciding to fly to Boston. Deciding to punch Eddie. So many bad decisions that never felt like decisions at all.

She gasped lightly.

Dr. Fox's eyebrows rose as if in anticipation.

"When I said earlier that I have to make all the decisions but have no power, I think what I meant was it never feels like I'm making decisions. It feels like I'm just making, I don't know, automatic movements within chaos."

"And you feel invisible when there is chaos."

"Yeah." Gemma nodded. "That's right. I feel powerless, invisible, and on autopilot."

Dr. Fox tilted her head left, then right. "Where's the chaos coming from?"

"What do you mean? From these chaotic events! Being run over by my brother! My sister's brush with rape! My brother dropping my baby!"

"But you said earlier you *always* feel powerless."

"Right," Gemma said firmly. "Right," she said again, softer.

"You're giving a lot of power to the decisions made on just two days of your thirty-five-year lifespan."

"No, it's just—"

"Or, maybe you actually feel you're on autopilot all the time because you feel you are in chaos all the time."

"I mean—"

Dr. Fox glanced at her watch. "We are nearly at time, but I want to know one thing. How do you plan to tell Calvin about what happened to him?"

Gemma frowned. "I don't know. I haven't given that any thought. He's just a baby. I don't even know how or why that would even come up."

"Right." Dr. Fox nodded. "If you want power over your decisions, maybe that's the one to start with."

Gemma met Dr. Fox's eyes and held her gaze. Dr. Fox shook her head, looking up at the ceiling as her hair fell away from her face. When her head tilted back down to face Gemma, she had a strange look in her eyes. Gemma watched her intently.

Dr. Fox cleared her throat. "Mom, I have a question."

Gemma's chin jutted forward in curiosity.

"My college girlfriend wanted to know where I got this scar," Dr. Fox said, pointing to her eye.

Gemma's face relaxed in understanding. She took a deep inhale and worked to keep her eyes from rolling.

"You've never told me about this scar, and I've always been curious," Dr. Fox continued.

"First tell me about this girlfriend," Gemma quipped. "Any tattoos?"

"Mom, I'm serious," Dr. Fox said, a stern expression on her face.

Gemma bit her lip. She tried to think of Calvin, her nine-week-old son, home from college. She suddenly felt overcome with sadness. *Where does he go to college? What's his major?*

Are he and Bo close? Did he do well in high school? What at-tributes of his did his teachers comment on at parent-teacher conferences? Who was his best friend in elementary school? Do they still keep in touch? Was he into sports? Theater? Is he silly, serious, sarcastic? Does he have freckles or curly hair or knobby knees? Did he have to have braces or wear glasses? What does his handwriting look like? What was his first word? A sob caught in Gemma's throat. *Did I ever feel bonded to him? Or was I so blinded by what happened, my decisions, my stress, that I missed truly seeing him?*

Gemma wiped her nose with her sleeve. "I'm so angry at my parents for the decisions they made on my behalf as a child, and here I am, on the verge of doing the same damn thing."

Dr. Fox relaxed into her chair. "That's parenthood."

A beat hung between them before Dr. Fox looked again at her watch and rose from her chair. "There are the decisions that are thrust upon us, and there are the decisions that we are lucky enough to make. I'd suggest giving thought to which ones are more responsible for all the things you feel right now."

Gemma walked out of the office and into the lobby, a warm sensation spreading across her chest. She wasn't quite sure what it was, but it felt a little like relief. The slight easing of her unrelenting sorrow. That last sentence had escaped Dr. Fox's lips so easily, and with such obviousness, that it almost seemed silly—unnecessary, even—to say. Yet Gemma would look back on that sentence years later, and only then fully understand that it was the beginning of her healing.

CHAPTER 25

Gemma watched as Anthony's car pulled into the driveway beside her sister's. "Okay!" she shouted. "He's here, let's go!"

Mary came around the corner with Bo at her side. "You want me to get Calvin?"

"Just get the diaper bag," Gemma said as she walked toward the pack and play in the middle of the living room. Calvin was kicking his legs and smiling up at Gemma. "Come here, you little chunk," she said, lifting him from the crib.

"Happy Thanksgiving," Anthony said softly as he came through the front door.

"Daddy!" Bo cried, running to him.

"We're going to take my car," Gemma announced. Mary looked at Gemma with an expression that Gemma couldn't read. She looked back at Mary, expressionless.

"Right," Mary said. "Bo, Anthony, you want to go ahead and get loaded into the car?"

Anthony nodded, extended his hand for Bo to take, and walked back through the front door.

"You okay?" Mary asked Gemma.

Gemma shrugged. "Yeah, why?"

"You didn't even say hello to him."

Gemma pursed her lips.

"Is this going to be awkward? Having him at Thanksgiving when you two are . . ."

"You sound like Mom."

Mary sighed. "Gem."

"It's fine. Let's just go."

When Gemma got to the car, she noticed Anthony had chosen to sit in the back, between the two car seats—a choice he probably would have made regardless of what was going on between them, but it hurt her feelings nonetheless. She clicked Calvin's carrier into place, glanced up at Anthony, who smiled at her briefly, and then climbed into the driver's seat. The car was eerily quiet as Gemma started the ignition and backed out of the driveway.

Mary broke the silence after three minutes of passing landscape. "At least the weather is nice today," she said sarcastically, leaning forward and peering up at the gray sky.

Gemma sighed, gesturing out the window. "Either rain or be sunny. I can't work with this."

Mary laughed. "They are calling for snow on Saturday."

"The Midwest isn't for the faint of heart."

Silence settled back in the car as Gemma's mind raced through an endless loop of thoughts. Her natural tendency on days like today was to make it good and fun for everyone. To control the room. To not bring up anything touchy, or act awkward, or let the mood be anything but up. But today she didn't have the energy for it. She felt low—on the verge of tears, as usual—and here she was in a car with her estranged husband, and she didn't know how to connect with him. And sitting next to her was her sister, who had finally confessed a trauma she had been through decades earlier, a revelation Gemma silently hoped Mary would one day be able to tell their parents and Eddie.

All the knowledge she now had about what happened between her and Eddie the day of his tryouts, and consequently what happened to Mary; the anger she felt toward her parents; and the empathy she had slowly gained for them with Dr. Fox—it all felt like too much to carry into a meal with everyone.

As she pulled into her parents' driveway, she let out an audible sigh.

Mary touched Gemma's arm. "You okay?"

Gemma glanced up at the rearview mirror to see that Anthony wasn't waiting to hear her response. "I'm fine," she grumbled as she unbuckled her seat belt.

"My darlings!" Irene exclaimed as she opened the door and saw Mary, Anthony, and Bo standing on the porch, and Calvin swinging in his carrier under Anthony's hand. "First," she said, extending a long finger with a thick gold band around it, "give me that baby. Then you may go inside."

Anthony laughed lightly as he handed the carrier to Irene, who moved her lanky body out of the doorway to let everyone else in. Out of habit, Gemma took note of every ring her mom was wearing.

Jack, wearing a black apron, came from the kitchen and greeted everyone: a hug for his daughters and a fist bump for Anthony. Irene explained that they were running behind on the meal, but that everyone should grab a drink—"Beer and wine in the fridge, or Jack can make a cocktail!"—and settle in for a bit while she finished up. Bo tugged at Anthony to follow him into the room where Irene kept all the toys. Mary offered to help Irene in the kitchen, while Gemma took Calvin out of Irene's arms and went to change his diaper on the living room floor.

As she finished, she looked up to find herself alone. With Calvin resting on her shoulder, she walked around the house in search of her father. He was in the den, apron still on, standing in front of the TV with his arms crossed. She smiled to see him like that—as if not fully committing to watching the football game in case Irene summoned him.

Gemma sat down on the couch and placed Calvin in her lap. "Good game?"

Jack, startled, turned around and clapped once. "Well, hello there!" He turned the volume down slightly and sat beside Gemma, watching as Calvin kicked his legs. "He's really growing, huh?"

"Yes. It feels like it's going faster than it did with Bo."

Jack nodded.

"But also, slower?" Gemma added.

"Yeah, I remember so much about Eddie as a baby, a little less with Mary, but it was honestly a blur with you."

Gemma laughed. "Thanks."

"A *wonderful* blur."

Gemma smiled as she turned her attention back to Calvin. She took great comfort in being around her father, despite how conflicted she had felt about him since her talk with Eddie.

"His eye looks good," Jack said.

A lump formed in Gemma's throat, as it did anytime she heard the word *eye*. A Pavlovian response to her deepest regret. But before she could respond, Calvin began to fuss.

"Is he hungry? Tired?" Jack asked.

Gemma hated how people did this when a child cried. As if the mother should always know instantly what her child needed. Or, worse, as if the person asking thought it inexcusable for a child to cry without reason. Gemma had been crying without a reason for weeks on end. *Sometimes you just need to cry*, she thought, bringing Calvin to her chest. *Or maybe he has a reason, but I don't know what it is because I'm just not a good mother to this boy.*

Jack stood up abruptly. "What about a walk?"

"Sure," Gemma said, between pats and shushes. "I'll need the stroller."

She made her way into the living room to get her coat. Jack exchanged his apron for a knit beanie and fetched the stroller from her car. Bundled in blankets as they moved down the driveway, Calvin grew calm.

"Good call," Gemma said to her father.

"Fresh air cures everything."

"I'm surprised you didn't want to stay and watch the game."

Jack shrugged. "It'll still be on when we get back."

Gemma's laugh took the form of a small cloud of cold air. "Boy, you've mellowed."

"How so?"

"We were told not to bug you when football was on. And as far as I could work out, football season was ten months long."

Jack laughed. "Who said you couldn't bother me?"

"Mom!"

Jack smiled as he pulled leather gloves from the pockets of his coat. "You know your mother. Always trying to keep everyone happy."

Gemma moved the stroller to the side of the street to let a car pass. "You've noticed that about her, huh?"

"Of course. It's who she is. She wants everything to be beautiful."

Gemma raised her eyebrows at this. Her father never spoke to her about her mother in any way but factual. He rarely complained about her and never offered insight into her motivations.

She'd never considered that before. Sure, her mother loved pretty things. Gorgeous clothing, luscious home decor, and, of course, jewelry. But Gemma had never considered that "beautiful" could be a worldview.

"And her quest for everything to be beautiful can sometimes—accidentally, of course—come across as controlling," Jack added. "Like bugging me when a game is on. The more beautiful she wants everything, the more ugly others can feel."

Gemma gasped. "Damn, Dad."

Jack shrugged. "I know she can seem critical. I'm sure you have felt criticized by her. Mary, probably, too."

Gemma stayed quiet even as her hands gripped the stroller more tightly.

"But she just wants things beautiful. A beautiful family. A beautiful life. A beautiful moment. I like that about her."

"Still, she could lay off my clothes and makeup," Gemma said with a smirk.

Jack laughed. "Fair enough. But she comes by it naturally."

"How so?"

"Oh, you know your grandpa. He was so proud to have such a beautiful daughter after three boys."

Gemma thought of her three uncles, burly men who all went into trade jobs. Their fingernails always had a dark line of dirt beneath them. Her mother always did seem out of place with them. A delicate rose among the bushes. "I never thought of that."

They walked in silence for a while. Waving at neighbors, petting a few dogs leashed to passersby. The movement of the stroller effectively rocked Calvin to sleep. Gemma broke the silence as they turned the corner next to a house already cluttered with Christmas lawn decor. "What about your dad?"

Jack exhaled. "Oh, you know Paps."

"As a grandfather, sure. What was he like growing up?"

Jack was quiet for several paces. "Mean."

"Whoa. Really?"

Jack nodded silently.

"Abusive?"

Jack winced. "No, nothing like that. Just, quiet. Gruff. Impossible to read."

"That must have been fun."

Jack scoffed. "The man didn't know the meaning of the word *fun*."

"Did you have fun as a child?"

Jack looked up at the sky thoughtfully. "Yeah, I suppose. As an only child it was kind of hard to find fun in the house. No siblings to play with, and Paps certainly wasn't going to play with me. And your grandmother was always busy with housework. But we had these neighbors, and they had five kids. Three boys and two girls. On weekends they would play touch football in their backyard." Jack laughed reflectively. "I watched them for a long time from my window, jealous and sulking. And then one day one of the kids—his name was Neal, he was the youngest—noticed me and waved for me to come outside. After that, I played with them every weekend."

"That sounds fun."

"Yeah, it was."

Gemma let the silence hang as they walked, her chest warm with affection for her father.

"And it was fun watching Eddie play."

Gemma's neck tensed. She nodded, quietly.

"Man, he was fun to watch."

"Are you sad he's not here today?"

Jack shrugged. "I didn't expect him to come. Sounds like he and Kat are off on another adventure."

"And Mom?"

Jack clucked his tongue. "She wants things beautiful."

Gemma felt her hands start to shake, a telltale sign of her nerves. She felt a question rising in her throat, but before she could ask it, Jack cleared his.

"Your mother tells me Anthony has been sleeping at a friend's place."

Gemma's shock at hearing her father say this paralyzed her tongue.

Jack helped lift the stroller up onto the sidewalk. "Everything okay?"

Gemma shrugged, still unable to speak.

"I won't pry into your business," he said, looking straight ahead. "But marriage is complicated with kids. I mean, it's complicated without them too. You take two people, with their own triggers and quirks, and have them live together, stepping over and around each other's triggers and quirks. But then, if you add kids, you put all those collected triggers and quirks onto brand-new people, and then pile everyone into a station wagon and try to enjoy a trip to the Grand Canyon."

"I lied to Anthony," Gemma blurted out, surprising herself.

Jack turned his head to look at her. "About?"

"About what happened that night to Calvin."

Jack turned his gaze ahead but stayed quiet as they walked.

"I told him—well, I told everyone—that I dropped Calvin. But it was actually Eddie. Eddie dropped him."

Jack's feet stopped. He rubbed the back of his neck and then shifted his eyes to Gemma.

She shrugged. "I know."

"Why lie?"

"Why do you think?"

Jack nodded, resuming his steps. "How did Anthony find out you lied?"

"He hasn't. He still thinks it's my fault."

"He moved out because he's mad that you dropped Calvin?"

"Among other things, yeah. He's just generally very angry about all things Eddie. I fucked up, Dad. I prioritized Eddie. *Protected* Eddie, not Calvin."

"Because you lied to protect Eddie?"

"Yeah. My kid, my *newborn baby*, was injured, and yet I had the capacity to think about protecting Eddie? Who does that? Who even has a thought in that moment *other* than helping their hurting child? I made the decision of a psychopath."

"Gemma . . ."

"No, truly. A psychopath lies and manipulates for personal gain. I lied to protect myself. They have parasitic relationship tendencies. Clearly I'm dependent on Eddie's approval. They are callous with emotions. And that's me. I mean, I can't even bond with—" A sob cracked in her throat before she swallowed it down. As she'd been trained to do since childhood, she wouldn't distress Jack with her emotions.

They walked on in silence. As they turned the corner onto Jack and Irene's street, Jack cleared his throat again. "Gemma?"

Gemma adjusted the blanket around Calvin. "Mm-hmm?"

"I get it."

"Get what?"

"Why you lied. Why you protected Eddie."

"That makes one of us."

"And I get what you're feeling with Anthony. How it's, you know, come between you two."

"How so?"

"Look, I don't want to get into anything too deep on Thanksgiving, but I get why you did what you did." Jack adjusted his gloves needlessly. "Hell, *I've* done what you did."

Gemma looked at him skeptically. Her father had refused to take Eddie to the hospital when he knew he had a concussion. He hadn't protected Eddie; he had put him in danger.

Jack looked down at his feet while they walked. "I destroyed evidence from a crime scene to protect Eddie."

Gemma's face twisted in confusion. "What crime scene?"

Jack let out a long breath, the cold cloud streaming from his lips. "The night that you broke your—" Jack's voice cracked.

"My collarbone. You mean the day of his football tryouts?"

Jack nodded.

"What evidence are you talking about?"

"Eddie crashed his truck that night. And when I got to him, I found empty beer cans on the floorboard. I got rid of them before the cops came over to the scene. And then I refused to take him to the hospital because I knew they'd test his blood. He shouldn't have been drinking and driving. Or drinking at all. And as furious as I was with him for what he did," Jack said, his eyes shifting to Gemma for a beat, "I just couldn't let him suffer the consequences."

Gemma stopped walking as the realization of what Jack had said washed over her. He continued a few steps before noticing, then turned around to face her.

"Eddie hadn't been drinking that day," she said.

Jack's brow furrowed. "What makes you say that?"

"Because it's the truth. I asked Eddie."

"When?"

Gemma closed her eyes and shook her head. "Last week. It's a long story. I flew to Boston and had it out with him. I wanted to know what happened that day. How I broke my collarbone. I deserved to know."

Jack's eyes, rimmed red, widened in surprise.

"Eddie hadn't been drinking that day," Gemma said again.

"There were empty beer cans in his truck."

Gemma shook her head.

"And the boys had been drinking in the locker room after tryouts. I didn't think Eddie had, or I wouldn't have let him drive you, but when I got to the scene and saw the cans . . ." Jack lowered himself onto a curb to sit. Gemma pulled the stroller over and joined him. "When your mom and I got to the scene, everyone—cops, EMTs, people in the store—all rushed to you, but I made a beeline for Eddie's truck. And when I got to him . . ." Jack's chin quivered, causing Gemma's eyes to flood. "I instantly sized up what had happened. I saw Eddie, I saw the cans, and I did what I did before everyone came rushing over to help."

Gemma leaned her shoulder into his and they both sat for a beat, looking at the cracks in the street in front of them. "The beer cans must have been from some other time," she said. "Eddie hadn't been drinking that day."

Jack shook his head, and a tear fell.

"Eddie got a concussion during tryouts. That's why he crashed."

Jack looked at her with such pain in his eyes Gemma thought she might throw up. "You didn't destroy evidence, because there was no crime," she said, putting an arm around him. "Just an accident."

Jack pulled off his glasses and buried his face in his hands. Gemma had never seen her father cry. Her heart ached for him as his gloves grew damp with tears.

"Dad," Gemma said softly. "You did what you thought was right."

"But I was wrong."

Gemma waited for a few moments, then extracted her arm and used the stroller to help herself stand. She extended an arm down to Jack, who grabbed for it and rose. They stood for a beat, looking at each other, before Gemma lifted onto her toes, opened her arms, and put them around her father.

As they broke apart, Gemma nodded toward the house. "Let's go in there and give Mom a beautiful moment."

Jack nodded and they walked, side by side, slowly up the drive. Once inside, Irene greeted them, holding a glass of wine and declaring, "There you two are!" Gemma noticed Irene had a mischievous grin on her face. Everyone took their places, and Mary got Bo into his booster seat. Anthony lifted Calvin from the stroller but seemed to be avoiding his wife's gaze. Gemma looked at Mary, who was smiling. Gemma's eyes scanned the spread in front of them. There was a beautiful turkey, a basket of rolls, green beans, mashed potatoes, cranberry sauce—which no one ever ate—gravy, sweet potato casserole. And, at the far end of the table, a familiar aluminum pan with a foil top.

Gemma's eyes widened and she looked up at her mother. "Is that . . . ?" she asked, pointing.

"It is!" Irene laughed, clapping her hands. "I wanted to

make up for us eating the pan Anthony got for you a few weeks back."

Gemma looked at Anthony, who smiled weakly, then back at her mother. "Mom, what a lovely gesture."

Irene swatted a hand. "I wanted to put it in a prettier dish than this tinfoil thing, but Mary told me it would read better in the pan you'd recognize."

Gemma laughed and shook her head. "It's the most beautiful thing I've ever seen."

She watched as everyone around the table, with all their concerns, and worries, and regrets, and hopes, dived into Thanksgiving dinner.

"You hear we're getting snow Saturday?" Jack asked, his mouth full of stuffing. Everyone at the table groaned.

"I'm not ready to give up fall," Mary said.

"Think anyone in the Midwest has a dinner where they don't discuss the weather?" Anthony asked.

As everyone laughed, Gemma lost herself in thought. The weather in Indiana fascinated her. It was always so predictably unpredictable. They could get a foot of snow overnight, and the next day, temperatures would be in the fifties. Her eyes moved around the table. She saw how Irene dazzled when she threw her head back in laughter. She observed how Jack's face and voice were softer than usual. She noticed that Mary seemed a bit lighter as she doted on Bo. She watched her husband gently holding her youngest son in one arm while using his free hand to bring a forkful of food to his mouth. She was sitting in a room with everyone and yet still felt as though she missed them. As if she were homesick for the very home she was in. *How is it possible to feel this close and this far away from people sitting next to me?* she wondered.

On Saturday, as predicted, Indiana would be blanketed with snow. On Sunday, the temperature would climb into the fifties and the snow would quickly begin to melt. During a trip to the grocery store on Monday, Gemma would notice how the mountain of snow and ice plowed into the center of the parking lot wouldn't show any signs of melting. The physics would befuddle her. It would eventually be sixty degrees and sunny that day, but that snow pile would linger.

Not unlike those gathered together on that Thanksgiving Thursday. The ice was piled so high that, despite the warming temperature and the shining sun, the glacier between them would take time to fully thaw.

CHAPTER 26

Gemma stared down at the heads of the people milling around the square below, between the falling snowflakes. The fact that Christmas shopping was already underway still seemed impossible. *Wasn't it just September?* she thought. And yet here she was, her first day back at work, a full twelve weeks since giving birth to Calvin. Her first session of the day was in twenty minutes, but she had come in early that morning, her nervous energy driving her like an engine.

At Thanksgiving, Gemma had felt a welcome shift inside her. Not quite peace, but something akin to acceptance. Irene had gone to such effort for her daughters, and Gemma noted that Eddie's absence didn't seem to overpower every room in the house. Instead the house felt pleasantly full, and happy, and loving. Her walk with her father broke something open in her, and she felt she understood her parents as well as any child ever can. They all stayed late to help Irene clean the dishes and dole out the leftovers, and though Gemma found herself enjoying the company, it was the first time in weeks she longed for her and Anthony to reconnect. Gemma was quiet on the car ride home, and neither Anthony nor Mary seemed up for talking. Perhaps they were all lost in the pleasantness around them, while still clouded by the darkness within.

Gemma tried to spend the holiday weekend doing a little clothes shopping, hoping new outfits might help her adjust to her new shape—smaller, yet lumpier—but the rush of holiday shoppers had brought her back through the front door less than an hour after Mary told her goodbye. "I'll just order online," Gemma said, shivering at the thought of the crowds.

She spent Sunday laundering what clothes she did have that fit, and taking a few long walks to center herself for her return to work. After her last visit with Dr. Fox, the Monday before Thanksgiving, they had agreed she might be ready to stop their sessions together, at least for now. Their conversations had forced Gemma to confront the past she'd spent her life both chasing and avoiding. And though she felt a calmness, relief even, about her relationship with her parents, she still worried about her relationship with Eddie. Perhaps out of habit, perhaps out of self-preservation, she refused to let herself expect their dynamic to be significantly different. He might never call or text with her the way he did with Mary. He and Kat might still visit at inconvenient times, and eat the food out of her fridge, and seem largely clueless about children, but Dr. Fox had said such a great line that summed it up for Gemma: "Everything in your life may *look* like it always has, but your emotional relationship with all those things and people will have changed."

Despite feeling stronger in some ways, Gemma still found herself crying regularly and growing more anxious by the day about her lack of a bond with Calvin. She had swept up so much of the sand seeping out of her closed fist, but she still felt that her opportunity to be a good mother was slipping through her fingers.

Gemma heard the chime of the office's front door. She waited a few moments until she heard Dr. Heinz unlock his office, then made her way through the lobby. Her heart rate quickened with excitement as she knocked on his open door.

"There she is," Dr. Heinz said from behind his desk, draping his coat on his chair.

"Hey, Boss!"

"How are you?" he asked, motioning for her to sit on his couch.

"Good. Strong." She smiled. "Strong*er.*"

He walked over to join her on the couch. "Good distinction. Tell me about your time with Dr. Fox."

"Oh, I don't think an employer can ask an employee what she talks about in therapy . . . ," Gemma said with a wink as he took a seat beside her.

"No worries. I'll just call her office for the session notes."

Gemma laughed. "She was, well, she was—"

"A character?"

"Well, that. Sure. But also, just so affecting."

"I thought you might like her style."

"Not at first. At first, I was kind of thrown by it. As if she was, I dunno, too casual? But in truth, I don't think I've ever been taken more seriously."

"Affecting and authentic."

"Exactly. She got me to dig into my issues with my brother. Because of the way he treated me, I have always thought he was mad at me. And I could never understand why. But he wasn't mad at me. His behavior was the product of a traumatic experience he endured, after which the emotional recovery was . . . well, bungled."

Dr. Heinz looked impressed and nodded. "Quite affecting indeed."

Gemma relaxed into the couch, nodding.

"How's Calvin? And Bo?" he asked.

"Both great. Calvin is even sleeping ten-hour stretches."

"He's the favorite child, then."

"It's shaping up that way."

"I'm glad you're back."

Gemma realized how much she had missed sitting and talking with Dr. Heinz. Their talks had always been her favorite part of the job. Seeing patients day in and day out was only possible because of her ability to consult with—and sometimes be consoled by—him. And yet she had been without his counsel since the day he told her she was not allowed back at work. The feelings she had that day toward him—the anger, the embarrassment—were now so distant to her that she could barely summon their memory. While he hadn't been there to guide her the past two months, he had sent her to the person who could. Now she was able to see what a remarkable thing he had done for her, giving her a chance at having something she didn't even know she needed.

She looked down at her hands. "I actually want to thank you."

"Oh?"

She felt tears welling up. "Shit, sorry, I'm still crying spontaneously."

"Maybe this isn't spontaneous," Dr. Heinz offered softly.

Gemma laughed as she caught tears with her pinkies. "Well, I certainly wasn't planning this."

Dr. Heinz sat in silence as Gemma grabbed a tissue and worked to keep her face dry.

"I promise I'm ready to be back."

"I have no doubts."

"I've been working really hard. With Dr. Fox, of course, but also just on my own. With all my family stuff."

Dr. Heinz tilted his head to the side. "Gem."

"Yeah?"

"I appreciate you working to intellectualize your problems. But I'm worried you can't see what else is going on here."

"What do you mean?"

He looked at her for a beat, opened his mouth, and then closed it again.

She sighed. "Just say whatever it is you're thinking!"

"You are suffering with postpartum depression."

Gemma sucked in air and squeezed her eyes shut. "I know."

"And what are you doing about it?"

"I just think if I can get some more sleep—"

"Gemma."

"It's temporary."

"What would you tell a patient who said that to you?"

"I'd say, 'You sound really smart and on top of things!'"

Dr. Heinz let out a laugh.

Gemma exhaled for a long time. "I can't separate what I'm going through with my family, with Calvin's injury, all of it, from what could be postpartum depression."

"Why do you need to?"

"Then I could know what to control."

Dr. Heinz's eyes went soft. "Gemma, it's never just one problem, one solution. We are complex creatures with complex concerns. As you well know."

Gemma nodded, unable to stop the tears. She pointed to her face. "This happens even when I'm not sad. They will just pour out of me, even when I'm feeling strong. Like I do today. Right now, I'm not crying because I'm sad. If anything, I'm crying because I feel grateful. For Calvin being okay. For Bo. For this job. For my parents and my sister, and even Eddie if you can believe that." She sniffed. "And I feel especially grateful for you."

He held up his hands and shook his head.

"Just let me say this, you *ass*." She sighed, then laughed. "I'm so grateful you suspended me from work."

Dr. Heinz's eyebrows shot up. "*Suspended* you?"

Gemma's face twisted in confusion. "Yeah?"

Dr. Heinz shrugged. "Seems like I just recommended you

take your full maternity leave. And maybe talk to someone while you were at it."

"No, you kicked me out of the office until I got better."

"And are you better?"

Gemma shrugged.

"If you aren't sure, why are you back?"

"My maternity leave is over."

Dr. Heinz winked.

"You are rewriting history here, Boss."

"Or you're splitting hairs."

Gemma looked at him intently for a moment before sitting up straight. "Okay, well, thank you for making me take my full maternity leave. And for recommending Dr. Fox. She was a great fit for me. And while I'm at it, thank you for the pasta from Rick's, and for taking a chance on me for your practice, and for being a good friend."

Dr. Heinz leaned forward, grabbed her hand, and squeezed it. "I say this with all the love and sincerity I have in me. It was *nothing*."

She laughed. Their hands released.

"At the risk of ruining a lovely moment of strength, may I make an observation?" Dr. Heinz asked.

"Lord."

"Why haven't you mentioned Anthony?"

"In the five minutes we've been talking?"

Dr. Heinz shrugged. "We listen for what we don't hear."

Gemma's eyes stung so instantly she wanted to scream. *Do the tears just line up in the trenches of my ducts like soldiers ready to storm the cheeks?* she wondered. "Anthony moved out."

If Dr. Heinz was surprised, Gemma couldn't read it on his face.

"This whole thing with Eddie, and my family, he just feels, well, he's always felt, that I don't prioritize him over them. And we got in a huge fight when we got home from the hospital after the eye surgery, and he left."

"Mmm . . ."

"What?"

"That doesn't sound like Anthony."

Gemma's mouth opened, but all she did was shrug.

"He has never struck me as a man who demanded priority *over* someone else."

"Well, shouldn't he get that? Shouldn't I be a good enough wife to give him that?"

"That's not how marriage works, exactly. Or any relationship. There isn't a scorecard. At least not in the healthy ones. You know this. And I know you and Anthony have always had a strong, mature dynamic."

Gemma's shoulders lifted. "I don't know what to tell you. He got mad at me because I was talking about Eddie with my sister instead of—I don't know—doing what I was supposed to be doing. Holding his hand? Holding the baby? Who knows! All I know is that he got mad that I was focused on Eddie, and we had a big fight that night and he stormed out with his suitcase. He's been gone ever since."

Dr. Heinz's eyes widened. "You haven't seen him since?"

"No, no. He comes by in the morning and helps get the kids up and dressed and fed and to day care. And he picks them up after school and brings them home and we all do dinner together and then he helps clean up and then he leaves."

"So, he's there every day?"

"Yep."

"So, when you said he moved out, what you meant is that he just sleeps somewhere else each night?"

Gemma sighed. "Right."

"The only part of your marriage he's not participating in is being alone with you."

Gemma's eyes narrowed. "I guess."

"Why do you think that is?"

"Because he's mad at me."

"He's mad at you, yet he's showing up every day to do his part in the marriage and in fatherhood, and only leaving when it's time to go to bed."

"Okay, well, it's not a sex thing. I *just* had a baby."

"I didn't say sex."

"What, then?"

"You know what the bedroom represents."

"Sex."

"Intimacy," Dr. Heinz said softly.

"Okay, so? He doesn't want to have intimacy with me."

"How do you know that?"

"He's not in our bedroom! You just said it! He's avoiding it!"

"Avoiding?"

"What else would you call it?" Her voice rose with her body off the couch.

Dr. Heinz leaned forward, his hands on his knees. "Gemma, what did you just say you learned about Eddie and his treatment of you all these years?"

Gemma sighed heavily as she paced the room. "That he's been like that to me because he had something pretty traumatic happen when we were younger, and he never really processed it."

"Right."

She threw her hands up. "I'm not getting it!"

"Hasn't Anthony had something pretty traumatic happen to him? Has anyone helped him process it?"

Gemma grabbed for the arm of the chair beside the couch, for fear she would collapse. A rush of remorse flooded her body. "Oh my god." Tears seeped from her eyes. "Oh my god, Anthony."

"He's not mad at you, Gemma. He's traumatized by what happened to his son."

"Oh my god."

"And you were too."

Gemma swallowed hard.

"Between that and this work you've done—alone—on digging into your past, well, there hasn't been space for Anthony in your room. So to speak."

Gemma wiped her cheeks with her hands several times as she nodded silently in agreement. "Jesus."

"You, better than anyone, know how a traumatic experience can set in motion an unintended dynamic. He left your house because his emotions were so strong, and he likely didn't know what else to do. But he *stayed* gone because . . ."

Gemma nodded. "I know."

Dr. Heinz nodded. "I know you know."

"But I also don't think that's entirely fair. How am I supposed to help him when I'm struggling as much as I have been? As much as I *still* am."

Dr. Heinz took a deep breath and looked up at the ceiling. "I suppose the goal is, whenever there *is* a struggle, you face it together."

Silence hung between them as Gemma thought back over Anthony storming out of the house months ago. *Anger is the bodyguard of sadness,* she reminded herself. Anthony may have appeared angry with her that night, but in reality, he was sad. Deeply sad, and Gemma had let him go. And worse, let him stay away.

She snapped out of her thoughts and glanced at her watch. "Okay. Um, do I look like I've been crying?" she asked, wiping her face and smoothing her hair.

"Absolutely," Dr. Heinz said, smiling.

She looked around, keyed up. "Okay, okay, I need to run to the bathroom and put some powder on before my session."

"Who you got?"

"New patient," she said.

"Well, it really is a day of fresh starts, isn't it?"

"Yeah, I guess it is."

"Proud of you," he said as he followed her to his door.

"You're making a fool of yourself."

He laughed as she walked across the lobby and to her own office, where she pulled a cosmetic bag out of her top desk drawer. On her way back to the lobby, she stopped at the doorway and unzipped her bag to make sure her compact was there and not in her purse. She rummaged through the bag, shifting the mascara and brushes around. As she moved two tubes of lipstick to the side, she heard her colleague, Dr. Rubio, call a name from across the waiting room: "Betty?"

Gemma, one hand in her bag, looked up to see her former patient rise slowly from a chair. Betty was looking directly at her. They held eye contact for what felt like an eternity. Gemma couldn't get her body to move or her voice to offer anything. All she could do was stare at Betty, a swirl of thoughts and feelings clouding her head. She watched as Betty put the magazine she had been reading back on the table, then bent forward and grabbed her purse. Still holding eye contact, she took a few steps toward Gemma, who managed to do the same. With ten feet still between them, Gemma opened her mouth to speak, but Betty put up a hand.

"Nice to see you, Dr. Sinclair," she said with a tight smile.

Gemma closed her mouth, smiled weakly, and nodded. Her hand still in her makeup bag, she watched as Betty walked into Dr. Rubio's office and closed the door.

CHAPTER 27

Gemma pulled into the driveway feeling giddy. She quickly unloaded the car. She had not one but two bottles of Anthony's favorite wine—the cabernet they had shared on the train in the Smoky Mountains—plus a bouquet of roses and, as was now the gesture of goodwill, a family-size order of the pasta dish from Rick's.

In the dining room she spread out a fresh tablecloth, placed new tapered candles in the holders, and set out their wedding china and silverware. She couldn't stop smiling to herself as she dimmed the lights, sent soft jazz through the Sonos speaker in the living room, and changed into a copper-colored knit sweater dress and knee-high boots.

Her heart raced when she heard a car door slam out front. She rushed to the door and threw it open to see a smiling Bo bounding up the walkway toward her while Anthony worked to unhook Calvin's car seat. As he withdrew his body from the car, his biceps flexing with Calvin's weight, he looked up to see her watching him.

"You're home early," he said, his eyes widening but his voice remaining neutral.

"And I have a surprise!" she said, practically yelling. She stepped onto the porch to lift Bo to her hip. "Come on in!"

She stepped back into the house and held the door open wide for Anthony. He turned left into the living room, set down Calvin's car seat, and lifted his messenger bag over his head, all while Gemma smiled at him.

"You're in an interesting mood," he said. He bent down to unbuckle Calvin and lift him from his seat. Gemma stepped forward and planted a kiss on top of Calvin's large, bald head.

"Come on, come on," she said, nodding her head in the direction of the dining room. "I have something to show you." Gemma quickly positioned herself at the far end of the table. When Anthony came around the corner with Calvin, she stretched out her arms toward the pan in front of her. "Dinner is served!"

"Oh," Anthony said, eyes narrowed.

"I wanted to do something special," Gemma said, smiling widely at him. "For you."

"Yeah, okay," he said, his expression unchanging.

Gemma's smile began to fade. "What?"

"Nothing, this is very nice." He shifted Calvin to his other arm. "Thanks, Gem."

"Seriously?" Gemma lowered Bo to the floor. "I'm really trying here."

"I know that, and I said thank you."

Gemma looked down at Bo. "Sweetie, can you go watch TV for a bit while Daddy and Mommy talk?" Bo shrugged and ran off toward the stairs. "Look, I'm trying to apologize," she said, turning back to Anthony. "To make up for . . . to *connect* with you."

"And I appreciate that." He sighed. "I really do. It's just . . ."

"It's just what?"

"It's just not as easy as dinner."

"You think I don't know that?"

"I honestly don't know what you think."

Gemma took a deep breath. "Okay, I get it. I do. Dinner is just the start. I'm hoping we can put the kids to bed early and talk."

Anthony nodded slowly.

"I want to hear about you. How you're feeling."

"How I'm feeling?"

Gemma nodded.

Anthony rubbed his neck. "Feeling about what, exactly?"

"Everything. You and me. Calvin."

He squeezed the baby to him. "What happened to Calvin, it really . . ." He snapped his eyes shut.

Gemma's stomach turned with shame. She leaned over and pulled out a chair for him, then sat down in the one beside it. "You're right," she sighed, patting the seat of the empty chair. "It was traumatic."

Anthony nodded, but he didn't sit. "And you left me alone in that."

Gemma inhaled sharply. Though that was likely how it felt to Anthony, it didn't feel exactly fair. "I didn't *leave* you," she whispered.

Anthony shook his head. "No, you just shut me out. And kicked me out."

"I didn't kick you out!" she said, jumping up. "You left!"

Anthony shook his head as his finger and thumb rubbed his tear ducts.

Gemma opened her mouth to add more but had no words. She collapsed back in her chair with a sigh. Anthony stared down at the table. Bo's show could be heard from the other room. Calvin began to squirm in Anthony's arms. Gemma looked up at him, but he stood motionless, still staring at the flame from one of the candles. After a few tense moments of silence, he walked over and handed her Calvin. Then he leaned forward and blew both candles out, put the foil lid on the pasta, took it into the kitchen, and slid it onto the shelf in the fridge. She watched him grab a clean bottle from the dishwasher, fill it with warm water and formula, shake it, and walk it back into the dining room. He looked at her, clearly in pain, but didn't hold her gaze. Instead, he walked out of the room without saying a word. With the silence trailing behind him, Gemma went upstairs to the nursery, sat in the rocking chair, and fed her baby, tears landing on his head while he drank.

———

Gemma stood in the hallway between the kids' rooms, not knowing what to do next. Bo was tucked into bed with his lamp on and his books piled around him. Calvin, in a fresh diaper and clean jammies, was kicking happily in his crib. She hadn't eaten dinner, but she had heard the tinkling of plates and forks from downstairs, so she knew Anthony had—and had fed Bo and would likely be headed back to his friend's futon soon. Her body ached and her stomach growled, but she couldn't muster the energy to go back downstairs, let alone fix herself something.

She let out a long sigh and shuffled toward her bedroom. Defeat pulled at her shoulders. Despite the light feelings she had enjoyed earlier while running around for the food and wine and flowers, she felt the heaviness she'd worked so hard to kick off crawling back on top of her. *Two giant steps back,* she thought, as she walked past the guest room and into her own.

Then something stopped her. She thought about Dr. Fox asking what decisions were made on that pivotal day of Eddie's football tryouts. That question had made her realize just how long-lasting the impact of a decision could be. She knew she had the potential to make a decision tonight that could have a lasting impact on her marriage, for better or for worse. And if that was true, any decision tonight that would continue to put distance between her and Anthony could ultimately lead to a chasm too big to be bridged.

She turned on her heel, marched straight downstairs to the entry table, and grabbed Anthony's keys from the bowl of loose change where he always dropped them. With her fist gripped tight around the metal, she stomped back up the stairs to their bedroom, slammed the door, and threw the keys on Anthony's side of the bed. She moved over to her side and sat with her arms folded, watching the door and waiting.

———

Gemma's eyes drooped and her head bobbed, but she forced herself to stay awake. The clock showed that she had been waiting on Anthony to come upstairs for two hours. She had passed the time by changing into her flannel pajama bottoms and one of Anthony's U of Penn T-shirts. She had braided her hair. She had even painted her toenails. *I can wait all night,* she thought, with a sinister half smile.

A few minutes later, the sound of feet hitting the stairs tickled Gemma's ear. She sat up straight again, suddenly fully alert. She heard the footsteps stop. She knew he was in front of Calvin's room. A few moments later she heard the steps again. They stopped in front of Bo's room. When she heard the steps again, this time stopping in front of the guest room, she felt a giggle bubble up. After a few seconds, she finally heard the footsteps again, this time approaching her door. Gemma's hand went over her smiling mouth.

There was a gentle knock at the door.

"Come in!" Gemma said in a chipper voice.

Anthony's head appeared. "Do you have my keys?"

"I do!" Gemma said, smiling and patting them beside her.

Anthony's eyes narrowed. "Okay, well, I'm really tired."

"Well then come to bed," she said, smiling.

He shook his head, but she could tell he was about to laugh. She wasn't sure if it would be a real laugh, or the kind of nervous laugh he always did when they fought, but either way her heart was full of hope. His nostrils flared as the faintest laugh she'd ever seen escaped. "Gemma."

She smiled, patting the bed. "Anthony."

He shook his head, his lips pulled into a straight line again. "What are you doing?"

"I'm kicking you back in."

Anthony's face relaxed into an expression Gemma couldn't quite read. He blinked and his eyes looked wet.

"In truth, you should have never left," she said, sliding her legs off the bed and standing up. "I shouldn't have *let* you leave."

"That's true."

"Futons are for bachelors," she said, taking a cautious step toward him. "But you, sir, are married."

"Also true."

"Whether you like it or not."

His lips twitched upward. "I like it sometimes."

Gemma smiled slightly, taking another step toward him. "That's better than never."

"It's definitely more than never," he said, taking his own small step toward her.

"That's a good starting place, don't you think?" she said, blinking away wetness until he released a smile big enough that she felt safe to throw her arms around him.

He embraced her tightly and they held each other in the middle of the bedroom, the room they hadn't been together in for nearly three months. Her body began to shake with tears, and he buried his face in her hair and held her as she cried.

"Okay, okay," Gemma said, breaking their embrace. "Keep it in your pants. We have talking to do."

Anthony shook his head with a smile.

"So, here's the plan." She walked over to the bed and hopped up on it. "We are going to sit here and talk everything out. Every feeling, every thought, every single grievance."

Anthony nodded.

"But there's one rule, and we both have to promise to follow it."

"Okay . . . ," he said, still standing in the same position.

"Neither of us gets to leave. No pushing each other away. No storming out. No walking out. No crawling out."

"Have I ever crawled away from you?"

"Just covering my bases," Gemma said, her hands up. "Can you agree to that?"

Anthony rubbed the back of his neck and nodded.

"Great." Gemma nodded once and patted the bed. "Now come here."

———

In the beginning, they sat with their backs against the headboard and their feet extended. She talked about how hard giving birth had been. The excruciating pain she had experienced at the hospital during Calvin's surgery. How frustrated she was at her body—she had lost so much weight but had never felt uglier. He talked about his shame for not knowing she was in so much pain, and for not being more supportive during her struggles—the enema, the fainting, the lack of sleep—in the hospital. He admitted his concern over her weight loss, and even confessed to asking one of his staff members if the dark circles under her eyes were normal. She agreed she had been so concerned with being perfect for her family's visit that she had kept her struggles quiet. He apologized for not pressing her to talk to him more.

They sat cross-legged facing each other as they talked about how scared they had been at the hospital. They went back over every detail of that night: the IV in Calvin's head, the bruising of his face, the tubes and cords connecting him to all the machines, the uncomfortable chair, the hard vinyl bench. She apologized for leaving him in the room with her parents and for talking with Dr. Heinz. He conceded that he had overreacted. She told him that the doctor had stopped her on the way to see Calvin in recovery to express his concern for her. Anthony apologized for not seeing in his wife what a stranger could. They held each other's hands as they both wept over each memory, tears of sadness and gratitude.

They were lying on their sides facing each other when Gemma admitted to throwing away Dr. Johnson's prescription for antidepressants. She rehashed her first day back at work and the embarrassing incident between her and Betty. Anthony's expression couldn't hide his surprise, but he listened intently, never interrupting her. She told him about her conversation with Dr. Heinz, and how she had not gone to work for several weeks, and that she had seen a therapist. To her relief, Anthony didn't seem upset. His eyes stayed kind. She told him what she had learned about herself—her tendency to push others away or to flee, her issues with avoidance—and how committed she was to changing her ways. She even promised to fill the prescription, conceding she needed the help.

Then, when they were stretched out on their bellies, their arms dangling over the side of the bed, she told him about her trip to see Eddie. He listened, his eyes facing forward, as she told him the entire story about Eddie's accident in his truck after backing into her and breaking her collarbone. That Jack took Eddie home instead of to the hospital so that he wouldn't get in trouble for driving drunk, even though that's not at all what had happened. How Irene had been at the hospital when Mary called, desperate to come home because of Todd's assault on her. And how all of this had splintered the McAlister family into silent shards of pain and guilt, leaving them unable to communicate with each other.

When Gemma finished recounting the story, Anthony sat up and faced her. She rolled over on her side to face him.

"You know what's crazy about that story?" he asked.

"Um, all of it?"

"Well, of course. The story is awful all around. I mean, so much hurt caused by so much unsaid for *decades*. Years of distance between all of you, and for what? For one terrible night." Anthony shook his head. "But what's craziest is that you did it."

Gemma blinked up at him. "Did what?"

"You got the truth. You got Mary to open up. You got your mom to notice she hurt you and make an effort to fix it. And more than that, you got Jack, Jack McAlister, to *talk*."

Gemma laughed. "Yeah, I've always been able to read my dad. But that walk? I didn't have to read him. He was an audiobook."

"It's funny to think about our own parents as kids. Or the fact that we were once kids and are now parents."

"Funny or horrifying?"

"Man, how are we messing up our own kids?"

"Well, for starters, I can't bond with Calvin."

Anthony's eyes shot down to meet hers. "What do you mean? You're great with Calvin. So loving. Affectionate."

She shook her head. "It feels like motions. I can't describe it. I love him. I promise I do, but I just can't *feel* it. In that visceral, all-consuming, overwhelming way I do when I even think about Bo. I am so ashamed."

Anthony put his hand on her back. "Hey, the feeling will come. It's just buried under the depression."

Gemma looked ahead, staring at the dust on the baseboard next to their bed. "Maybe so."

"I promise. Go easy on yourself."

Gemma sat up on the bed, took a long, deep breath, and nodded.

"You know what else I find so interesting about the day of Eddie's tryouts?" Anthony asked.

Gemma shook her head.

"Eddie wanted to be with you. He wanted to take you for ice cream."

Gemma's eyes went soft. "Yeah, how 'bout that."

"You had a good relationship at some point."

"Yeah . . ." Gemma looked off. "Until we didn't."

"God, that sucks."

Gemma shrugged, sadly.

"He was doing all the right things," Anthony said. "And then one day, literally one single day, it all changed. That really makes me feel for the guy."

"I guess."

"What?"

"Eddie still needs to take responsibility for how he is. Don't forget he left for his marathon when our kid was in surgery. Nothing excuses that."

Anthony's eyebrows lifted. "True. But to be fair, he did stay around and take care of Bo."

"With Mary's help!" Gemma rolled over, got off the bed, and paced around the room.

"Wait, I thought you felt good about Eddie now."

Gemma's insides twisted and tightened. "Yeah, I do. I mean, I don't know. It's complicated."

"I get it," Anthony said with a shrug. "I just understand him a little better."

Gemma kept pacing around the room, biting her thumbnail as she walked.

"Gemma? You look like a person who's about to walk out of here."

She glanced at him briefly but didn't stop pacing.

"And you know the rules," he added playfully.

She came to a stop, her body facing him. Maybe it was because Anthony had been so kind, so understanding, so forgiving with all she had revealed during the last few hours, or maybe she didn't like that he was now seemingly defending Eddie, but Gemma was overcome with the urge to tell him the truth. "Eddie dropped Calvin."

The moment the words left her lips, she was filled with regret. *Did I just undo everything we accomplished here?* she wondered.

Anthony stared at her, a confused expression in his eyes. "Eddie dropped Calvin when?"

Gemma looked at him, waiting for her words to sink in. She watched as his eyes widened in horror. He stood slowly and ran his hands aggressively through his hair.

"He fell asleep with Calvin in his arms."

Anthony shook his head, his eyes squeezed shut.

"I was unloading the dishes and then came into the living room to see he was sleeping and holding Calvin."

Anthony kept running his hand across his forehead as if trying to calm something inside his brain.

"I sat down on the couch, and I was on my phone and not watching, and I guess his hand relaxed, and Calvin rolled off—"

Anthony put up his hand to stop her. "I know what happened next." He stood up and walked to the window on the other side of the room. After a few moments of quietly staring out into the darkness, he walked back over and sat on the edge of the bed.

"I'm sorry I lied," she said, walking over to him and putting her hands on his shoulders. "Old family habit."

"Why the hell would he fall asleep holding a baby?"

"I know, I know."

He looked up at her, his eyes dark. "I want to punch him in his smug face."

"No need," Gemma said, smiling slightly.

"Don't protect him now," Anthony said, looking at her intently.

Gemma put her hands up and backed away. "Oh, I'm not. I'm just saying, there's no need to punch him. The man's been punched."

"What?"

"Yeah, I punched him. I clocked him hard, actually."

"You *what*?"

Gemma's shoulders lifted. "I punched my brother in the face."

Anthony let out a one-syllable laugh. "When?"

"When I flew to Boston. He opened the door and I just . . . I just punched him."

Anthony crossed his arms and looked up at her.

"I don't know what came over me," she said. "But I just saw his face and thought it needed my knuckles on it."

A smile spread across Anthony's lips as air escaped out of his nose. His chest began to rise and fall with the quickened breaths of laughter.

"It was a real 'eye for an eye' situation," she said with a sly smile. Anthony's laugh faded and he looked at her with an expression she'd never seen before. She frowned. "Too soon?" He shook his head so slightly she almost didn't detect it. She struggled to translate the language of his face. Not quite a smile. Not quite a scowl. "Anthony? Say something," she choked out after several seconds of silence had passed between them in the darkened room. *Why did I make a joke in this moment?* she asked herself. Anthony was just then learning about what truly happened to Calvin, and now she was joking around. *Another distancing mechanism Dr. Fox would pounce on.*

"Our whole relationship, I have felt that I came second to

your family," he finally said. "Not that it was a competition, just that, well, you know. It just felt like you were a McAlister. And always going to be a McAlister. Even after we got married." Anthony looked down at his hands resting in his lap. "And I'm not talking about taking my last name or anything. I mean, it was great that you did, but I would have been fine if you hadn't. I guess it's just like you never quite saw the two of us as *your family*."

Gemma nodded. "That's fair. For whatever reason, I've always felt caught between the family I was born into and the one we created."

Anthony pursed his lips. "I can't explain it, but you punching your brother, which I know was out of anger over Calvin—anger over a lot of things—helps me see things, see *you*, differently."

"How so?"

Anthony shrugged. "I guess you doing to Eddie exactly what I wanted to do to him—punching the guy, for Chrissake—makes me feel we are on the same side. Us versus everybody."

"Shame on me for taking so long to make you feel that."

"I shouldn't need to feel like we are against other people."

"I don't know, maybe you do. Maybe that's kind of what marriage is supposed to be. Maybe not being against others, but maybe being *for* each other. Above all else. Making *this* family our top priority, even when it upsets everyone else."

Anthony nodded. "Still, the guy didn't deserve that."

Gemma shook her head "No, he didn't. But at the same time"—she smiled as she walked toward him and grabbed his hands cautiously—"that punch seemed to fix a lot of things."

Anthony laughed as he pulled Gemma into his arms. "*Fix* is a strong word. Maybe it was more that you were hitting the reset button."

"Yeah, I clocked it something good."

CHAPTER 28

"Gemma," the nurse called from the open door at the back of the lobby. Gemma nodded to her and then bent down to grab her diaper bag, purse, water bottle, keys, and the carrier in which Calvin lay with his eyes open, kicking his legs in quick, jerky motions.

"How's Mama today?" the nurse asked Gemma, though she was looking at Calvin.

"Good!" Gemma said automatically. "Ready for the holidays?"

The nurse nodded as she extended her hand toward an open door at the end of the hall. "I haven't even started my shopping."

"Nothing reveals the invisible labor of women like the holidays," Gemma quipped.

"Ain't that the truth. Especially when you still have believers in the house," the nurse said, nodding toward the carrier.

Gemma swatted a hand. "Oh, we don't do Santa."

The nurse's eyes went wide.

Gemma shrugged. "I'm not signing up for a man to get credit for my work."

The nurse looked at her for a beat and then threw her head back in laughter. "Oh, Mrs. Sinclair, you had me going for a minute."

It's Dr. *Sinclair,* Gemma corrected her silently. *And I truly do want the credit.* But she played along with a laugh. They didn't deny Bo—and now Calvin—Santa. They just kept Santa a small deal, leaving only one unwrapped book on the fireplace from him.

As the nurse closed the door, Gemma unbuckled Calvin to release him from the carrier. She had put him in fuzzy, red footed pajamas, and he felt so cuddly and looked so cute, Gemma couldn't stop pressing him close to her. "My little chunky chunk," she said, lifting him up so that his head rested in the nape of her neck. *Why am I commenting on this baby's body? Why do I call him 'chunky'? I would never say that to a baby girl, would I?* Gemma wondered as a heavy knock on the door jolted her.

"Come in!"

The door swung open and there was the surgeon. Gemma felt taken aback, likely from associating his face with such a horrific episode. "Hi," she squeaked out. If he sensed she was acting weird, it didn't show on his face.

"How's the little guy?" he asked, seating himself on a rolling stool.

Gemma leaned forward with her son reclining in her arms so the doctor could take a look at his eye. He used a series of tools and lights, and even with all the poking and prodding he did on Calvin's tiny face, the baby seemed to go with it. Calvin's head jerked just a little at some moments, but Gemma took note of how easygoing he was in the moment. *What a cool kid,* she thought with a twinge of pride.

The doctor scooted back from Gemma. "This fella is as calm as they come, huh?"

"Yeah," Gemma said. *How am I just now noticing that?*

The doctor took out a pen and began scribbling on some paperwork on the counter in the exam room. "Well, Dr. Sinclair, from the looks of it, this little guy is all healed."

Gemma's chest expanded with air. She squeezed Calvin tighter to her. "What does that mean? Specifically."

"All the ocular nerves look great—no detectable damage. Put another way, if I were examining him without knowing what happened, I would not know it had."

Gemma exhaled loudly. "Except for the scar."

The doctor cocked his head to the side as he slid back over to view Calvin's face. "As he grows, that will fade. I'd wager that by the time he's six months old, you won't even be able to see it if you aren't looking for it."

"So just don't go looking for it."

The doctor clucked his tongue with a finger gun and a wink. "Best advice I could ever give a patient. Or a parent." He hopped up and turned to the door. "Just don't go looking for it."

———

Back in the car, Gemma clicked the carrier into the cradle and looked at Calvin for a long time. *See your kid,* she told herself as her eyes traced the outline of his face, around his eyebrows, down the slope of his nose, and over and around his little bow lips. "You're beautiful," she said, smiling at him. "Absolutely perfect. I'll never see anything in you that makes me feel otherwise. And I promise I will never go looking."

On the drive home she felt something she hadn't felt in months. Relief. *Likely from the good news at the follow-up,* she told herself. But she had already known in her gut what the doctor just told her. She had watched for any indication that Calvin's eye was failing him—milky appearance, lagging movement, seeping. Everything was fine. Nothing left behind but the fading scar.

While she was happy to receive the good news, it couldn't be the true source of the relief she felt in this moment, stuck in holiday traffic on College Avenue. Sure, she'd been on the medication Dr. Johnson had prescribed for a week, she'd been walking every morning, she and Anthony had resumed their intimacy, and thankfully her appetite had returned.

And she felt good about her family. She and her mother finally had another lunch, a much more pleasant experience than their previous one. They didn't talk about anything particularly deep, but Gemma enjoyed their time together and felt herself relax around Irene in a way she never had before. Gemma didn't even wear makeup to the lunch, a fact that raised Anthony's eyebrows. Beyond that, Irene stopped by each week to hold Calvin and kiss all over Bo. She always brought a bag of groceries and some sort of casserole that Gemma could just reheat. Gemma was now able to see this as a gesture of love and not as an indictment of her ability to feed her family. Irene's love for all things beautiful didn't mean Gemma was ugly.

Jack and Gemma had texted most every day since their Thanksgiving walk. They didn't directly address that conversation, but they didn't entirely avoid it either. A few of the exchanges had called back to Jack's insights on his own father, which Gemma took to mean Jack was continuing to assess his own role as a parent. Other than that, their texts were mostly about what Jack believed was Bo's predilection for football over baseball, and strategies for how they might handle this when he got to high school. Gemma took comfort in his humor, even though part of her longed for the closeness, the vulnerability, that they shared that brisk day on the streets of Jack and Irene's neighborhood. That moment was the most she had ever seen her father, and the most she had ever felt seen by him. But those changes in her relationships with her mother and father didn't inherently give Gemma relief. She felt reflective, thoughtful, empathetic, maybe even guarded. But not especially relieved.

Perhaps her relief was in some small way because of how she and Mary had grown closer. Since living with Mary for a few weeks, and uncovering a deeply transformational moment in her past, Gemma felt she could see all sides of her sister. Even though Mary had not yet shared the truth with their parents, Gemma was relieved that her sister hadn't closed back up to her. They continued to talk about what happened, and Gemma noted that something in Mary was shifting. A few nights earlier, while they were watching *Succession* after she'd joined Gemma and Anthony for dinner, Mary leaned over and asked, "Is it just me, or is Kendall kind of hot?" Yes, her newfound depth with Mary certainly felt good. The relief that came from guaranteed closeness—something Gemma didn't know if she'd ever feel with Eddie.

She had exchanged only one text with Eddie since she saw him in Boston. A week or so after Thanksgiving she got this message:

The coffee in Rio de Janeiro is next level.

She spent a few hours wondering how to reply, but then ultimately got busy preparing for the holidays and going back to work. Only when she got a package the next week—a bag of coffee beans from Brazil with a note that simply read, "Next level"—did she respond.

This isn't enough coffee to survive the holidays with the kids, but it's a start.

He didn't text back and she hadn't expected him to. Perhaps that was bringing some of her relief: letting go of what she hoped she could have with Eddie, and instead appreciating what she did have with him. After all, his thinking enough about her to buy, package, and mail something felt as close to getting ice cream with him as she'd felt in thirty years.

A car honked behind her, startling Gemma from her thoughts. "I can't move, asshole!" she said into the rearview mirror. She caught a glimpse of Calvin's reflection in the mirror that was adhered to the seat in front of him. He was smiling. "Oh! Not you, baby! You're not an asshole! Oh my god, why would I say *asshole* in front of you? Oh! Dammit, I did it again! Shit! Oh my god, Gemma, shut the fuck up!"

She clasped a hand over her mouth and laughed into her palm. Something felt strange in that—a feeling her body remembered but her mind couldn't recall. A tiny laugh bubbled up from behind her. She craned her neck to look back at her son. "Calvin?" He was quiet again. "Were you just laughing at Mommy?" And then his mouth opened to reveal two rows of pink gums that let through the tiniest giggle she'd ever heard.

The car behind her honked again.

"Oh, fuck you!" she yelled as she let her foot off the brakes now that the car in front of her had lurched forward a few feet. Calvin giggled again.

"Calvin!" Gemma laughed as she yelled his name. "Don't tell anyone I said that!"

He giggled again, which made Gemma burst into laughter, and all the way home they took turns making each other laugh.

———

"Mom!" Bo called as Gemma came through the front door. "Dad! Mom's home!"

Anthony came around the corner, a dish towel over his shoulder, and leaned in to kiss her on the lips. "Tell me," he said. His eyes looked heavy with concern.

"He's perfect," she said, dropping her bag to the floor

and bending down to hug Bo. "No detectable evidence of the injury."

"Oh, that's such a relief!" Anthony said, pulling her in for a hug. "And you!" He squatted down to look at Calvin in his carrier. "What a champ you are!"

"Yeah, you should have seen him. The doctor was practically turning the kid's eyeball inside out and Calvin just went with it."

"I've always said he is the chillest baby."

"Said that to who?"

Anthony shrugged. "Coworkers, mostly."

Gemma smiled at him, appreciating his ability to see what he saw in others. She noticed she didn't feel her typical pang of guilt for not seeing it in Calvin sooner.

Anthony nodded into the living room. "Tummy time?"

Gemma took off her coat and scarf as Anthony gathered Calvin from the carrier and placed him on a stretched-out blanket on the floor. He turned and motioned for Gemma to sit on the couch.

"Without wine?"

Anthony smiled and walked back into the kitchen while she kicked off her shoes and hung up her coat. He returned with a glass of chardonnay.

"That's better," she said, taking the wine and motioning for them to both sit. They watched silently as Calvin alternated between lifting his head and lying down, while Bo was absorbed in an episode of *Daniel Tiger* Gemma could recite from memory.

"How was work?" Anthony asked.

"I saw two patients today," she said after taking a sip of the cool, pale liquid.

"And did you curse any of them out?"

"Not a one."

"Well look at you."

"Between those good sessions and the appointment this

afternoon, it was actually a really great day," she said, her eyes on Calvin's bald head. "I felt relieved."

"Relieved?"

"Yeah. That's the only way to describe what I've been feeling all day."

"Because of Calvin?"

"I mean, I'm happy about the news, but I also suspected that was the case."

"Relieved to be back at work?"

Gemma bit her fingernail. "Maybe? I don't know. It's just a funny feeling. Maybe it isn't relief. It's like . . . well, it's kind of like that feeling you get when you've forgotten something that you know was good, and as you're trying to remember it, you get excited because you know it's going to make you happy all over again?"

"Like that time I couldn't remember what I wanted to tell you but I knew it was good news, and it took me hours to remember that I won those Snow Patrol tickets?"

"Yes! That! I've felt like that all day. But I can't remember what I've forgotten."

"Well, enjoy the ride for now."

Gemma turned her body and stretched her legs out over Anthony's lap. "I actually have a new patient."

"And?"

"Young mom."

"Nice."

Gemma nodded. "It's weird, but the minute she walked in I knew I was going to approach her differently."

"Differently from what?"

"My last decade of patients."

"Why? You're a great therapist."

She put her hand on his. "I appreciate that. But I think I've just learned so much going through the process myself that I want to borrow."

Anthony smiled as though he understood. Gemma looked over at Bo before turning back to her husband. "I'm now going to say the most obvious thing in the world, and you just have to let me say it and not react," she said. "Deal?"

"Deal."

"Doing the job is nothing like they teach you in school."

Anthony laughed.

"I am well educated," she said. "But the past two months, I actually *learned*."

Gemma and Anthony watched quietly as Bo played happily with his toys on the floor.

"You know what they say about librarians?" Anthony asked, breaking the silence.

"That you didn't have prom dates?"

"Besides that."

"What?"

"That you can't truly be good at it until you've read all the books."

Gemma grinned at her husband as he rubbed his hand up and down her leg. "Well, you're closer than most."

"The work you did with Dr. Fox will make you that much better at taking others through it as well. *You're* closer than most."

Gemma took his words in, her face relaxing into the feeling she'd had all day. She closed her eyes for a moment, squeezing them tight to try and conjure up the elusive sensation. *Stay close*, Gemma thought to the feeling.

Suddenly her eyes popped open.

Stay close.

Relationships were about closeness. Proximity. Intimacy. Audacity. Confronting your parents. Showing up for your sister. Punching your brother. Stealing your husband's keys. *Stay close.* A relationship was simply an array of tiny moments that moved you either closer to or further away from where you wanted to be with that person. Closer to or further away from the person you wanted to be. And everything in life was about moving little by little in the direction you wanted to go. Gemma's eyes lowered to Calvin on the floor. *The only way to bond with Calvin is to move in that direction,* she realized. *Get close and stay close.*

She swung her legs off Anthony, leaned forward to set her wineglass on the coffee table, and stood up. Bo looked up from his toys to watch his mother's movements.

"Where are you going?" Anthony asked.

"To get a little closer," she said.

She stepped over to the blanket on the floor and lowered herself down onto her belly, putting her nose within inches of Calvin's. When he sensed her, his eyes fluttered open. He studied her face, his eyes scanning over her hair, down her cheek, to her chin, and back up to her eyes. She studied his face in return, this time not taking note of the tiny incision under his eye.

"Hi, my giggly boy," Gemma said.

At the sound of her voice, Calvin's eyes began to lift, the fog of sleep clearing, and his face became a wide, toothless grin. He let out the giggle from the car. There was that feeling again. Relief. Or something like it. She looked at her baby boy and felt a tug from within. Her mind raced to trace its source in her body. To track down the thread, hoping to grab hold.

She closed her eyes for a moment and found it. There, deep down, was a ribbon of warmth. Gemma sensed something within her shift and roll, every unraveled strand—all the parts of her she once was, she still was, and everything she was trying desperately to become—working to lift and move toward all the other detached tangles.

And for the first time in a long time, Gemma felt close.

According to the National Institutes of Health, postpartum depression (PPD) will affect one in seven women within the first year after childbirth. Half of these cases will go undiagnosed. If you or someone you know is experiencing symptoms of PPD, call or text the National Maternal Mental Health Hotline, 1-833-TLC-MAMA, for free, confidential support.

ACKNOWLEDGMENTS

Blinking back tears. Eye strain from writing too long? Tears of gratitude?

The space is warm.

Sunlight pours in.

A Frenchie and a golden retriever lie together in a beam of light.

Claire's email appears. If she's a book agent, why does her email read like she's the strongest of champions?

A child runs into the room. Blond curls. Lowery. She's laughing.

What she is laughing at suddenly appears next to her.

London. Blond bangs and a twinkle in her eyes.

There is a story they need to share.

The phone rings. John and Debbi want to FaceTime. Loving, supportive figures hovering, as if ethereal, between parents and grandparents. Their faces fill the screen. Laughter fills the speaker.

Another chime. Another email.

It's the team at Girl Friday. Sara, Kylee, Allison, Brittany, Adria. Do they ever stop working hard?

Black coffee steams in a hot-pink mug on the desk.

A text chimes. Amanda. The screen is blurry. A sisterly text blending into the text of a best friend. Which is it? Which is she?

Curly and Bangs exchange the phone for a hug.

She breathes them in. They are oxygen.

Another text. Kris. A friend checking in on the very project she pushed for and helped launch.

Can't answer. There's someone at the door.

Katie. With paperwork. Only she doesn't look like an irreplaceable assistant; she's dressed like a cheerleader.

An Oklahoma sunset.

Somewhere in the distance an iPad plays YouTube.

Instagram notifications chime. Why does it sound like clapping? The thunderous sound of a supportive group.

He walks into the room and stands behind her.

Her breath catches in her chest.

He watches the words dance across the screen.

He points to a sentence that needs changing. He bends down to kiss her. He grabs the pink mug.

She needs a refill.

He needs to know.

He's the highlight of every waking hour.

She refuses to acknowledge that this all might just be a dream.

ABOUT THE AUTHOR

Meg Myers Morgan is a bestselling and award-winning author whose books speak to the nuances of womanhood, motherhood, and self-worth. Her collection of essays, *Harebrained*, won the gold medal from the Independent Publishers Book Awards. Her career development book, *Everything is Negotiable*, is a bestseller and has been translated into multiple languages. *The Inconvenient Unraveling of Gemma Sinclair* is Meg's debut novel. Meg earned her degree in creative writing with honors in English from Drury University, and she received her master's and PhD from the University of Oklahoma. She is currently an associate professor at the University of Oklahoma. Meg, her husband, and their two daughters are all citizens of the Cherokee Nation and live in Tulsa.